FIGURES IN A LANDSCAPE

Brigid Murray is a water-colour artist and writer. She helped to run a pottery and craft centre in Ireland and was an advisory teacher for maladjusted children, before moving to the North Pennines to paint and write poetry. She has two previous published books; on Irish pottery and glass. *Figures in a Landscape* is the first novel in a proposed trilogy. The second is to be published in 1993.

FIGURES IN A LANDSCAPE

Brigid Murray

CHAPMANS

Chapmans Publishers Ltd
141–143 Drury Lane
London WC2B 5TB

ISBN 1 85592 065 4

First published by Chapmans 1991

This paperback edition first published by Chapmans 1992

Printed in Great Britain by Clays Ltd, St Ives plc

For All Survivors

My special thanks to Terry Harris
and Sue Rayner
for their endless patience and help.

ONE

Outside, it was getting worse.

Karin rubbed three fingers across the window and saw a bleak, rain-blasted landscape through the small colourless arc, then watched despondently as beads of condensation trickled down to distort the view.

Her throat was beginning to hurt, even when she didn't swallow.

It wasn't supposed to be like this. Tracy said that hitching was easy. You just stood near a roundabout and stuck your thumb out. They had to slow down at roundabouts, so you caught them before they speeded up again. Dead easy, kid, Tracy giggled. Karin wished she was with her now. Tracy was her best mate and a good laugh. She could do with a laugh.

It was all the bloody driver's fault. Naw, it wasn't, it was her own, back at that roundabout near Durham; that was her own stupid choice. She should have stuck it out. But she had been standing nearly an hour and was soaked by the time he stopped. Up till then, every driver had just rushed past, windscreen wipers swinging, looking straight ahead, pretending to concentrate on the road. They didn't want wet clothes in their cars.

She wasn't even looking when he pulled up.

Where a' you going? sne yelled up at him.

That was what Tracy said you had to ask. If you told them where you were going, they could say they were going there as well, couldn't they; then you'd be in bother, wouldn't you? she had reasoned patiently.

To Lancaster, he shouted down to her.

I'm going to London.

I can take you as far as Scotch Corner.

Not to Scotland, to London, she shouted back.

Scotch Corner's on your way but it's up to you, suit yerself. I have a delivery to make in Middleton first. You might get a better lift if you wait. The engine was idling noisily, the lorry shuddering, impatient to be moving again.

It was his indifference that had decided her, that and the rain running down her neck. Scotch Corner sounded better than where she was, anywhere did, so she climbed into his lorry. It reeked of diesel and old rags and the stink got worse when he switched on his heater for her and she sat in its blast with steam rising from everywhere.

When he wanted to talk she turned and pretended to look out of the window. Once he nudged her elbow and offered her a fag. She turned back to the window and smoked it in silence and he stopped bothering her after that.

That was ages ago, before the lorry started to make funny noises and he pulled off the road into a layby and jumped down to investigate.

Now, what seemed like hours later, Karin was still in the layby and fed up. Without the heater, her wet clothes had chilled again. She'd been on the road since morning. Tracy said you could get to London in three hours, four at the outside if you got the right car. At this rate, it would take days. The clock on the dashboard showed three o'clock. It was getting dark. And another thing, she was feeling a bit funny. She leaned forward and wiped a small circle in the windscreen. The view was no better than that through the side window: just mist rolling back to reveal more mist. Better get out and find the driver and ask him what he was doing

– and have another of his fags. There was no point in smoking her own.

She pushed the heavy door open awkwardly, then stood on the wheel hub and clung to both the door handle and side handle before launching herself backwards to the ground. At the rear of the lorry, the tool-box was lying open on the wet gravel but there was no sign of the driver. He must have gone to get help. Why had he said nowt? Funny bugger.

Karin knew she could stay in the lorry until he came back, but that might be hours and then it would be dark before she even reached Scotch Corner. No, she'd have to move, she decided, and leaned into the cabin to reach her bag. The front of her skirt and jacket got soaked again. I was soaked anyway, she shrugged, and turned to face the mist.

She hadn't been taking any notice when he'd pulled into the layby, so had no idea of the direction. She'd been imagining fat chips being dipped into the runny yolk of an egg when he'd squealed to a halt and jumped out. Middleton must be somewhere back there, and Scotch Corner as well; but where? It didn't really matter. If she chose the wrong side of the road first time, she'd just cross over and get a lift going the other way. She should still get to Scotch Corner before it got dark and get a lift going all the way to London.

There was no traffic in either direction. At first, Karin stood staring into the mist, willing a car to emerge, afraid that if she took her eyes away, she would miss one. Half an hour later, she gave up and started to walk, to try to warm up.

The small bus took her by surprise. The wind had sounded like a distant engine so often that she had stopped listening.

It pulled up quietly and the doors hissed open.

'I nearly didn't see you.' She said nothing, waiting. 'Well, get in if you're coming,' the driver said.

'I'm going to Scotch Corner.' Her voice surprised her. It was hoarse.

'Aw, we're miles away from there. I'll drop you at the next crossroads.'

Karin climbed into the empty bus, paid her fare, ignored the driver's smile and walked to the back. It seemed only seconds later when he pulled to a stop again.

'D'you know where to go now, then?'

'I can read, can't I?' she tossed at him and got off.

At the junction, there were five roads and only four signs on the post and none of them was for Middleton or Scotch Corner. The weather was changing, getting colder, the road slippery. The mist still clung to her but the rain was needling tiny pricks of pain on her face and fingers. Breathing hurt her now and in the centre of her forehead there was a sharp pain surrounded by a dull ache.

Karin started to walk, aimlessly this time, head down, watching her feet moving past each other, defining her field of vision. Behind her, she heard an engine change gear to come round the bend, but she kept moving. The exhaust gave a couple of snorts and coughed to a halt: a Land Rover. She knew she was being scrutinised and tilted her chin, prepared to wait. At first, neither of them moved, then an arm reached across and yanked a stiff window open.

'Are you going far?' The voice was slow, probing, suspicious. She sensed trouble.

'Where are *you* going?' Karin countered, remembering Tracy's formula.

'That's what I asked *you*,' maddeningly slow.

This was a smart arse. She would have to compromise. 'Just up the road, that's all.' She spoke to the open window. Still he did not open the door.

'Why, there's only Dave Barnett's place up there and then mine.'

'Yes, I know.' That was daft, she thought. If you'd told him where you were going, he might have put you on the right road.

'Why, if that's where you're heading, I can save you a trip. He's not there.' His voice was irritatingly soft, almost lazy, a different voice from her sharp, clipped tones. His gave him time to think as he was speaking, whereas she had to do the thinking before she opened her mouth. This was her chance to say aw, all right then, ta, and turn round. Instead, she heard herself say: 'Yes, I know, he's left me a key.'

She was getting in deeper. It was a stupid thing to have said. It wasn't the lie itself that worried her; she told them all the time. It was simply that this lie wouldn't hold. She usually stuck closer to the truth. This was dangerously far from it and she knew he wasn't taken in. Being left a key was wishful thinking. It was because she was tired.

Maybe that was why she was sweating as well as shivering. It wasn't just rain running down her back. It was all mixed up. She was hot and cold and shivering and sweating and every footstep was pounding in her head. It was time to stop for the day, and Dave Barnett's place would have to do, wherever it was. She'd find somewhere to sleep. Tomorrow, the weather might have improved and she'd be feeling better.

Karin stood, shifting from one foot to the other, ready to run, expecting him to face her and call her a liar. Both of her feet were numb. Her fashion boots were soaked and crumpled at the toes.

Come on, y'old fool, she thought to herself, standing there, her face impassive, showing nothing. She gave an involuntary shiver that made her clench her fists in her fingerless mitts. The bag handle had stopped hurting ages ago. Her hands were as numb as her feet.

'Aye, well.' He leaned over and opened the door, pushing it towards her with his fingertips. She pushed her bag beside the gear stick and climbed in stiffly. The torn edge of the leatherette seat caught the top of her legs and they squeaked as the Land Rover swayed from side to side. Only her bottom remained still, stuck to the seat with her wet skirt.

They bumped endlessly over ruts in the road, past verges stark with bare branches whipping in the bitter wind. The trees thinned and gave way to stone walls as the road snaked up the moor, along escarpments that were linked by hairpin bends. It was now three thirty on a mid-January afternoon and the light was nearly gone. Another hour and it would be totally dark.

'Well, it was lucky I was passing. It'll be dark soon and you would've been caught out. What would you've done then, eh?' he shouted above the engine noise, not taking his eyes off the road.

Karin was ready. She'd decided what she was going to say before she'd got in.

'I know, thanks. I was getting worried. I was supposed to be here earlier but I missed the bus. I was just going to turn round and go back when you came. I would've had to go home and come back again tomorrow.'

The last bit was overdoing it, too friendly, confidential. That was the great thing about sticking closer to the truth. You could afford to be more off-hand. And people believed you more easily.

The driver looked at his arms resting on top of the wheel; then he hunched his shoulders and frowned.

'Funny, Dave Barnett said nowt to me last week about anyone coming. Just said he was shutting the place up for the winter.'

'Yes, but he called to see me. He's my cousin, see. And I said it would be better than leaving it empty because of burglars and that. He hadn't thought of it until I said it.'

'Bit young, aren't you?'

'How d'you mean?'

'Why, it gets rough up there. That's why he left, afore the next lot o' snow.'

Trust the old bugger to mention it. But he was right. She wasn't sixteen yet and small for her age. She'd been expecting this as they'd bumped along. Still, if he had his say now, mebbe it would save him from brooding and going to the police later.

'I'm not that young; I'm doing my A levels. Anyway, my sister and my mam'll be up at the weekend.'

12

'Aye, and what are you going to do when you get snowed up, eh?'

'Same as everyone else does.' Laughing, sounding confident; thinking: pick the bones out of that one.

'Aye.' He was still suspicious, she knew. He wrenched the wheel to avoid a deep rut and with a tearing sound, her skirt released its hold and Karin slid away from him, along the seat, banging her elbow on the door. Her vision blackened. She bit her lip and then the inside of her cheek, before risking a sideways glance at him to see if he'd noticed.

An ordinary-looking bloke, probably old enough to be harmless. Flat cap, waxed jacket, deeply cracked at the elbows and armpits, the bottom of it rubbing the tops of his wellingtons, cow shit past the ankles like thick socks, dried now. Harmless, just nosey, she decided.

'I thought you had to be at school to do exams?'

And like a bloody terrier, she thought.

'Yes, you do, but I failed mine last year.' Then on sudden inspiration, 'I took them a year early and I'm having to do them again on my own, so I thought this place would be good for a bit of peace 'n quiet, like.' Clenching her eyes against the headache.

She was out of her depth now and struggling, although the last bit about working on her own wasn't a complete lie. When she'd been suspended from school, she'd had home tuition and the tutor had set her work to do. She hadn't done it, of course, but she'd had it set. She wished he'd stop asking her questions. Apart from the danger of being found out, it was hurting her to talk now.

He started to brake again and this time, instead of nosing round another bend in the road, he cranked slowly to a stop. The interrogation was at an end but so was the lift and she could see nothing. Karin steadied herself.

'Here you are, then. I take it you know the way?' She eased her wet bottom off the seat and slid one foot tentatively out of the door, straight into a drainage ditch. Standing on one leg, up to her ankle in water, she leaned in to take her bag.

'You've not got much with you?'

Wearily she turned back to him, 'No, I told you, my mam'll be up at the weekend.'

'Aye, well, you've got your torch?'

'Yes.' Her other foot groped for ground, then sank into the ditch as well. She tried to slam the door but it bounced open.

'Leave it, I'll shut it from the inside.'

She heard the click of a latch and saw his arm go back to the wheel.

The Land Rover shuddered into gear and as the wheels spun they threw a muddy spray high above her head. She shut her eyes as it showered down her face.

Once he was out of sight, Karin stepped out of the ditch and looked around. If she needed a torch, Dave Barnett's house must be off the road. The fell was now colourless, the heavy sky allowing only a thin slit of grey on the horizon. She supposed that the darker lines were walls. She didn't want to lose her bearings. With a bit of luck he'd dropped her at the nearest point to the house, wherever it was.

Peering ahead of her, through the dusk, she saw a track wind away down the valley.

It's better than climbing, she told herself as her boots slithered, their tiny stiletto heels driving through the shale. But her cheerfulness soon died. There was no house in sight and she was tired. Her feet were trailing and her eyes wouldn't focus through the pain in her head. 'Aw, bugger,' she croaked as she stumbled for the umpteenth time, this time badly, only saving herself with her bag. Sobbing, she groped on the ground to steady herself before getting up.

'Shut up, Karin Thompson, y'idiot,' she said savagely, and putting each foot down carefully in front of her to test the ground, she moved on safely until she reached a farm gate.

Two chains and a piece of baler string were intertwined.

She climbed over, balancing perilously on the top in her tight skirt and clutching her bag. As she thudded to the other side, she felt one of her heels break.

Sod it. She stopped to rip it off and a few steps further on, stopped again and kicked the other heel on the ground.

'Come on, break, blast you,' she muttered. It wouldn't.

She limped on towards a gap in a wall and through that, towards what she took to be a building: Dave Barnett's house, she supposed; she hoped.

Mansell Jowett swung the Land Rover in a wide arc in the yard behind the house, pulling up as close to the back door as he could.

Three weeks of persistent rain had raised the level of the cow slurry and he hadn't got round to unblocking the drain, despite Maggie's nagging at the muck tramping into the house. Mebbe if she nagged a bit less, he'd feel more inclined towards things, he thought slowly. Light flooded the yard as he pushed open the door and in closing it, he shut out the noise of the generator pounding in the barn. Maggie was standing at the Aga with her back to him. As usual, she didn't turn round or lift her head.

'There's tea in the pot. Your dinner'll be another half-hour. I've just finished the milking. I couldn't wait for you.'

He grunted. That was as good a way as any to answer her when she was in a mood. He padded across the floor in his stocking feet, poured himself a mug of tea, then pulled out a chair and sat crossways on it, leaning one arm on the table.

He sat for a while, looking at the floor between his knees before clearing his throat.

'I gave a lift to a lass just afore there.'

'Aye.'

'Aye, she said she was going to stay at Dave Barnett's place.'

'Well?'

'She was a townie. She wasn't dressed for it. She only had

a bit of a bag and anyway, she was too young, no more than fifteen.'

'Aye, well, we have enough to do here without worrying about her; or Dave Barnett.'

'She might be in bother.'

'I doubt it. How old did you say she was, fifteen? She's old enough to take care of herself. Some of them are raising a family at fifteen these days.'

Maggie lifted the pan lid and stabbed one of the potatoes. Satisfied, she turned to the sink and began to drain them. Her words reached him from behind the steam.

'Anyway, Dave Barnett's affairs are none of our business and you know he hates callers.' The potatoes clodded against the lid as she shook the last drops of water out of the pan.

'Aye, you're right, and it's all shuttered up anyway.' He spoke to her back as she bent to open the Aga door and lift out a roasting tin. A haze of blue smoke from the scorching fat hung between them. She scored the parboiled potatoes, cut them in half, packed them into the tin and slammed the door behind them.

'There now.' She pushed a strand of greying hair back from her sweating face. 'Another half-hour. We're just waiting for them taties now.' She turned back to the sink and began to wash the pan.

'Leave it, lass, I'll do it with the rest of the dishes afterwards.'

That's because he left me to get on with the milking, she thought.

'Naw, I cannot abide a cluttered sink and besides, it'll be one less for you to do.'

His face fell. She was going to take him up on his offer. She was a hard woman.

'I know what you're thinking and I have to be because you're too damn soft.'

He picked up the teaspoon and dawdled it around his mug. It was no good looking out of the lavatory window tonight. He'd see nothing at Dave Barnett's with the shutters closed, but he'd look tomorrow morning. If she did have a key and was staying there, like she said, she'd take the shutters down. She'd have to – to see.

But why had Dave Barnett put them up in the first place if she was coming? Still, two years ago he'd gone away at Christmas, shuttered everywhere; then come back one day later and had to take them all down again. He was a funny lad. Maggie was right. He was scared of people getting to know him. No one ever got across the door. Hail, rain or snow, he kept you standing on the step. Not like his aunt, Cissie Barnett. When she was alive, her door was never shut. A kinder woman never walked. If Dave Barnett was going to live in the Dale and in her house, he had a lot to learn about being a good neighbour.

He stared at his tea. Dave Barnett had never mentioned any other family. Not that they'd ever talked much, but somehow Mansell'd always got the impression that he hadn't any. And why would he go out of his way to visit relatives in Newcastle when he was on his way south? That young lass wasn't Dave Barnett's sort of person. She was too common. He brought his hand down to the table and his spoon jumped. A levels, she'd said. She was as likely to be doing A levels as he was. Well, she wouldn't get in. The house was shuttered as well as locked. It would serve her right. She'd been bloody insolent. With that sly little fox face and those earrings in one ear. Maggie was right. She'd have to fend for herself.

Why didn't I think of a torch? Why the bloody hell don't they have pavements and paths? Stumbling across the field to the house, Karin walked as wide-legged as her tight skirt would allow, with both arms stretched out in front like a player in blind man's buff.

Her bag weighed a ton. She swapped every other minute from one wrist to the other, not able to carry it in the crook of her arm, needing ten outstretched fingers as radar.

She stumbled and then, without warning, touched wall. One minute she was groping darkness and the next, there was solid wall: a house wall, with a bit of luck. It stretched above her reach. She allowed herself a moment to rest her head on the stone before starting to feel her way around. A windowsill jutted out at hip level but there was no glass in the space above, only wood. The next was the same. Then came a door which was locked. There was another shuttered window; then the wall turned a corner. There was a guttering above her head now, so a single storey, probably a porch. The wall was blank, until it reached another pair of shutters, this time, with a bar across them. She swung it out of its catch and when the shutters didn't open, she prised her fingers underneath, her nails scraping on the stone sill. Pulling was useless. Something was holding the shutters from the inside.

Aw hell, I'm soaking and famished and cold. The last word brought sobs that came out as high, dry gasps. She fisted her hands and pounded her rage on the shutters until she realised that they were bouncing. She stopped and grinned. An inside bar, same as the outside one. A cinch! She poked in her bag and brought out a knife. Carefully she felt for the crack in the centre of the shutters and slid the blade in and up, making contact with the metal, willing it to lift. One final burst of breath and it gave. Dead easy: a beginner's job.

It must be a log shed, she decided, feeling the wood, rough and wet and filling the entire opening. By the time she'd thrown out ten logs, she couldn't control her legs, but it was all right by then, there was a space big enough to get in. Balancing on two logs and leaning on her bag, she hitched herself up. Once inside, she found the shed was only half full. Logs tumbled away from her as she clambered and slid down the pile. She reached the floor and her breathing slowed. She felt around again; wall, right-angle turn, wall, another corner, and in that corner, a piece of old carpet and what she took to be curtains, velvet stuff, stinking damp.

18

She'd earned a fag. That would clear her head, then she'd be better. Leaning against the wood, she groped in her bag. The fags were sodden; so were the matches.

Stop snivelling, you silly bugger, or you'll go soft in the head. You've got somewhere better than the roadside and it'll have to do you.

Into her bag again. A can of Newcastle X and her Walkman. Gingerly she eased the carpet over to a couple of logs; then lifted the curtains and draped them around her shoulders. She ripped the headphones off and tossed them away. The Walkman was rain-logged. She snapped the ring-pull on the can and softened for a moment at the familiar hiss of the beer.

You can still go to London in the morning, when it's light, can't you? she reasoned with herself, coaxing, comforting. Anyway, there was nowt she could do as long as it was dark. Except . . . She checked herself. She wasn't going to think about home any more. They could sod off. They all could. Every rotten one of them.

The wind had dropped. No amount of listening brought any sound. She shifted uncomfortably. Her bum bones were sticking through the carpet. That was one of the first things that Tracy's mam said when they were moved next door for being behind with the rent: Ee, you could do with a bit of our Tracy's bum. Just look at her, our Tracy: her bum's like two hard-boiled eggs in a handkerchief. Then she pealed with laughter, her chest wobbling.

Don't take any notice of her, Tracy said. She doesn't mean it.

She could see their kitchen quite clearly. She had squeezed in through the back door and was standing sideways between a pushchair, two bicycles and a pile of very stale dirty washing that was wedged between the top of the machine and a shelf above it. Mrs Taylor was standing at the cooker shaking the chip basket. The smell was everywhere, at first competing with the washing and the smell of cat before wafting triumphantly past both, to reach her.

Mrs Taylor turned round. It's just a bit o' fun, pet. Then she said, You're not one of them picky eaters, are you?

Does that mean she's going to feed me? Karin wondered. She might be all right here. She'd have to wait and see. She tried not to hope. She'd learned long ago that when you hoped for things, you only got disappointed. Better just to wait and see.

Naw, I eat anything, she said off-handedly.

The cat jumped onto the table and started to wind itself between the sauce and the milk bottles, picking its way among the crumbs and stepping over the margarine, mewing. Mrs Taylor turned round, scooped it up with one hand and turned back to the stove. Karin gripped the inside of her cheek in her teeth and stared at the sauce bottle.

Our poor Mitsy – just a hungry auld puss and she wants her tea, that's what, Mrs Taylor commiserated.

The cat was purring ecstatically. Mrs Taylor rubbed her cheek against its unprotesting head and shook the chip pan with her free hand. Then she turned, balancing the cat expertly on one outstretched hand. Will you take her . . . ? Her voice tailed off. She stood, arm outstretched, the cat quite still. What's wrong with you? Why've you gone white like that?

Nowt, Karin mumbled, pushing the memory away.

Mrs Taylor closed her arm and brought the cat back to her shoulder, where it began to sharpen its claws. I'm not running a Chinkie takeaway. I wasn't going to put her in the pan. Then she wobbled with laughter again at the thought.

Karin forced herself to grin.

Ee, that's better. We've never been so desperate that we've had to cook the cat. We've come close, mind you. Seeing Karin's face, she added, I'd rather the cat had her tea than us. We can understand why there's nowt. She can't.

Karin started to breathe again and brought her shoulders down from her ears. She might be all right here.

Anyway, your tea's ready. Pull out that chair, our Tracy's won't be a minute.

She had plonked that plate in front of her, piled high with lovely fat chips and two brown-edged fried eggs, all speckled black with bits of burnt fat, before turning to lower the basket and settle it to a steady sizzle.

She knew then almost for certain that these new neighbours were going to be all right and she slapped the bottom of the OK Sauce bottle with a brief defiant joy before reaching into the bread bag for a slice of thick-cut white. She might even be able to tell them about her mam and Debbie.

She pulled herself together. Stop it, Karin Thompson, or you'll be bawling next.

Dreaming wouldn't get her anywhere and memories wouldn't feed her. Now that she was here, in the middle of nowhere, she'd have to keep her wits about her.

She shifted again on the log, but it was no use. Clutching the curtain and her bag, she got up carefully and turned round to double the piece of carpet over and sit on it again before it sprang back.

There was nowt else she could do and she was lucky to have found this. She might even get some sleep.

With these thoughts, she pulled the curtain around her as tightly as she could and, shivering and sweating by turn, she settled down in the silence to wait for daylight.

TWO

Her mam was opening the stove door and swinging the bucket of coke towards it with a well-practised aim. He came up behind her, dangling two kittens by their necks. They were mewing helplessly, their backs curled and claws spread. Elbowing her aside, he tossed them both into the embers and slammed the door shut.

You'll never get it going without some kindling. If you need any more, the rest of the litter's out the back.

The fire behind the thick glass door blazed for a moment; then the spray of sparks that had lit the edges of their fur collapsed as the kittens shrunk and charred, their eyes bursting from their heads before they melded into blackening sizzling lumps.

Then her mam changed into Mrs Taylor. She knew that as soon as she turned round because she moved towards him, big and unafraid and intent on murder. Karin watched her swing the coke bucket backwards and forwards with deliberate aim, and saw the coke shower slowly past him, leaving him untouched, laughing, taunting. Mrs Taylor lunged at him with her hands and caught his neck, then staggered back. She hadn't killed him – nobody could do that – but she'd made him mad and now he'd get his revenge and he'd take it out on her or Debbie or the cat and the rest of the kittens; all of them if he could.

She turned and found herself taking giant strides in her rush to get to the kitchen – wasting precious time, weeping as she floated between each step. Blackie was nursing the other kittens on the draining board; then it was Debbie, perched cross-legged, cradling the kittens in her lap. She was still floating, trying to force herself to land and screaming, Hurry up, Debbie, he's coming; trying to pull her towards the stairs, and Debbie was wailing, Leave me alone, our Karin, they're my Barbie dolls.

No they're not. Come on or he'll get you, and she was lifting Debbie and the kittens and struggling with them to the stairs.

As soon as the stairs began to move, she realised that they had no support but there was no choice but to go on, each step tilting or crumbling or moving as she reached it. And he was behind her, following, roaring, and she couldn't escape, could only push Debbie and the kittens out of reach before resigning herself to turn round and face him.

The stairs moved under his weight. Then each step became a log which tumbled over and over until they buried him. She clambered down to where his hand clawed air. The logs threatened to engulf her as she leaned forward, holding darkness with one hand and trying to reach him with the other. Then the logs closed in, cutting her off from his hand that was still opening and shutting helplessly, grasping nothingness.

She woke briefly. She was making a thin, dry gasping sound. It hurt. There was pain everywhere, whenever she breathed or moved. Her hair was plastered to her head and trickles of sweat were running down her face.

The logs continued to move towards her, inching forward at first, then avalanching, burying the hand that had now ceased to move, leaving only the fingertips exposed. The logs touched her, moulding themselves to her body, paralysing, suffocating. She would have to burn them, like leeches, to loosen them.

She was running now, in the old flats, leaping from joist to joist, the ground hundreds of feet below her, the joists charred and crumbling. It had been an accident. She hadn't meant to burn everything. Mid-leap, she realised that the joist she was aiming for was unsupported, suspended in space from one wall. There was a second's resignation before she landed and began to tilt slowly downwards, pitching head-first to the floor.

Now she was sinking, drowning; and trying to break the surface, to swim. The ground floor of the flats was flooded, almost to the height of the ceiling; and the water was still rising, leaving no headroom. She reached up to a joist and sank again, her gasp at the air filling her mouth with slime.

The dawn came reluctantly, the blackness greying by degrees, until by eight o'clock there was the dull light of a snowcast January morning. It seeped into the log shed through the cracks in the shutters and through the small window behind her, that was only partly hidden by logs. Karin's eyelids opened very slowly.

Her skin was too tight. She was too hot. Her mouth was cracked and her tongue was too swollen to move around her mouth. It was difficult to suck air past it and when she did, it spread like flames in her chest. Her neck couldn't support her head and there was something inside it, hammering, filling it with a slow, annihilating beat. It lolled back on one of the logs and she let it rest there while her small sticky eyes tried to focus.

She was somewhere with piles of logs. She'd been going to London. Mebbe she was there? Naw, she couldn't be. She'd come to the wrong place. She'd better get moving. Couldn't: too heavy; must have turned to lead. Mebbe she was dreaming

There's sommat the matter with me. Mebbe if I had a drink. She remembered that there had been two cans of

Newcastle X in her bag and wondered if she had finished them both. Her bag was on the floor, out of reach.

I must have flu or sommat. Small tears pushed through the crust around her eyes as she realised her predicament.

I'll have to try and reach my bag, she thought but closed her eyes.

Move.

I can't, I can't.

You have to.

She eased her hand down her leg until it reached the floor and her head fell forward.

Aw hell, it's going to drop off. I can't stand it, it's pounding. But neither could she straighten up. She sat with her head on her knees, trying to absorb the pain before toppling forward to lie on the floor. Reaching out with one arm she touched her bag and pulled it towards her. The can was there but the ring-pull could have been a manhole cover. Her fingers were unable to grip or pull. She groped in her bag again for her knife, levered it under the ring and jammed the can against a log. She pushed with her whole arm until she heard the comforting hiss of the ring's release and put her head briefly on the floor as a reward. She lay, shaking, trying to hold the can, to co-ordinate her mouth and the little hole, feeling the beer trickle across her cheek before spilling in a sudden flood into her throat. Two ping-pong balls and assorted razor blades were blocking it. She coughed and the pain shot everywhere. You're up shit creek, Karin Thompson.

She had better put the can somewhere safe, and try again later. She stood it carefully on the floor, still within reach but safe from an accidental knock.

Her eyes closed.

Outside, a helicopter swung down the valley and tilted inquisitively over Jowett's farm. The noise of its engine reverberated in the snowy silence. The sky and fell were the same dull white. Here and there, a dark line met another where the tops of stone walls that were still visible veined the landscape. Nothing moved. It hovered for a few moments longer and then veered off down the valley, leaving the silence to close behind it.

Giant bluebottles were crawling up the walls. One of them noticed her and as he turned towards her, the rest followed, their noise filling her head as they approached. They were going to lay their eggs on her and there was nothing she could do. She couldn't move.

Mansell was in a foul mood. He'd had to dig his way into the byre and he'd have to take hay to the sheep at Upper Myers if the snow held. The forecast was bad. Chances were he wouldn't find them, not with Jess. She was too old for that kind of work now.

And Maggie wouldn't do owt. She'd just said that he should've brought them down days ago when the snow was forecast. But sometimes you could get through January without snow; at least that's what the old ones said. He always thought it was worth the chance – and one year he'd be proved right. Anyway, if you brought the ewes down aforehand, you had to feed them and then let them up again and there'd be another blizzard so you were no better off. Let them take their chance, he always said. What chance? They've got none, nowt has here, she'd reply.

Dave Barnett had just got out in time. That lass must've gone back down the road after he dropped her. There was no sign of her this morning when he looked out of the lavatory window. Pity, it would have taught her a lesson to get caught out up there.

He crossed the yard and stamped back into the kitchen, dropping snow off his wellingtons with each step.

'The Aga's gone out in the night and I'll have to clean it afore I can get it going again.'

'You shouldn't leave it so long.'

'Aye, well, if you cleaned it now and again, it would get done twice as often, wouldn't it?' She turned to the cupboard under the stairs, nursing one arm.

She was going to make a fuss about her arm again. He knew it. Every day the same: I shouldn't be doing the milking; I'm only doing it to save the cows from exploding.

There was silence while she rooted at the back of the top shelf for the Primus stove.

'There, get some meths in that and get it going so we can get a cup of tea at least; and listen, don't let today go by without unblocking that drain in the yard, d'you hear me, or else the slurry will be in the kitchen here when that snow melts.'

It's getting too much for both of us, he thought as he pumped the Primus stove. Time was when it didn't take a budge out of either of us but not now.

To run a hill farm, you needed money and muscle, he decided, and they had neither. The money was still a bone of contention between himself and Maggie. She'd put her father's money into that boarding school for Joan. He'd argued till he was black in the face. What was the use of a fancy education for a farm lass? It would only fit her for a city job. But she's not interested in farming anyway, Maggie had insisted. No, but she'll not meet a local lad either. But why should she have to meet someone local? The world's full of nice lads. She'll have her pick and let that be an end to it.

And what an end. Joan was gone. She was Head of Languages at a big London comprehensive and not married and never likely to be if her letters were anything to go by. So no chance of a son-in-law to give a hand with the farm and the money that might have helped with machinery or buying in help had gone in school fees.

'What a' you thinking?' Maggie demanded suddenly.

'You're standing there, pumping and you're miles away.'

'Nothing; just about our Joan.'

'What about her?' she snapped.

'How you were right to give her a chance,' he soothed.

'On days like this I sometimes have my doubts.'

God would be abdicating next, he thought. 'Well, it's done now and you did what you thought was best and she's gone.' He didn't want an uproar.

'Aye, she would have gone anyway,' she agreed. 'At least she got a good job and a bit of security, thanks to me.'

The abdication was only a rumour. He hid a little smile as the Primus roared into life.

'Them ewes in Upper Myers will need feeding or else bringing down. What a' you going to do? Will you take hay up to them and wait and see how the weather is next week, or what?'

'I'll just have a cup of tea first.'

'Aw, that's champion, Mansell. Be sure and get your priorities right, won't you? There's that much to do, I don't know where to start and all you can think about is your belly.'

He concentrated on balancing the kettle on the Primus and sat in silence while it boiled, letting Maggie bang on inside the Aga, ignoring her clattering and the grunts.

'I've poured you a cup of tea.'

She didn't answer.

'Did you hear what I said just then?'

He gritted his teeth. She was leaning into the Aga and he knew if he didn't get out, he'd push her into it.

And no breakfast.

He was shaking as he slammed out the door and crunched through the half-frozen slurry, past the stained snow, tossed to either side and banking the narrow path to the byre. Once inside, breathing the soft smell of the cows and their dung which he'd piled in one corner, he felt himself calming down. He stood in the warmth of the gentle breathing, watching them swish their tails and snatch at the hay. There was no point in getting himself worked up, he decided. A woman like Maggie could ruin a man if she was given let.

The next time Karin woke, it was late afternoon. Her eyes travelled unfocused over the logs, across the shutters that she had barred after climbing through, towards the dim light glowing through a small window behind the logs and then to a door. As she lay and looked at it, the handle swelled and faded, the door crumpled and folded; then fell forwards: sometimes squeezed between the two supporting walls, sometimes being crushed by the roof.

She stared, focusing and re-focusing. There was no key-hole, only a handle, a thin metal handle catching the remaining light. That meant it would be bolted on the other side. That meant a chisel job unless she could kick it in and get her hand through the hole.

I'll have a look at it in a minute. Her eyes closed again.

Now.

Naw, later.

Now. The light's going.

She turned and put her hands under her shoulders, pulled her knees up, and crawled towards it.

The handle was too high.

If she lifted one arm, the other wouldn't support her. Sit down, back to the door; now lift one arm. Nearly. Arm dropping.

Another effort and this time, it opened. Just like that. Never bolted.

Buoyed with relief, Karin concentrated on crawling through the doorway and walking the can of beer ahead of her, inches at a time along the passageway ahead.

Half an hour later, she lay in the kitchen and lifted the Newcastle X carefully to her mouth. Slowly she let a tiny sip trickle in but waited until it found its way round the obstacles and down her throat. She wouldn't risk coughing.

The kitchen was almost dark. Its window was shuttered

so the only light was from the window in the woodshed, fading as it stretched along the passage.

Far above her head, the edge of the sink and the taps caught the last gleams of daylight, strangely disembodied in the surrounding darkness. She pushed a chair towards them; then pulled herself up one of the legs and on to the seat. Leaning over the sink, she grasped a tap with both hands and turned until it was open, fully open: and there was no water.

Idiot! She'd forgotten the stopcock. She should have remembered that from the time she'd flooded the old flats. That time, she'd had to saw through a bit of pipe because the stopcock had been sealed.

She lowered herself carefully down the chair leg to the cupboard under the sink and crawled inside. There was a saucer holding a candle and a box of matches. Lying full length, she scraped one of the matches and held her breath when it flared; then steadied the flame above the candle wick until the two flames rose in unison. She lay for a moment in the glow and slight warmth. The stopcock was stiff. She turned it slowly, a fraction at a time, for ever, before she heard it opening, drop by drop. Satisfied, she eased herself out of the cupboard, and put the candle under the chair for safety.

On the second expedition to the taps, the ascent had steepened, but the water gurgled encouragingly. Then it was running everywhere, over her face, her hands, her hair, down her neck and a small, safe trickle worked its way into her mouth when she turned her head. Now all she needed was somewhere to lie down and some way of taking more water with her. Still hanging on to the edge of the sink with one arm, she crashed about the draining board with the other. An empty milk bottle toppled towards her. She filled it and turned off the tap.

She lowered the bottle to the ground and crawled, moving both the candle and the bottle, towards another open door: and lino, she hoped, not sisal matting, which was hurting her hands and knees. Better than that, the next floor was carpeted; and the bottle, the candle and her knees all slid easily over the wool velour surface.

She was only feet from the sofa when she felt herself giving in, as though someone had finally switched her off. She knew she must be dying and she didn't mind. She was surprised but she wasn't frightened. It was just a pity after coming all this way. She put her face on the carpet and closed her eyes.

Get up, now.

Straightening her elbows, bracing her arms, pulling first one knee then the other up beside it, she swayed towards the sofa, still edging the bottle and candle forward: following the light and the water and still not bothered about dying. Not feeling that she was bothered, yet knowing that she wouldn't allow herself to die. Funny, all muddled: not being bothered and not allowing herself to give in. Funny, that.

She stood the milk bottle carefully near the arm at one end of the sofa and put the candle and matches beside it before snuffing it out. With a last effort, she rolled onto the cushions away from the edge; then lay, unmoving; and the tartan rug that had been draped across the back slithered down on top of her, unnoticed.

THREE

Maureen Wilson wished she could feel hungry. It would justify her greed. Her elbow was the problem. Whenever she
bent it, her hand arrived at her mouth. It meant that dry-
roasted peanuts and salt and vinegar crisps could be eaten on
automatic pilot while writing or reading reports or watching
television. To lose weight would require a new body job
with her mouth in the back of her head and her elbows
attached to her ankles. All diets failed simply because they
all allowed her left hand to have access to her mouth.

Years ago, she promised herself to sort out her eating. It
was obsessional and it worried her. She was a competent and
shrewd social worker and had no reason to be overweight
except that she liked eating. She liked it better than food,
although her eating wasn't entirely indiscriminate. A packet
of biscuits could be followed by a tub of cottage cheese to
provide low-calorie protein, and several slices of bread and
jam would demand a salad as reparation. But there was
something spartan about salad. It was duty food and deserved to be followed by a pudding or two or three.

And as all the world's puddings could be found in this
North London borough, she took equal shares of them all.
She knew every restaurant in her area, and routed home
visits to include her favourites.

When she accepted the paradox of her professional competence and private chaos, she stopped dieting and settled to a steady eleven and a half stone. At five feet two inches it was heavy but at least it was constant. The starve/binge days had been much worse with the regular agony of losing seven pounds and the inevitable gain of ten pounds in retaliation. Now she just ate and accepted that it would always be more than she needed, and on most days a lot more.

The office was hot and the air stale at the end of a day of many cigarettes and bodies. She played with a chocolate biscuit wrapper: folding it precisely in two, then four, before pushing it through her pen clip. It was dark outside and she was clearly reflected in the window. Dumpy, she decided then changed her mind: fat fool was more accurate. There was no longer a paradox. Now she was in a mess both privately and professionally.

The High Court hearing for the Barnett children was in a month's time and the affidavit wasn't ready. The file lay bulging on her desk. If the press ever got wind of it, a spokesman for officialdom would excuse its tangled tale of misery as a regrettable chain of circumstances.

But its contents were safe. Nowadays, a child had to die before social workers hit the headlines. Cut-backs in funding didn't count; nor the reduction in staffing that led to health breakdowns, delays in care proceedings, bungled fostering arrangements and the waiting lists for any kind of therapy.

Too few doing too little for too many, she thought.

She read the reports carefully:

11 p.m. 2nd February – Place of Safety Order granted and Anna and Megan Barnett received into care at Springfields.
16th February – Case Conference. Recommendation that children be made Wards of Court.
28th February – Children warded.
17th March – Directions hearing with registrar – Wardship confirmed. Case set down for hearing.
9th May – First hearing with judge: Welfare reports to be

submitted. Continue interim care and control to Local Authority and discretion over access to allow period of assessment of children and family.

At this point she noted that efforts were still being made to contact the children's father, David Barnett, and reports were still pending on the mother, Sally Barnett.

And now, nearly eleven months later, still nothing had happened.

In June Sally Barnett was given an appointment for 11th August to see Dr Lamb, consultant psychiatrist.

In August Sally Barnett missed her appointment.

And in September an irate David Barnett arrived to demand the custody of his children.

In October a date was set for the High Court hearing: 22nd February.

She sat and stared at her reflection in the window. October had been the start of the downward spiral: Andrew McArdle, their team leader, had gone on extended sick leave and she had 'acted up'; taking on his responsibilities as well as her own case load.

One of those responsibilities was the supervision of Anne Stevens, bright but inexperienced, and the Barnett children's social worker. Maureen had basically left her to get on with it; Anne Stevens had seemed confident and cheerful. Until December, when she had given in her notice. She was overworked she said. Aren't we all? Maureen had snapped.

Would she have resigned, as Anne Stevens did, given the same circumstances? Probably not, but then she had had a better boss in Dick Turner who had taken her out for a drink regularly during her first year. What God didn't give them, you can't. If you remember that, you'll do okay, he said.

She sat there, the reflections of the filing cabinets like miniature tower blocks behind her. I wasn't fair to her, she thought, she deserved better, even though she scared me.

Everything about Anne Stevens was bright and beautiful or had seemed so at the time and simply because she was thin. Maureen knew that no amount of ability or seniority could compete with that and instead of admitting it, she decided that the woman was competent, and needed minimal supervision. Now she had to cope with the backlog of cases caused by Anne's Christmas resignation. They all needed urgent action, at a time when her own case load automatically increased after the holiday. So now she was trying to do interviews and visits during the day and catch up on the paper work at home, even when it meant working till ten at night and most weekends.

Ah well, you're learning the hard way, girl, she thought as she resumed her reading.

David Barnett had been to the office four times yet was described as 'disinterested'. She crossed it out and wrote 'uninterested'. Each visit had been dated and each request for custody of his children had been noted. The school report described Sally Barnett as a caring, concerned mother, actively involved with the PTA; yet the file comment was *unco-operative*. It represented nine months of incompetence on the part of Anne Stevens, exacerbated by her poor supervision.

There were too few details about David Barnett. He was thirty-two, born on 28th June: which made him a Cancerian, she noted. He had been at Sussex University, but there was no mention of his degree course or subsequent work. He was married, with two children, Anna and Megan, aged nine and seven. He had left his wife two years ago and the children had been taken into care a year later. He had moved North and was now self-employed as a toy maker. That was unusual, she thought.

She glanced at the clock above the door as she reached for another biscuit. There were fifteen minutes left before his appointment, barely time to re-check the list of missing details: his parents, siblings, early childhood, degree, jobs, wife's background – all the threads that connected him to

family, friends and society, and without which she was helpless.

One rough note of his first visit of 4th September read:
*Says his childhood was the same as anyone else's. Refused to elabor-
ate. Met his wife at university. Said that everyone else was smarter
and more successful, found college a struggle. Says he is only aver-
age and a plodder.* In the margin was written, *Suspected clinical
depression*; then in the notes, *Refused referral to Dr Lamb.*

You were lucky he only refused and didn't leave you with
your legs knotted behind your neck, she thought. The arro-
gance of the diagnosis irritated her, as well as the change of
tenses. The girl couldn't even write decent English. Why
were there no further details? He had made three more visits
which showed great persistence and determination for someone suspected of clinical depression. More likely it had been
the writer's own accurate self-assessment.

This was David Barnett's fifth visit. Maureen reached for
her notebook and pencilled in the date, 16th January, brushing away biscuit crumbs as they fell.

It would be easy to recommend long-term care, with
limited access, if at all. But if David Barnett didn't care,
why did he come every month? If he did care, why didn't
he talk? And why had an unco-operative mother been a force
in the PTA?

The biscuit packet was empty. She scrunched it and
pushed it into her bulging wastepaper basket. There was
nothing left to eat. She checked her drawers again; then resigned herself. As soon as this interview was over, she would
pop to the nearest supermarket. She lined up her notebook
parallel to her pencil holder and then turned one at right
angles to the other.

Her desk was as far from the door as possible. That couple
of extra seconds clients spent walking across the room gave
her the chance of a little unobtrusive scrutiny.

This was the last appointment in a long day and likely to
be difficult. She was glancing at the clock again when he
knocked.

He wasn't her usual sort of client: he was of medium height, with medium brown hair, and wore a conservative grey suit. His trousers had immaculate creases and his shoes were well polished; the edges as well as the tops. Possibly a new shirt, or very well ironed. A dark tie.

He closed the door carefully behind him and walked towards her, looking at the floor.

'Mr Barnett, I'm Maureen Wilson. You met my predecessor, Mrs Stevens, last time you were here,' stretching her hand across the desk.

'So you are in charge now?' He slumped into the chair, not noticing her hand.

'Yes, for the moment, although there can be no guarantee that I'll be dealing with the case permanently.'

He was sitting with his hands on his knees, palms upward and fingers interlaced, looking at them. She still hadn't seen his eyes.

'I've read your file and there are a few things I'd like to talk about in more detail.'

His mouth stretched from cynicism to resignation.

She ignored it and went on. 'I see from the records that you've been here four times already.'

'Because Social Services won't do anything; so what can I do?'

'Well, I've just taken over, but my first impression is that Social Services can't do anything because they don't know enough.'

'I don't see what more you need to know. I'm their father and I want them back now that I'm able to look after them. There's nothing secret or special about me.'

'Have you always found it hard to talk about yourself?' she asked. There was a pause before he nodded.

'That's all right then, we can start with someone else. What about brothers and sisters?' She couldn't let him off the hook at the outset or the interview would be at an end; and if he mistook kindness for weakness, he'd just clam up.

He nodded again in answer to her question. 'One sister.'

'Older or younger?'

'One year younger.'

'When did you last see her?'

'Twelve years ago, just before I got married.'

'Where was she living?'

'In Wales.'

'Was she married?'

'Yes, she'd got married at seventeen, the year after she left school. She couldn't have done much else. She had no qualifications of any sort.'

'So what was she doing in Wales?'

'She had two children, and was breeding Kashmir goats.'

'Sounds interesting.'

He had been gazing into a corner of the room and turned back and looked at his hands. No, he thought, it wasn't that: half-way up a mountain; no road; her children were running wild, and there were goats everywhere. It never stopped raining, but none of them seemed to mind, except the goats. They were delicate, she said, and rain didn't suit them so they were kept inside. Meals were haphazard. He was staggered when she said they had applied to Social Services to be long-term foster parents, and a social worker had already been out on a preliminary visit and had seemed very happy with them.

'No, it wasn't interesting, it was squalid.'

'Ah. And her husband?'

'A business studies graduate drop-out. He's five years older than Gwen, but just as irresponsible.'

'How long did you stay?'

'Four days. I was glad to leave.'

'What about when you were children? How did you get on then?'

He lifted his head for the first time and stared out of the window. It was dirty, he noticed, the corner of each pane like a Roman serif.

'We didn't. We never got on.'

'What about holidays?'

'They were the worst of all. We usually went back to the North to stay with our grandparents. Gwen, that's my sister, was like my father. She loved the allotment and the pigeon loft and hens and rabbits.'

'And what about you?'

'I hated it.'

He stared at his hands again, seeing the bare ground with the hen and pigeon and rabbit droppings everywhere.

'So was it very different from home?'

'Yes.'

He remembered the outside lavatory with newspapers stabbed on a nail behind the door and the single cold tap in the scullery where his father's unmarried brother used to come in from work every night, strip to the waist and stand with his braces dangling around his knees, getting washed in an enamel dish on an old chair.

He could remember him sloshing the water over his head when he rinsed his face and the snorting noises as his hand groped for the thin hard towel. It puzzled him that his uncle still smelled of sweat, even when he'd been washed and his blue-scarred, greasy white flesh repelled him. He watched with awe as he made a careful parting in his wet hair, first combing it all forward then flattening it on either side, peering into a little mirror that hung from a nail above the sink.

'It was squalid,' he added.

That word again, Maureen noticed. 'And Gwen; how did she get on?'

'She was fine.'

Within a day Bossy Boots had got everyone organised. She was feeding the hens, collecting the eggs, winning approval and playing skippy in the back street. Even there she was in charge, deciding who would run in first and who would turn the rope.

'And you?'

'I just used to sit and watch.'

He slumped at the memory: Does the lad take after his mam, then Jack? and his father saying, Yes, he's the quiet one; but bright, same as her. All his mam's family are bright. They were all made to stick in and it paid dividends; all teachers now; except his mam: and she was due to go to college when I met her. Did I ever tell you that? Well, she was. She doesn't like London much but we're happy enough.

He knew it off by heart.

'So why did your father come to London?'

'He joined the police. He was married during the war and his first wife left him a year after he was demobbed. I suppose the police offered better prospects than the pits and then there was accommodation with the job. He married my mother in 1954.'

'And were they happy?'

'No. My father could never see it, but my mother told me.'

He clenched his teeth at the picture of her sitting on the side of his bed, weeping, her weight pinning him under the blanket: I was going to leave him and then when you came, I had to stay. I had no choice. But it will all be worth it in the end, you'll see . . . kissing him good night, her voice breaking; the bedroom door ajar and the wedge of light from the landing inviting escape; and treachery.

Maureen took a deep breath. 'And your wife: where did you meet her?'

'At college.'

'Was she in your year?'

'Yes, but she read English and History; I did Maths and Computer Science.'

'So how did you meet?'

'At a disco. I bought her a drink and we just talked.' He paused, his eyes unfocused. 'I was happy,' he volunteered simply.

Happy was an understatement. He'd been empowered. There was nothing he couldn't do, nothing he wouldn't achieve for her. She was perfect for him, laughing, always trusting, never worrying. He felt as though he would shed all the cares of his life; even grow wings. He was her prince and for his princess, nothing would be impossible.

'And then what?'

'And then what? I've told you enough already.'

'I'm sorry if you've told all this before but for some reason it's not in the file. What happened after you met your wife?'

He shrugged; then relented. 'We continued to see each other and decided to stay together. I got a job in computers at first and Sally got into the Civil Service. We lived in my flat to begin with. Then when we were married, we scraped together the deposit on a house.' There was a pause. He turned his head slightly and looked at the floor. 'It was very dilapidated, and a bit far to travel, but I felt we were on the ladder.'

'Did Sally?'

'I don't know: she always saw things differently from me.'

'How did you feel?'

'I liked it at first. It was such a change from anything I'd ever known.'

'You said, "at first": so afterwards?'

'Things started to go wrong.'

'Such as?'

'Oh, cooking and housework. We ate takeaways mainly, because we were both working and when I suggested we could take it in turns to cook, she said no, because it would still mean that she had to do it every other night.'

'Ah.' She waited for him to continue.

'When we moved, I repaired and cleaned and decorated best part of the house. I even built a kitchen from DIY units. She said, "Marvellous: what a clever man I've got."' He mimicked her, sneering. 'But the kitchen didn't tempt her to cook.'

He had a memory of sorting a load of washing and putting it into the machine; then bounding upstairs to where she was waiting for him. She was lounging on the bed and said, I'm going to call you Eeyore. It suits you better than Prince.

42

That sounds like demotion.

Don't be silly, darling. Donkeys are very endearing.

Then you're Piglet.

'Sorry, what were you saying?'

'I said, and when you discussed these differences?' Maureen picked up a pen and breathed very gently.

'She wouldn't. She said she was stuck with me, a stodge, and so I would just have to accept her. She would never change to be the person I thought she should be.'

'And did she?'

'What?'

'Did she change?'

'She got pregnant. When she told me and saw my face she just giggled.'

'And you?'

'I was devastated. We weren't ready, we hadn't the money. Worse, she stopped work and then just sat around all day eating peanut butter and bacon sandwiches, or toast and marmite, just letting the house rot.'

He looked at the floor. There was no conflict for Sally. All her energies had always been spent guiltlessly on herself. She was beautiful and loved herself more than anyone. After herself she loved Anna, their first child; her first doll and an excuse for more clothes.

'After Anna was born, how were things then?'

'She did breastfeed her, which surprised me: except that it appealed to the exhibitionist in her, I suppose, but she insisted on disposable nappies. The quantity doubled when Megan arrived, two years later, because Anna wasn't potty trained and Sally refused to be bothered about it. She just said she'd use the toilet when she was ready.'

'So what did you do?'

'I took on extra assignments for the money, and it gave me an excuse to stay late at work. I was making kitchen units by that time and it paid better than computing. I'd enjoyed making our own kitchen and it seemed a natural progression.'

'But the toy making? I thought you made toys?'

'That came later, when there was too much competition in the kitchen unit business.'

'Ah, I see,' she paused. 'So, you had two children and your wife seemed to organise everything to suit herself on a budget beyond your means. How did you feel?'

'Not much at first.'

Except murder, she thought. It's getting late and I'm tired and please don't let him start denying anything. There's so much to sort out.

'That was at first; then what?' she persisted.

'I felt angry most of the time but bottled it up.'

That's more like it, she thought.

'And when the bottle was full?'

'We had rows eventually.'

'When was the first really serious one?'

'Megan's first Christmas.'

'Do you remember what it was about?'

'Yes.'

'Tell me.' That was much too direct but it was nearly the end of the interview and she needed the rest of the background to the marriage breakdown. To her relief, he continued.

'We went to stay with my mother for Christmas. Anna was two and a half and Megan six months. My father was dead by this time and so my mother was living by herself.

He had never mentioned his father's death. She made a mental note underneath 'squalid'.

'When did your father die?'

'The year before, in November. I wanted my mother to stay with us then but couldn't face her reaction to the mess we lived in. The next year I asked if we could go to her for Christmas. I thought it might bring her out of herself and show Sally how a house should be run.'

That would thrill Sally, she thought.

'And what happened?'

'Sally upset my mother.'

'How?'

'She let Anna run wild – and she was breastfeeding Megan.'

'Why did that upset her?'

'Sally just pulled it out anywhere. She enjoyed people's discomfort. My mother was embarrassed. She said it was ignorant and bare-faced cheek. Sally heard her.'

The palms of his hands were sweating at the memory.

Bare-titted is what you mean, Sally yelled. You haven't got any and never had.

Stop shouting at her, Sally; she cannot cope.

She needs to hear, she needs to know what an uptight little boy she's produced.

'So what happened then?'

'Sally yelled at my mother and then we left. She said that it was worse than trying to live in a furniture showroom.'

'What did you think?'

'I was furious. We rowed all the way home. I said Sally was angry because she knew my mother was right about Anna being uncontrollable.'

'And Sally?'

'She said that it was just Anna's natural, intelligent curiosity, not the work of the devil as my Welsh Chapel mother thought. I resented that.'

Sally just sees her as a misery guts, he thought. My mother's strict, but she's fair and honest and hard-working, even if she isn't always laughing like Sally. No, he thought, like Sally used to laugh. How did marriages die before you even realised they were terminally ill? After that Christmas there had been nothing there except the two children and now, not even them. He was soaked in misery. He stared at the window and closed his eyes.

'We'll have to leave it there for today, Mr Barnett; but I have a suggestion and I'd like you to think about it. It would mean finding somewhere to stay near here, or at least within a day's journey.'

'That's all right, I'm staying with my mother here in London.'

'For how long?'

'Another month, maybe six weeks; until the worst of the winter up North is over.'

Maureen Wilson leaned back in her chair and weighed her words carefully. She threaded her pen between her fingers and said slowly, 'As you know, there is going to be a full hearing in the High Court in about a month's time. The Social Services will be applying for care and control of Anna and Megan. If it's granted, it could last until they're eighteen.'

She twirled the pen slowly backwards and forwards, weighing her words again. 'If you could come once a week until then, I'd be in a better position to assess your claim; if you're serious about wanting the children, that is.'

He looked up. 'You mean?'

'No, it's not a promise. All I'm saying is this: I'll be dealing with your case, and if you want a fair hearing I need to know everything I can about you.'

'And who else will need to know?'

'Apart from your solicitor and barrister, only a probation officer who'll be making a Welfare Report to the court. You'll see a lot of me before the case comes up but there's only five weeks; and if you want me to help you, you'll have to work with me.' She nearly said 'trust', but stopped herself.

He sighed, a short breath down his nostrils that betrayed his anger.

'I've got no choice really.'

'Oh, you have. Be very clear about that,' she said quickly. 'You have two choices: either you can continue to make demands without giving us any good reason why we should grant them, and then spend the rest of your life blaming us for losing your children; or you can try my suggestion.'

'And I still might lose them?'

'Yes, you might. It's like anything you try: you have fifty

per cent chance of failure and an equal chance of success. And if you don't try, you have a hundred per cent guarantee of failure.'

She knew she was being pompous. She could feel herself flushing and hear her voice getting too loud. It would be the final irony to have got this far with him and then wreck the whole session just because she was tired. After thirty years she should be used to this sort of attitude.

It was the usual cop-out; and now that they had reached the crunch, it looked as though Dave Barnett was going to take it.

Damn him; I'm not his fairy godmother, and if I had a magic wand, I'd rustle up . . . there was a moment's hesitation . . . I'd rustle up a hot pork pie.

She brought herself back to Dave Barnett, her brief resentment gone. She sat, quite still, re-centred and focused on him.

'I think I've always been scared to try for things in case I wouldn't get them,' he said quietly.

She closed her eyes and smiled inwardly. It was more than she had hoped for.

He sat, lost in the memories of his mother's hopes for him: a First, like his Uncle Owen; then a Ph.D.: dreams beyond his ability. Then there was Sally. And in the end, she'd been just the same. She had expected him to be some sort of wonder man as well. He had failed as her Prince and been demoted to playing Eeyore. He looked directly at Maureen Wilson for the first time.

'I've always been a coward,' he said with resignation.

'And who do you think are the heroes?' she asked very gently.

'People who aren't afraid, I suppose.'

'Oh, I think they are. I think they're even more afraid and still do what has to be done, in spite of it. That's why heroism gets medals. You can't qualify as a hero unless you've been afraid.'

He looked down. She remained very still, hoping he

would understand what she had said, understanding the opportunity it offered.

She sat quietly for a few more seconds. This was the last step, and the timing, the tone, were crucial. She took a long breath and said steadily, 'So shall we meet again next week?' hoping it betrayed no expectation of refusal, and yet did not sound as though his acceptance was a foregone conclusion. 'I'm sorry to have to hurry it like this but the interview has run over time and the caretaker will be waiting to lock up.'

He sat, looking at his hands again. She found herself holding her breath and forced herself to exhale slowly. Then quite suddenly he said: 'Will it be at the same time each week?'

'Yes, it could be, if that would suit you.'

'That would be all right.'

They both rose and she put out her hand.

'Thank you,' he said and took it; then turned and left the room.

As soon as he had gone, she sat down again. The tip of her tongue was curled to the roof of her mouth and she breathed out deeply, rilling the air through her teeth before letting her mouth drop open and allowing her clenched jaws to relax.

She could have done better, she decided, but at least she had made a start and had the reprieve of a second appointment in which to improve. With good management there might be another two after that, before she lodged her affidavit with the court.

She pulled her notebook towards her and wrote rapidly; *squalid – twice – mother? father's death skimmed, Gwen – v. independent. Mother's influence on David considerable.* She added *unhealthy?* but crossed it out.

It was beginning to take shape, but she wouldn't presume to know it all until she saw Sally Barnett. She held the missing pieces, but that was tomorrow's work. If the records were correct, Dave Barnett had walked out on his wife and children and had simply disappeared for three months without a trace. Sally Barnett's statement said that he had left no forwarding address or contact number. Now he said he cared but he certainly hadn't cared then. And he hadn't asked how they were. He'd never mentioned them! He'd presented Sally as being uncaring and irresponsible, but what about him? The next meeting would be more painful. She would have to ask these questions and he would have to answer.

But with hard work, it could still be sorted out in time for next month's hearing.

Satisfied that she had noted key facts and queries, she tore the page off the top of the pad and put it in the front of the Barnett file, then locked it in the cabinet.

In the cloakroom she wrapped her scarf twice round her neck and tucked the ends into her coat.

She melted at the thought of going home. Her little flat would be waiting for her, warm and cosy; and puss yowling and winding himself around her ankles. It was the sum total of all she had worked for.

An icy rain storm was waiting outside, the thin sharp lances glittering diagonally in the street lights. She put up her umbrella; then raced for her car, her short legs spread wide as she skipped across the puddles.

FOUR

Maggie Jowett turned wearily from the Aga. 'What's the use of grumbling when it's your own fault for letting the diesel run out?' He was at it again, 'on the winge', she called it.

'I doubt we'll have to milk by hand,' he said again.

'Of course we'll have to milk by hand, unless you're planning to do it by foot.'

The generator had stopped at lunch time when the diesel was finished. The television had gone off during *News At One*. So now they had no electricity, so no milking machine as well as no TV, and now a Tilley light to be carted everywhere.

'This happens every rotten winter. You let the diesel get down instead of getting the tank filled before the weather sets in.'

'I thought we could take a chance on it. The snow didn't look as if it would lie.'

'In the middle of January?' she snorted. 'It's here for weeks and well you know it. If you don't know by now that we're always snowed up from early January till at least the middle of March, solid, then you need your head looking at.'

He said nothing and they set off, one behind the other, across the yard to the byre, each with a Tilley light.

He hasn't even the list to dig a path more than a spade's width, she thought to herself. He's getting old.

'They'll not take kindly to it, I doubt,' he said as he hung his lantern above the first stall and stood gazing at the cow's udders.

'They've not got much choice, have they, poor beasts? It's either this or bust. The sooner we start, the sooner we'll be finished.' She stomped over to fill a bucket and start washing them down. He stood, wondering why the weather had suddenly turned so hard. The first wet snow had frozen and this lot was dry and powdery.

God give me strength. He's like something from another planet, she thought, turning round and seeing him standing. He must have got dumped off by a visiting UFO. They knew what they were doing. Joan always said they were more intelligent than earthlings. He must have failed their entrance exam. She moved to the next stall. 'There, get started; Julia's ready. I'll wash Betsy. Come on, man, get a move on or we'll be here all night.'

'All right,' he muttered and squatted down at Julia's rear. He gripped her teats and began pulling and squeezing; then stopped abstractedly. Julia shifted uneasily.

After all these years and he's still cack-handed at milking. She was so exasperated that she was on the point of saying: Come on, I'll swap you: you wash them down and I'll milk; although it would kill her arm; when Julia lifted her tail.

'Mind!' she yelled.

Too late. He was covered as the liquid dung squirted out horizontally and Julia swiped her tail twice across his face in case she'd missed a bit.

'I'll have to get myself cleaned up,' he said, getting to his feet.

'Why don't you just go into the yard and take off your clothes and roll in the snow like they do in Finland and them places?'

He turned at the door to look at her. She was a bloody queer woman, a mystery to him. There was nowhere to hang a Tilley light in the yard so how would he see? Besides, he'd get his death of cold. She was definitely going soft in the head. It was old age.

That day, Karin stirred occasionally. Each time, she reached for the bottle of water without opening her gummed eyelids, resting it on the edge of the sofa and tilting it very carefully to allow a sip at a time to trickle into her mouth. She finished by pursing her lips in the top of the bottle and tipping it up until they were wet, before lowering it carefully to the floor again.

The fever had leached her. She no longer knew where she was or how she got there. That day, all that was left was the knowledge of the water bottle and her small remaining store of energy was rationed to taking a sip and wetting her lips whenever she woke.

The next day she stayed awake for a little longer. Now she could remember that there was a tap in the kitchen and that was where she had found the bottle.

All her limbs, and her head, still ached. Her chest still exploded like a Catherine wheel if she breathed too deeply, but she wasn't cold any more, nor sweating, and her throat felt better. The bed was quite comfortable, and there was no one shouting at her to get up and no one trying to make her do anything. It was all right here, wherever it was. She wasn't well, she knew that, but if she could just stay where she was for a bit, she'd be okay.

On the third morning, she started to pull the crust off her eyelids, rubbing a wetted finger along each, picking off small crumbs, pulling the bigger ones down through her eye lashes until she had broken the seal and could open her eyes.

From where she lay she could see two open doors. The first, she knew, led into the kitchen. Light was stretching from somewhere beyond the far one.

Maybe an outside door was open, but she wasn't cold. It must be warm outside.

She lay for a while, trying to work out how to move. She tried to lift her legs and couldn't. Her arms weren't much better. It was all she could do to reach for the water bottle. She would have to think about that; and soon. There wasn't much water left.

It must be summer, she decided as she drifted off again. It was very hot.

The terror returned. At first, he approached slowly, from behind, from where he could not be seen. But she knew him, recognised her old dread. She had to keep moving, keep ahead of him. He was always only one corner behind her. If she stopped he would catch her. Worse, she was lost.

She had once known these streets but now either they had changed or she had forgotten them. Here and there was a familiar turning, once, a corner shop she knew, but each time it was followed by a long line of alien houses and blank-faced people standing in front of them, staring at her. She saw a woman standing, planted in a doorway, her arms folded across her chest, and raced towards her in relief to hide behind her. But it wasn't Mrs Taylor, and the woman leaned against her closed front door, blocking her refuge. Along the side of the house was an assortment of broken toys and old cars. Thankfully, she climbed into one and crouched, listening, trying to get her breath back. Then the car door opened and she scrambled across the seats to the other side, groping for the handle, opening this door, still ahead, still winning; until the door was slammed behind her, like a gin-trap and she hung, suspended by one leg. Inside the car was laughter and all the people from the houses joined in. There were screams of delight as she pulled at her leg; then crawled away, dragging her stump and leaving a spreading pool of blood behind her.

The artificial limb centre was in a bus station behind a flimsy curtain. Someone took a cast of her remaining leg; then presented her with an identical artificial limb.

But that means I've got two right legs.

It's the best we can do: there's a shortage of left 'uns.

Aw, all right then: just give me a wooden one and two aspirins.

You'll have to be quick; you're on next.

The curtain was pulled aside to reveal a nativity play and a stage filled with children in angels' costumes.

Where's Mary? a voice boomed and the limb fitter pushed her forward.

Jean Caspar was perched on a stool and as she was wearing bigger wings than everyone else, Karin knew she must be the Angel Gabriel. She looked down her nose to her joined hands and hissed, What are *you* doing here, Karin Thompson?

No good asking me; I don't know; I'm supposed to be at PE.

Have you lost your strip again?

No, one of my legs.

Well you can't be Mary with one leg; and where's baby Jesus?

I don't know. Our Debbie's in the wings. She'll do.

How can she, she's a girl? And anyway, she's too big – how'll you carry her on?

I'll think of sommat. It's either her or her Barbie doll and that's so small they'll wonder where the incubator is. Aw Jean, be a pal and think of sommat to say while I go and fetch our Debbie. I can hide her under my dress and walk back on.

I can't do that: I've learned my lines now.

Aw go on, or I'll be in trouble.

You're never in owt else. Oh, all right then. She straightened up, spread her arms wide and pursed her lips. Behold; I bring you glad tidings. Today is born to you a saviour who is in an incubator and will be arriving shortly.

Mrs Taylor wiped tears of laughter from her face and tilted her chair back, squealing and screeching as she fell over. Karin groaned.

A solemn procession of school governors, led by the headmaster, approached the stage.

Go and take those earrings out and come back with Jesus, he ordered.

She blundered into the wings. What'm I going to do? I never had a Jesus.

The artificial limb man was reassuring. I've got a cardboard cut-out. I can sellotape it into place.

And what about my wooden leg?

No problem. As soon as the nativity play's finished, rehearsals start for the panto. It's *Treasure Island* so you can be Long John Silver. He arranged the cut-out doll on her shoulder. I'll just give it a few feathers and then all you have to do is turn it round to be a parrot.

Ee, I would never have thought of that.

Well, you have to be flexible. That's the first rule, the only way to survive, isn't it?

She groped her way back on to the stage, clutching the cardboard infant on her shoulder and faced the audience.

That's her. His voice rang out from the back of the hall. I know because I've got her leg here and if you try it, you'll see that it fits.

You've no right to have my leg. Give it back, she yelled into the darkness.

What's it worth to you?

I cannot give you anything more; you know that.

Well, I'll just have to have Debbie as well, won't I?

And the audience murmured in agreement.

She woke with a start, craning her neck to see the back of the audience; then realised what she had done. She slowly lifted her legs. She grinned and her top lip split, but she didn't mind. She lifted her arms above her head and lowered them until they touched the arm of the sofa behind her. She had no pain now, except for her throat: and the remaining ping-pong ball there was shrinking.

She sat up slowly, swung her legs down the side of the sofa, stood up and promptly collapsed.

Aw, bugger; it'll have to be hands and knees again. And she set off as she'd arrived, walking the water bottle with one hand and the candle in the other.

She was half-way across the room when she saw it: a wooden mouse on wheels. It had huge black eyes and a cheeky little grin. She laughed.

I'll collect you on my way back: promise!

She came back from the kitchen with the mouse in tow. She propped the bottle of water carefully near the arm of the sofa and rolled back onto the cushions, still clutching the string of the wooden toy.

Karin Thompson, you must be going mad. Mebbe it's the water, she giggled.

She'd have a sleep, she thought, then try sitting up again. She'd been all right sitting up, it was just standing that was the problem. Funny that, because she was a good runner. They put her in the school sports every year if she was there. The PE teacher said she could be in the school team; maybe even represent the North of England if she behaved herself. But she had to miss all the practices after school.

She had to be at home, to be there when the minibus dropped Debbie off; and she couldn't explain to anyone. There was a brief unguarded memory of Debbie hugging Mrs Dobson, the bus driver; then waving at the other children and standing, clutching her bag of wet knickers, still waving after the bus had turned the corner out of sight. She shut it out.

Training, that's what she'd do to get herself walking again. She knew enough to do it. Nobody had ever said she was thick, only badly behaved. She was cleverer than girls who had gone on to do GCSEs; some of the boys as well. The cleverest delinquent I've ever met, one teacher said.

But she couldn't train on an empty belly. Even Superman probably sneaked a hamburger when he was putting his knickers on top of his tights in the telephone box.

That had been a great night! Her and Debbie and Tracy and Tracy's mam had all gone to see Superman and just as he stepped out of the phone box, Tracy's mam said, If I tried that here, he'd be arrested, and laughed that great big laugh of hers.

Tracy and her had nearly weed themselves. It was better than the film.

Tracy's mam wasn't like a mam really, not like hers, anyway. Tracy called hers Supermam. Mebbe she was the way that mams were supposed to be. She wasn't fussy whether the house was clean or not. That made Karin feel better straight away about her own house and the mess it was in. Tracy's mam only bothered about things that made them happy. Being happy was a better way of spending your time than being clean, she said. Eating was important for being happy, so she cooked. The memory of Mrs Taylor's chips whetted Karin's appetite. If only her mam . . . She stopped herself again.

It was getting dark. The chips could wait. She wouldn't die of starvation for one more night.

The sofa was deep and when she sat with her back resting against it, her legs were sticking straight out over the edge. I'm like Minnie Mouse, she thought as she took off her boots. Soon her eyelids began to close and she slowly slipped sideways until her cheek was resting on the seat. She snuggled down under the tartan rug.

First thing tomorrow she'd have to start training so she could get up and get a drink whenever she wanted one and have a look round and find something to eat. Once she was busy, she wouldn't have time to think and then she'd be all right.

But it wasn't too bad, even now. She was getting better and for the moment, she was safe. Soon she'd be fit again and then she'd be free.

FIVE

Maureen threaded her way skilfully through the morning traffic swirling round Archway; then turned off Holloway Road and made her way past Hornsey Road to Muswell Grove. Job advertisements usually described the area as lively. What they meant was that there were thriving yuppie settlements shoulder to shoulder with pockets of poverty, alienation and loneliness. She had got used to reading house fronts.

Most of Muswell Grove Road was respectable. Occasionally there was a house without a well-painted front door and window frames, and with the tiny patch of grass overgrown; but very few.

Number 23 was still cared for; just. The paintwork was ready for renewal and the grass needed cutting, but someone had bothered with it until quite recently. The doors and windows were dark green. The house front had been rendered, and painted eau-de-Nil. The garden railings and the wrought-iron handrail leading up the steps to the front door were also dark green. They had been painted with a textured, metallic, rust-proof paint.

Not her taste, Maureen decided, but then maybe not Sally Barnett's either.

She rang the huge brass bell in the centre of the door and

satisfied that it was working, moved down two steps so as not to seem threatening.

There was no answer. She could be out, of course.

She rang again. She might be in the garden. It was worth a try. These houses had long back gardens but no access except through the house. She rang the left-hand neighbour's bell and a neat, elderly woman came to the door.

'I'm trying to get in touch with Mrs Barnett and I wondered if she was in her garden and couldn't hear me. It's such a lovely day, she might have been tempted outside.'

The woman smiled, 'Oh yes, isn't it? Almost like spring. We've both been tempted. Yes, she's outside, or was, just a moment ago, because I saw her picking jasmine. Would you like to come through and have a word with her over the fence, or shall I tell her that you're here?'

Ah, difficult one, this. Sally Barnett couldn't be expected to talk with a neighbour hovering around, but would she come to the door if she knew who the caller was?

'Would you ask her to come out? I believe she has a room to let and I would like to see if it is still available.'

'Yes, of course. Who shall I say?'

'My name is Maureen Wilson.'

She returned to the steps of Number 23. The January sun was so welcome, she thought, as it penetrated the back of her coat with its thin warmth.

Her face was cold. She wanted to turn it to the sun but didn't want to risk presenting her back to Sally Barnett.

In the garden, Mrs Jolly delivered Maureen's message.

'She's quite mistaken, Mrs Jolly. I've never advertised a room to let.'

'Well perhaps you should go and tell her, my dear. It's not really any business of mine.'

Sally Barnett laid the branches of jasmine on the kitchen table and walked into the hall.

The caller could be anyone, a con for a burglar, anything;

a double glazing saleswoman: or she might simply be mistaken and be in the wrong road or at the wrong number.

She opened the door. It was part of Sally Barnett's inheritance to be thin and long legged. Generations of men in her father's family had been the same and like her, they had all been tall.

She had a sallow skin which complemented her faded mousy hair and left huge brown eyes to distract attention from a very small and unattractive down-turned mouth.

She is too old for that face now, Maureen thought, and much too old for a pale pink tracksuit. She smiled, 'Mrs Barnett? I'm Maureen Wilson. I'd appreciate it if I could talk to you. If it isn't convenient at the moment, perhaps we could arrange another time?'

She was from Social Services, Sally Barnett knew that, and not just because the woman knew her name. It was something about her: a firmness, a confidence that came from years of dealing with people. And a courtesy. At least she wasn't standing on her toes on the top step. And at least she was discreet: she hadn't said anything to Mrs Jolly. She didn't look angry and Sally knew she would have to face it some time: so why not now?

'Come in. I'm free at the moment so we might as well talk now.' She stood aside as Maureen reached the top of the steps. 'Just go through the hall, the kitchen's at the end. It's the warmest place.'

It was filled with the scent of jasmine. The branches were lying on the table, each blossom a tiny flake of light in the dark, north-facing kitchen. Dark and cluttered: that was the best description. The jasmine was lying among crumbs, two pots of marmalade and half a wholemeal loaf. There were two newspapers and a magazine and the top of one of the marmalade jars was sticking out of a book.

Maureen's first instinct was to cut herself a slice of bread and dollop some marmalade on it before Sally Barnett joined her; but she restricted herself to licking a finger and picking up a few breadcrumbs on its tip.

Although clutter overflowed from every surface, not all of it was rubbish. There was an exquisite porcelain bowl on the dresser: Famille Rose, she guessed. It held rubber bands and paperclips and several keys. A volume of Milton's *Paradise Lost* was tilted dangerously against it, threatening to push it over the edge. Protruding from it at an odd angle was an airmail letter. She could only make out part of the address: Booligal, New South Wales. *Grimm's Fairy Tales* and a book of verse for children were lying on one of the chairs. They hadn't been planted; Sally Barnett didn't know she was coming. They must have been there for nearly a year. It was only a scrutiny of seconds before she joined Maureen.

'Sit down. Would you like tea or coffee? Can you find a seat? Just move those magazines.'

But where? She lifted the pile and finally balanced them precariously on the dresser, propping them with a jar of apricot conserve that was growing a vigorous green mould.

'Tea please.'

'Tea bag, Earl Grey or I've got some China somewhere?'

'Earl Grey.'

'I haven't any lemon.'

'That's all right. I usually drink it just as it is, but preferably very weak.'

Sally Barnett made it in a small, wicker-handled teapot; then got a delicately fluted china cup and saucer from the dresser cupboard. She put a spoonful of instant coffee in a mug and joined Maureen at the table, balancing the mug on top of one of the newspapers.

'Oh, I'll just put the jasmine in water before I forget. I love the scent. It reminds me of Kenya!' She filled an empty wine carafe, inserted the five stems; then brought it back to the table, easing the loaf of bread out of the way to make room for it. Maureen deftly uprighted one of the marmalade jars.

'Oh thanks; there's a lid somewhere,' Sally Barnett said as she sat down. She looked directly at Maureen, 'You're from

62

Social Services. Mm, I thought so. So where do you want to start?'

Maureen sipped her tea. 'I don't mind; just wherever you feel most comfortable.'

'Have you seen Dave?' she asked sharply.

'Once, yesterday.'

'So I suppose he's told you all about me?'

'No, not really. We talked mostly about himself.'

'I'm surprised. I thought he would have had a good long moan.'

So it wasn't just him. She hadn't mentioned the children either. She could have been expected to open the conversation with, have you seen Anna and Megan? Are they all right? But no, it was, Have you seen Dave? and unless the file was incomplete, she'd never made an application to visit them.

She sipped her tea again. 'I've just taken this case over from another social worker who left and I was struck that in a year of reports from everyone, there was very little about yourself. I wondered if you'd had much of a chance to talk to anyone?'

'I haven't been away, if that's what you mean.'

'So did anyone call from the office?'

'Yes, once. I was in bed with a migraine one morning and had just been sick when the doorbell rang. It wouldn't stop. She must have been standing there with her back to the door, leaning on the bell with her elbow, looking up and down the street to fill in time while she was waiting. She announced she was from Social Services and in a hurry.'

'And?'

'I just said that in that case, she could hurry away because I didn't feel like talking.'

'And did she?'

'She apologised and started to blather. I just interrupted her and said if she didn't leave, I'd help her out. She probably thought I'd been drinking and might get violent because I was swaying on my feet. Anyway, she left.'

63

That sounds like dear Anne, Maureen thought. 'Did she ever come back again?'

'No, or at least, never when I was here.'

She had probably been scared witless. There was a momentary sympathy; then almost a smile, as she remembered her own early days on tiptoes, standing on doorsteps with one foot turned out, ready to run.

'Is your tea cold? Tip it out if it is and pour yourself another cup.

'Here . . .' She reached across the table, got the cup and tossed the slops carelessly into the sink behind her; then put it back onto the saucer.

'Thanks.' Maureen poured herself another cup, wishing there was the offer of a biscuit. Obviously Sally Barnett wasn't a biscuit fiend. She probably didn't eat cake or sweets either.

'So that's the only contact you've had with Social Services since the girls were taken into care?'

'Yes.'

Maureen sat looking at her tea, then the jasmine; waiting.

Sally Barnett sat idling her finger around the handle of her coffee mug. 'I do care about them, you know. Just because I haven't been in touch doesn't mean that I don't care.'

'Yes, I know that.'

'How can you know that? How can you know anything?'

Maureen's reply was slow and quiet. 'I know you used to help a lot at school. If you hadn't cared, you wouldn't have done that. And as well as that, I think it's possible to care so much that you feel too helpless to do anything about it.'

'Yes,' she said slowly, 'that's it: that's it exactly.' She gave a long sigh, then said, 'Because I know I was a good mother.' She stopped, tried to say something further, and without warning tears started to rain onto the table in front of her. There were great stomach-heaving sobs and she put her head on her arms and howled.

Maureen sat in silence until the first rush of sobbing subsided. When Sally Barnett began to cry more steadily, she got up very carefully, walked over to the sink and refilled the kettle.

Sally blew her nose. 'I'm sorry about that.'

'That's all right,' Maureen replied, sitting down again and easing the mug of coffee towards her. She watched as she took a tiny sip and put the mug back on the table, cradling it with both hands.

'I –' she began. 'Oh, what's the point? What difference does it make? You know everything already.'

'Not really.'

'Does it matter?'

Maureen didn't answer.

'I'm not sure if talking won't make things worse. Anyway, I don't know where to start.' She blew gently into her coffee. 'I told you I was born in Kenya?'

'No, you said that the jasmine reminded you of Kenya.'

'Ah, well I was. My father was a planter. My mother played bridge. She . . . Look –' There was a sudden anger in her voice, 'I don't want to talk about any of this; not about me, not about anyone – okay? I shouldn't have started. I shouldn't have let you in.' She was almost shouting.

Maureen got up and fished in her bag and put her card on the table. 'That's all right. If you want to get in touch, give me a ring at the office.' She hesitated for a moment. 'I'm sorry, but could I just use your loo before I go?'

Sally Barnett forced herself to say calmly, 'Yes, of course. Up the stairs, first on the right.'

'Thanks. I'll let myself out.'

There was no reply. She was sitting winding a piece of hair around her finger, staring at the coffee.

Upstairs, Maureen shook her hands dry and thought, well, no worse than a public lavatory.

When she came down, Sally Barnett was waiting for her in the hall.

'I didn't intend to be rude just then. It's just that, well, part of me wants to talk and another part of me is so angry when strangers think they have a right to turn up on my doorstep and –'

'You mean me? Of course I have a right to call on you, the same as you have a right to refuse to talk to me.' She turned towards the front door.

'Just a moment,' Sally said and hesitated, 'I might as well tell you everything now, if you have time, that is. Have you?'

An hour later they came out of the kitchen again.

'You've still got my card? Give me a ring if anything crops up. If I don't hear from you, I'll come next Wednesday, in the morning. And if I ring and get no answer, I won't lean my elbow on the bell. I'll assume a migraine and let you contact me.'

Sally Barnett smiled for the first time.

'Don't worry. I don't get migraines very often; and if anything crops up, I'll let you know in advance and save you a trek.'

Maureen stood on the steps and turned her face up to the sun, now at its best. The air was sparkling, even here in London. She took a long deep breath and smiled; then walked down the steps, and turned right out of the gate and along the pavement, to where she had parked her car discreetly at the end of the road.

Inside, she settled to make rapid notes:

Born in Kenya. Only child. Mau Mau movement 4 years old and security precautions very tight. Sent to boarding school in England at 6. Parents came to England later same year when independence agreed for Kenya. Won a bursary at 13 – enabled her to continue her education. Her father inherited money from his mother which he invested in the commodities market and lost. Trust fund set up for Sally that could not be touched until she was 21.

Read English and History at Sussex where she met Dave Barnett. Married him a year later. Father died same year, 5 months after being declared bankrupt. Mother re-married and went to live in Australia. Anna born following year. Megan born two years later – marriage already in trouble.

She opened a bar of chocolate and sat, brooding over the interview. At one point Sally Barnett said, It's all so obvious now. If I'd had as much foresight as hindsight, none of this blasted mess would have happened.

It might have been different and it might have been worse, she replied.

Sally Barnett spun round. That makes me sound like a complete idiot and lucky to have only a broken marriage and two children in care.

I didn't mean that, she said.

But I did, she thought; that's exactly what I meant. I don't like the woman. What does she do with her trust fund income? She looks a mess and the house is a pigsty. Why did Dave Barnett have to work overtime to keep them all? It doesn't add up. But at least there was food in the house, she thought with relief. So maybe the report had been wrong. Maybe Anne Stevens had exaggerated? The food was stale, true, but it was there and better than nothing.

She started the car, checked her driving mirror and pulled out.

Sally Barnett watched her from behind the lounge curtain until she disappeared from view; then went back to the kitchen and took a bottle of gin out of the bottom of the dresser. She found that morning's tumbler on the draining board and poured herself a triple. She did get migraines; she hadn't told lies. She just hadn't told everything and that was going to be the problem. She began to cry again.

Maureen Wilson couldn't possibly know the whole story or she wouldn't have been so nice. By next week she would have found out everything. Then she'd tell her what she thought of her. She couldn't face that. She'd have to ring her office and say that she had changed her mind and didn't want to see her again. Maureen Wilson wouldn't be able to say anything, because it was she who had offered her the choice in the first place.

SIX

The next morning, Karin sat up almost as soon as she woke. Encouraged by this, she held the side of the sofa and stood up; wobbled for a couple of seconds; then sat down again.

I'm getting good at this, she said to the mouse as she set off again on hands and knees to the kitchen.

She wanted a drink, a big drink, and lots of drinks from now on; then she would pee properly. She must have narrowly avoided being dehydrated, she thought.

Mr Littleburn had gone on once about people lost in deserts or shipwrecked. He said that some of them had to drink their own urine to survive. There was uproar in class and yells of, Ugh, Sir, and some of the lads made jokes and refused to repeat them and were sent to the Year Head.

That quietened them, and he continued: Yes, people have survived by drinking their own urine. Does anyone know why that is better than drinking sea water?

Jean Caspar put her hand up.

Yes, Jean.

Please, Sir, is it because you don't want to drink all the fish pee?

There was another roar from the class.

That's an interesting point, Jean, but can anyone tell me

what else is in sea water, something that makes it easy to swim in the sea?

NaCl, Karin muttered.

What? asked Tracy.

Salt.

Go on, tell him, then.

You can tell him; and Tracy put her hand up.

Stop talking, Karin Thompson. Yes, Tracy?

Salt, Sir.

Yes; good girl: salt. Thank you very much, Tracy. As well as increasing buoyancy, salt increases thirst and dehydration.

Again she drank an extra half-pint at the sink before filling the bottle. Her throat wasn't hurting any more and swallowing was easy.

Back at the sofa, she lay and worked out her strategy. How long had she been here? She knew she'd set out for London on 15th January. She had probably been ill for three or four days. If today was the fifth day, it was 20th January. She would have to go before next weekend. No, it was impossible. She'd never be fit enough to leave by then. Couldn't. Not a matter of couldn't. She would have to: it was no good moaning. Life was never what she wanted. It was just what it was and she would have to get on with it. Once she was in London, she'd be okay.

Right, no time to waste. Up you get, you lazy bugger, get your candle and bottle.

She drained the rest of the water and set off again.

In the kitchen she collected more candles, a tin-opener and cutlery from one of the drawers and reached for a mug and plate from a cupboard.

There were only two other cupboards. He might have taken all the food and gone to stay in a caravan, even in the middle of winter. Some people were daft enough to do anything. She knew that from experience. There had been that field trip with Mr Littleburn in Northumberland last February. It sleeted down all the time, and they were soaked; and

Mr Littleburn kept saying that if they made up their minds they could still enjoy it.

By the end of the third day, no one had any dry clothes left and Mr Littleburn had lost his voice. Tracy told him that none of them would mind if he just cancelled the rest of the week and went home, even though they had paid for it: just in case he got really ill. It was a master move and they all cheered when he whispered for a show of hands and it was unanimous.

We're just worried about you, Sir. We're tough, younger than you, Sir. They had nearly trampled each other to death to get on the bus.

Sir, were you ever shipwrecked? Tracy asked him. He shook his head.

Aw, it was just that I was wondering why you enjoyed it with the sleet and everything and being wet all the time and cold. I thought if you'd been shipwrecked, then it still wasn't as bad as drinking your own pee, like.

They all roared with laughter and Mr Littleburn managed a thin smile.

Both cupboards were full of tins, neatly stacked in sections, but there were no baked beans; he must have taken those with him, the greedy bugger.

Karin mooched through and decided to open the chicken in white sauce and the peas. It would have been better with some tomato sauce but she could look for that tomorrow. Half-way through, she felt full. I'll take the rest of it back with me and have it later.

She melted the bottom of a new candle onto the saucer and, pushing that with one hand and the remains of her meal with the other, she set off back to the sofa.

She dozed for a while and when she woke, it was dark. She lit the candle and finished the food. If you were real, I'd feed you as well. The mouse regarded her solemnly, his eyes gleaming in the candlelight.

Back on the sofa, she felt satisfied with her day. She was in charge again, making the best of things, getting better; and tomorrow she'd walk because she'd decided to, and she had always been able to do whatever she'd decided had to be done.

By the second day without diesel, Maggie Jowett, thankful that the paraffin tank was still more than half full, had quickly adjusted her routine to the Tilley lights. She lit them both by torchlight; then, once it was daylight, refilled them and cleaned them, ready for the evening.

Despite her arm, she did the milking out of sympathy for the cows. She could barely move it by the time she had finished. There was no point in going to the doctor's with it. He'd only give her some fancy sort of aspirin and tell her she was growing old. Then, like as not, he'd probably ask after Mansell. 'Not growing at all,' she muttered to herself. 'Stunted from birth.'

'What's stunted? What are you talking about, woman? None of the ewes have lambed yet?'

'It was nowt for your ears, pet.'

He padded round uneasily. 'Pet': there was something up. 'Have you heard owt from our Joan recently?'

'Why are you asking?'

'I was just wondering, that's all.'

She had got a letter last week and had hidden it in the old blanket box. She had read it until she knew it off by heart:

Dear Mam & Dad,

How are you? I was watching the Weather for Farmers today and saw the snow forecast for the North. I always think of you when the weather is bad.

I want you to come for half term. I know it's difficult for you to get away at this time of the year, and it is cold travelling, but I have a very special reason for wanting you to come;

*and the enclosed cheque is for train tickets so you don't have
to sit for hours on a draughty bus.*

*Not much news here. We are nearly two weeks into the
new term and the timetable is working well.*

*Nothing much else happening. The Operatic Society met
last week to decide on our next production and narrowed it
down to three but didn't make a final decision.*

No more for now. I hope you are both OK.

Much love, as always.

Joan

The letter wasn't dated. She could show it to him later. That
bit – *but I have a very special reason for wanting you to come* –
that had jumped out as soon as she'd read it. Then Mansell
had come in from the yard before she'd had time to think
about it so she'd stuffed it quickly into her overall pocket.

I saw the post come. Did he bring owt?

Just one of them gift catalogues. Here, have a look at it; I
haven't got time.

The post Land Rover had called twice since then; giving
her two chances to produce the letter and say that Joan had
written. Why hadn't she? To punish him, she thought. To
get my own back for being stuck on this God-forsaken farm
and thinking myself lucky to get down to the village once a
week.

It hadn't been so bad two years ago when she'd helped
Dave Barnett with his office work. Then someone sent an
account back because she'd made a mistake and he said he'd
have to check through all the others. And shortly after that,
he said his business wasn't going so well and he didn't need
her any more. It might just have been an excuse to get rid of
her. Funny lad, she still knew nowt about him after working
for him for more than a year. He'd say good morning or
good afternoon, tell her what to do and leave her to get on.
He never asked how she was; never said anything that wasn't
connected with work. And she'd never asked questions. It
was more than her job was worth. He'd never said as much,

73

but he didn't need to: he had that way about him. He was cold.

Compared with him, Mansell was just soft, no, mindless, she decided: There's never a birthday or an anniversary present; only a fiver shoved into my hand at Christmas and being told to get something for myself. And as far as he's concerned, that's enough. I'm mean with him, I know, but there's no encouragement to be kind.

Joan got where she is thanks to me. If I'd listened to him, she'd have left school at sixteen, worked in a shop; then been married at seventeen to a lad at the foundry with no prospects and no security.

She wasn't talking about getting married, was she? That wasn't what she meant by a very special reason, was it? What would a lass in her position want with getting married? Besides, she'd promised: Mam, as soon as I get a bit bigger flat, you can come and stay for as long as you want.

It had been a freezing November day at the coach station. She had turned to Joan and said, The time's always too short, love; I hardly get here before it's time to go back. And then Joan said it, she *had*: she'd said, Mam, as soon as I get a bit bigger flat, you can come and stay for as long as you want.

She said it again to herself, wrapped in the warmth and promise of the words.

It'll be no more than my due, she thought. Joan won't drudge her life out and it's thanks to me.

That very special reason was either a bigger flat or a promotion and probably both. Why not? Joan had the brains to get to the top and she hadn't got them off the road, or from Mansell.

'Did you hear anything from her?' He interrupted her reverie.

Had he found her hiding place and was testing her? Now what should she say? Nowt. Just say nowt and he'd give up.

She was ready to go the moment Joan asked her. She had everything she needed laid by in the chest upstairs; every blouse and skirt and cardigan Joan'd ever sent her, all there, all ready: and every last penny in the building society. She wouldn't have to keep her.

That's not why I gave you an education, I'll tell her. She'll put her arms round me and say, you should be Chancellor of the Exchequer, Mam, you're a marvel. And I'll say, of course I am; who do you think you got your brains from?

'I asked you five minutes ago if you heard anything from her. You still haven't said owt.'

He wasn't going to give up. It was the terrier in him.

'Why are you suddenly so interested in our Joan?'

'Why wouldn't I be? She's all I've got, all you've got, for that matter and I was thinking it might be nice to go down there for a holiday this year.'

She gripped the rail in front of the Aga.

He must have found the letter.

'She's asked you till she's sick of asking you and you've never bothered. I doubt whether she'd be interested now. She probably gave up the idea years ago.'

'Naw, you're wrong there. She'd be very pleased if I said I was thinking of going.'

'So why don't you write to her and say that then?'

'I'm going to, just as soon as I get a minute.'

That'll be when you've unbunged the yard drain, she thought with relief.

SEVEN

Roserill Road in South-east London was 1930s respectable.

Dave Barnett lay and watched a small ripple of sunlight at the top left-hand corner of the curtains. The wind must be moving the tree outside the window, he decided, before closing his eyes again.

He was still tired. The traffic had settled down to a background hum around one o'clock and increased steadily again from five o'clock onwards.

And now, the sour taste of vomit rose in his mouth. He turned quickly on his side and hung his head over the bed. The smell of fried bacon, scorched fat and over-ripe tomatoes was coming from the kitchen. He lay and swallowed several times, willing the nausea to pass. When it felt safe, he tilted his head back to the pillow and forced himself to focus on the dappled curtain again.

'David. David!' the voice persisted.

'Yes, I'm coming,' and satisfied with the silence that followed, he turned over.

'David, it's eight o'clock. Your breakfast's going cold and your egg will be hard. There's only yourself to blame. I called you half an hour ago.'

The voice was at the bedroom door. With a jerk, he flung back the blankets and stumbled to his feet. Why did she always cook breakfast an hour before he got up? Why did she cook it at all when she knew he hated it?

He began to shiver as the cold penetrated the small bedside mat. The bathroom was worse. It was on the north side of the house and even more spartan. His feet stuck to the cold linoleum.

His present of a bathroom mat set had been accepted, but judged too good to use.

I'll keep it for when Gwen comes, she said and put it on top of the wardrobe in his room next to the good fireside rug. He had persisted at first.

Why don't you put the bathroom set down?

Because it would only get wet.

But it will get wet when you put it down for Gwen.

But I'd like her to see it before it gets wet.

So it remained in its polythene bag, wrapped in brown paper to keep the dust off it.

Back in the bedroom, he struggled to pull his socks on his frozen feet, as unco-operative as a small child's.

'David, I won't call you again,' the voice shrilled upstairs.

'If only you were a woman of your word,' he muttered, yanking the heel of the second sock underneath his foot.

Downstairs, she put the plate of congealed bacon and egg in front of him and poured his tea.

'What about yours, Mum? Aren't you having any?'

'I had mine ages ago. I've been up for hours; and besides, I don't need a lot, you know. A slice of bread is enough for me now.'

He looked down at the table.

'David, are you saying something? Why is your mouth moving? You'll be talking to yourself next. Come on now, cheer up. The day's only started and you haven't made your mark on it yet. Another slice of fried bread, and finish your egg, eh?'

He pushed his plate away, knife and fork deliberately crossed.

'I don't want it. I've told you that I don't like a cooked breakfast.'

'You don't know what's good for you, that's what.'

'So how do you know what's good for me if I don't know?'

'Because I'm your mother.'

'That's like saying because the sun comes up, it's daylight, but it's not the same.'

'I don't see what the sun has got to do with me knowing what's best for you.'

'One is only an opinion, the other is a known fact.'

'Well, I always thought the sun was a fact as well.'

'You amaze me,' he said.

'Do I? Well, that's nice. Here now, wipe up your egg with this half-slice of bread.'

'No.'

'Oh, you certainly got out of bed on the wrong side this morning. Come on now, eat your breakfast; then you'll feel better.'

Give in, you mean, just give in. That's it, he thought. They were in a predictable orbit, each always presenting the same face to the other, neither turning nor changing. He was trapped and her meddling and manipulation would only get worse if she found out about the children.

'You're at it again, your mouth's moving. What are you trying to say?'

'Is there any cereal in the house?'

'No, I only get it if Gwen's coming: for the children, you know. They like it better than anything else, although it takes such a lot of milk. Gwen doesn't seem to mind, and of course, I don't say anything.'

She has her own ways, he chorused silently.

'She has her own ways and always did have.'

She was always a strong-willed child, he waited.

'She was always a strong-willed child.'

Not like you, now. You were always the good one, was the next line.

79

'Not like you, now. You were always the soft one.'

He looked up from his tea. 'That's a change. I was always the good one.'

'Oh yes, good as well, but I still have to worry about you, and Gwen can stand on her own two feet. I'm not getting any younger and Gwen has gone from strength to strength. She's even started to worry about me now. In fact, she wrote last week and said I was to go down and stay for a while.'

He knew.

'What did you say?'

'Nothing.' His face began to flush as he remembered the letter:

. . . I know you worry about Dave, you've always worried about him but he must muddle through somehow when he's on his own. Don't let him manipulate you.

Ha, that was a good one, he thought.

You have your own life to lead, you can't spend it waiting on Dave. You did enough of that when he was small. Leave Dave. I know you worry about him because he's delicate, but he's never needed to be anything else because you were always there.

At that point, he had heard his mother open the front door and quickly stuffed it back into the biscuit barrel on the sideboard with three pages unread.

Gwen only had one side of the story. What about his mother? For years she'd said: I don't know what I'd do without you, Dave. Gwen won't be told. She worries me sick. I think I'd die if you were as headstrong as her. In the end, he'd even hidden Gwen's letters. Her exuberant accounts of living rough in the Welsh hills were more than his mother could cope with, so he had protected her.

And then his father had died: You're the man of the house

now, Dave. So he'd put her first. He'd even sacrificed Sally and the kids to her tyranny.

And for what? Gwen had won, after all.

Bloody Gwen. Arrogant, bloody know-all. He stared intently at one red square of the tablecloth.

'There now, you're sulking. I knew it. Will I fry you another egg?'

He closed his eyes and the red square danced in front of them.

'Well then, will I?'

Behind his eyelids the red expanded, flowing, filling, threatening to overflow, beating at his ears.

'Will I, David?'

'Will I what?'

'Fry you another egg?'

'No.'

'Now that's just the sort of thing that gets me worried about you. I don't know what to do. I have to go. Gwen insists, and says she'll speak to you herself if I don't. I've no choice really. She says you'll have to stay with Sally and travel from Norfolk every day, or get digs, if you think it would be too much to try and look after yourself here. I told her it would be, of course, but she insists that it's not my job now to look after you. So what can I do? I can't upset her, can I?'

He dropped his head further and stared at a white square on the cloth until his face was fixed.

'Now, you see. I told her you'd be upset but she says if I don't go, she'll come and get me. It puts me in a very awkward position. I wish that firm of yours would pay for you to stay in a hotel and put my mind at rest or give you a job in Norfolk so you could stay with Sally. Mind you, I'm not saying anything against Sally but I do think it was a ridiculous thing to do, to decide to have the whole house decorated and move out with the children and go there, of all places, just when you had been moved back to London. But it's none of my business so I'll say nothing.'

No, don't, he thought: then said brightly, 'Well, it looks

81

as though Gwen is determined to have you there. Maybe you'd better think about it at least.'

'I'm past the thinking stage. I've done it. I've bought my ticket for tomorrow and I cannot get a refund now, so I'll have to go. As much as I want to stay here and look after you, I cannot, you see. I cannot just do what I want.'

'Well, I'll just have to manage as best I can, won't I?'

'Would you give me a ring and let me know how you are?'

'Oh, all right, then.'

'Would you? Oh, that would put my mind at rest. Dr Jackson always says that if everyone was as conscientious as me, there'd be no problems in the world. I could worry myself to death, he says.'

And everyone else as well.

'Your mouth's moving again, David. Now, don't start any new problems just as I'm going; please, there's a good boy.'

She got up and began to clear the table, wrapping the bacon rinds in a piece of greaseproof paper.

'Are they for the birds? I'll put them out.'

'Of course not. I'll render them down first before I leave and top up the dripping jar. The birds can have what's left.'

'You're very good to them, you know.'

'Oh well, I wouldn't go out of my way to be nice to them, but I wouldn't deliberately harm a bird.'

'That's what I mean. Anyone else would just feed them the fatty rinds and then they'd die of coronaries.'

'Well, I never thought of that, to tell you the truth; but it's true: I usually think of everyone else before myself.'

His face flickered but he controlled it until he got upstairs and into the bathroom.

He sang tunelessly under his breath, smiling at the steam. He hesitated for a moment; then shook the drops into the hand basin as well before zipping his flies.

Tomorrow, when she'd gone, he'd dribble on the floor.

Karin lit the candle and lay listening to her stomach rumbling. She fancied beans on toast.

Come here, mouse, cuddle in for a few minutes.

She jerked the toy towards her but the mouse ran backwards. How did you do that? she wondered and pulled it again, cautiously. The mouse moved forward obediently.

If she had beans on toast, she'd eat the melting soggy bit in the middle first, where the margarine and bean juice mixed, leaving the crusty edges of the slice to be cut into pieces, then turned on their sides and made into brooms, speared on the fork prongs, to chase the remaining beans and juice around the plate. What a mingy bugger to take all the baked beans with him.

She wanted hot food. But bread, she wanted some bread with it as well. Did you eat all the bread? The mouse stared at her unblinking. I can tell you're used to being in trouble with an expression like that! Take that look off your face Mouse Thompson, this *minute!* She grinned.

Right, up you get, before your belly thinks your throat's been cut. Cautiously she stood up and took a step.

Once she could do a Homo Sapiens to the kitchen, she could find the light switches. She daren't open the shutters in case anyone was watching the house, but she needed decent light to find her way round and use the cooker.

She made her way slowly to the doorway and the light switch.

Naw, naw; it cannot be. She clicked it up and down twice. Hang on, think; if the kitchen one's off as well, it'll be the fuse box, not the bulbs. He'll have switched it off at the box.

She'd try the back porch first because he'd put the candle and matches in the kitchen; and besides, there was the light from the passage to help her.

She couldn't remember being there between the woodshed and the kitchen. She recognised nothing of it. You must have had only one oar in the water, she thought. She grew serious at the vague memory of her struggle that night at the sink. Her legs started to tremble violently.

She switched the lever up and rested for a minute. I'll just go and try the light; then I'll see what's outside that little window in the woodshed.

The neon flickered; then shone steadily. Nothing else will ever be a problem again, she decided; now I can see and I can walk again. She massaged the top of her legs and shivered, remembering that lesson with poor old Mr Littleburn.

When Captain Oates left the tent and said, I may be gone some time: what was that an example of, do any of you know?

Constipation, she whispered to Tracy, who shrieked; then buried her head in her hands.

Tracy Taylor, this is not a laughing matter.

She's not laughing, Sir, she's crying. She can't take any more of the story; she's like that, Sir, sensitive. She always cries at sad films as well.

All right, then. Try and pay attention, Tracy. These men were paragons of all that is best in human nature: generosity of spirit . . .

Sharing their last bottle of brandy, I bet. She muttered.

Tracy sobbed again, her head on her desk.

I don't think she can take much more of this, Sir. It's nearly time for the bell. Can we draw a picture?

Oh Sir, let's Sir, the rest of them chorused.

Why are you in this class, Karin Thompson? Have you ever thought how selfish you are, how unfair it is to the rest of the class? I'm going to see your Year Head about getting you moved to a much higher stream, where you'll have to work.

Her daydream came to an abrupt end. Something must have happened to her eyes. It couldn't be, it just couldn't: she must be seeing things. She knelt awkwardly on a log, shivering with one arm resting along the top of the small window. Outside, it curved away, rising to a pure white wind-rippled crest: snow; mountains of it. She was trapped. She couldn't get to London until it thawed. And the prospect of slushy snow was worse because she couldn't risk waiting until it had all gone and the roads were dry. She'd have to get going before that and her boots would be soaked again.

Don't be daft. That's not a problem yet. The problem now is to organise some hot food and find the loo and some heating. Your boots can wait.

Back in the kitchen, the shivering gradually subsided sufficiently for her to be able to open a tin of stewed steak, and fish out the pieces with a fork.

The toilet must be working because I've turned the water back on. I bet it's upstairs. Aw hell, Edmund Hillary and Scott all in the same day.

The lounge light showed an open staircase. She went up slowly, step by step, on her bottom; then pulled herself to her feet on the landing. The bathroom door was open.

Thank goodness he's left me a toilet roll, she thought as she sat down.

She'd have to find out what sort of water heating he had and get herself a bath and wash her hair, even her clothes. But that would depend on being able to dry things. He must have some sort of heating, surely.

At least she didn't have to worry any more about washing Debbie's sheets and getting them on the line before she went to school. She felt a lump growing in her throat at the memory and quickly switched her attention back to the bathroom.

In the cabinet above the hand basin she found an old toothbrush and a new tube of toothpaste.

The hot mint scoured her tongue. She poked it out at herself in the mirror. It was still thickly coated but her mouth felt fresher.

She stared at herself dispassionately. Her bright red hair

stood up in tufts at the back of her head. Her face was pale than usual and her hazel eyes larger.

There was a towel on the edge of the bath and a scrap o soap on the hand basin. She washed her face, gasping at the icy water. She opened the cabinet again. At the back of the bottom shelf was a small jar of Vaseline. Better than nowt It would help the flaking dryness around her mouth and or her cheeks. She put a large dollop on her lips. The split ir the top one was still painful and the cracks at the side of her mouth still opened whenever she ate or drank.

Downstairs again, she returned to the kitchen. It was a gas cooker. That was funny: she hadn't noticed a gas meter nex to the fuse boxes. Of course not; the house was too far away to be on the mains: he'd be running it off a Calor Gas cylinder. She would have to go outside and turn it on.

At the back door, she hesitated. It might be completely snowed up. The snow might all fall in on top of her when she opened it and someone might notice the door had been opened. But at the prospect of endless cold meals she sho back the top and bottom bolts.

Nothing; there was no snow. It was another porch and no gas cylinder at the point where she judged the cooker to be. only a lever on the wall at right angles to a pipe. The connecting valve? She turned it in line with the pipe and shu the door gladly behind her.

The top cupboards yielded tea bags, dried milk, sugar. jam and a packet of bread mix. She wouldn't risk the over in case there wasn't much gas left in the cylinder. She would make herself some sort of flat bread pancake on the frying pan.

The outside was scorched and the inside not quite cooked. but slathered with jam and washed down with a cup of tea, it seemed like the best food she had ever eaten. It was better than egg and chips. It even beat beans on toast.

EIGHT

Maureen knew that she was dreaming and willed it to continue:

The take-off was just a running jump. She stretched her legs wide over the puddle and rose effortlessly above it. Exhilarated by the height of her first leap, she floated slowly to the ground, tapped it lightly with one toe and rose again, this time over a house and then, by extending her legs a little more, over row upon row of houses.

She could relax now that she knew how to do it. The controls were simple: breathe in to rise and out to descend.

It's easy, she assured the child who was watching from below; just jump up and once you're up, just move your legs, look, like this . . .

The slam of a car door interrupted. She felt the dream slipping away and tried to hold it but there were voices outside and the sound of a front door opening and more voices before the car moved off.

When she couldn't re-enter her dream, she lay and fretted. The clock showed ten past four. She might as well get up and write some more case notes. It would be better than lying worrying about them. It was Saturday. She could always go back to bed later.

At half past nine, she stopped writing and began to pack,

humming to herself: shampoo, body scrub, moisturiser; some small change for the scales and her locker; a comb, two apples, oranges and bananas, two Kit Kat bars; or would one be sufficient? No, another bar of chocolate would only affect her happiness, not her size.

I'll take a couple of magazines, just in case there's no one to talk to, she thought. She skipped down the steps to the car. Her bottom wobbled happily in her baggy tracksuit.

When she arrived at the baths, Lil was there as always with the towels.

'Here you are then, luv. They're nice and warm. Got change for your locker, have you? That's right. What about your scale money? Are you going on the scales before you start or not?'

'Oh, seeing that it's a new year, I'll be good.'

Lil laughed again.

'Good job you don't believe all the rubbish they say about Turkish baths. It's them little skinny ones I feel sorry for. You can see 'em, totting up the weight of each glass of water, on and off the scales like little fleas, and all of them put together wouldn't make a pan of soup. What misery, eh? What do you say, Dot?'

She turned to a tiny, bird-like woman who had joined her behind the counter, but Dot only smiled.

The locker rooms were empty. Maureen undressed and wrapped herself in two towels; then padded over to the scales.

Eleven and a half stone: not bad, she decided, considering all she'd stuffed in the last week. The Barnett case had prompted an orgy of eating almost as bad as her binge days. She knew why she was doing it but that wasn't much help.

She showered, then worked her way through the warm rooms until she reached the steam room. This was the bit she loved. She thankfully loosened her towels and lay down on the bench, letting her fat flow and settle where it wanted. Trickles of sweat ran from the mounds of her belly and thighs. Her short hair clung in tiny curls all over her head.

She abandoned herself with utter joy to the melting, tasting the salt on her lips and shutting her eyes against the sting.

The door to the steam room opened cautiously and the jets hissed menacingly. Maureen kept her eyes closed.

Sally Barnett entered and moved slowly to the opposite bench, took off her towel, lay down, and draped an extra towel, soaked in cold water, over her head. It did little to ease the throbbing. She was a fool to drink so much. She willed her body to start sweating. She'd have to go and get another drink of water. Red wine always dehydrated her and the gin hadn't helped. Maybe this time the water would stay down.

Ten minutes later, Maureen got up, went for a shower and into the cool room again. When she returned to the steam room she could just make out the figure of another woman lying on the bench opposite.

One of Lil's little skinny ones, she thought.

That suggested a snack. Another ten minutes here: then 'll try the plunge pool and have a cup of tea and a biscuit, just in case I've lost any weight, she grinned.

But the thought of the café prompted her body to get up off the bench and grope its way to the door. At the little tea bar, Dot was waiting with rows of cups neatly stacked in front of her, the tea urn bubbling and the shelves stacked with chocolate biscuits.

'Feeling peckish, luv? I'm not surprised. You've been in here nearly half an hour already. Here, give me those wet towels and I'll get Lil to give you a couple of dry ones: then you'll be more comfortable. Is it tea? The usual? Two sugars?'

In the lounge she paused for a moment; then decided. She'd have a banana and one of the Kit Kats, then see how he felt. She was just starting her second Kit Kat when Sally Barnett came in.

They looked at each other for a moment; then Maureen spoke. 'Hello. I hadn't expected to see you until Wednesday.'

Sally Barnett froze; then laughed nervously, 'No, that's right. I often come; at least, not that often and only for a

89

massage, sometimes more than others; sometimes not fo
ages; then sometimes every week for several weeks in
row . . .' She tailed off, looking miserable.

'Don't worry; I often meet people I know here and
when I'm not wearing my work hat, I just switch off
Besides, I have difficulty getting it to fit, as you can see,
she smiled.

Sally Barnett giggled nervously, then tried to control it.

'Oh, don't worry. My size and I reached an understanding
some years ago. Now we coexist quite well. Are you having
anything to drink? I've got a bit of chocolate biscuit left o
an apple or an orange. You're welcome to any of them.
only bring fruit to make me feel virtuous.'

Sally Barnett felt her stomach heave, 'No, thanks, I jus
came out to cool down for a bit. I couldn't eat anything, bu
thanks.'

'A bit early for you, is it?'

'Mm, I had quite a lot to drink last night.'

Why was she telling this woman? This dumpy littl
cherubic-faced woman sitting with a half-eaten chocolat
biscuit who didn't flicker.

There was no sign of disapproval nor, what would hav
been even worse, any gush of professional understanding
just total acceptance, as though she'd said that it was quite
nice day for late January. Damn her, she got inside one'
defences so easily.

Maureen smiled at her. 'I usually unwind on a Friday nigh
by stuffing myself silly. I just come here because I enjoy it
not to try and undo any damage. I think I'm beyond that
I'll never change. I love eating too much. I only just manageo
to stop myself from cutting a slice of bread in your kitcher
on Wednesday. It looked so good and I fancied a piece. It'
an obsession with me.'

Now, now was her chance.

'Actually, I was going to give you a ring about next week
I want to cancel Wednesday morning. I thought about it after
you left. It's nothing personal. I think you're very fair and

uncritical. It's just that I don't think there's anything more to say.'

'There is just one thing.'

'Oh.' She tried to sound non-committal.

'Yes, something I forgot to tell you and you might have been worrying about it. I didn't think about it until I'd left you.'

'Oh.'

'Yes, I should have told you that I've seen the photographs. It occurred to me that you might think I hadn't because I was new to the case and that I might return on Wednesday like the avenging angel.'

Sally Barnett sat down. Her face became very old and tired.

'Ah! As soon as you'd gone, I thought you couldn't have seen them or you wouldn't have been so reasonable with me.'

'I'm sorry about that. Anyway, if you still decide to cancel Wednesday, could you try and let me know by Monday? It's up to you. I'm not into coercion,' she looked down at several mounds bulging from her towel, 'as you can see,' she smiled gently.

'So if I don't hear from you by Monday, I'll see you on Wednesday as we arranged. I'm going to get myself another cup of tea before starting the rounds again. Can I get you anything?'

Moments later she returned with the tea and a Perrier.

'There you go. One of my oranges would help if you think it would stay down. I'll leave it for you. You might manage it later.'

Sally Barnett sat clutching the Perrier bottle in one hand and the empty glass in the other. 'I'll never get the children back,' she said suddenly. 'You know that already, don't you? I drink too much.'

Ah no, not on a Saturday morning, please, Maureen thought. I've been up to the ears in it all week. I came here to get it all out of my system.

'Why not wait and see how you feel about Wednesday before saying any more?'

'I'm sorry. I've no right to intrude on you like this.'

'No, it's not just that. If I really wanted a nine-to-five job, I could do something else. I just don't want you to say things to me that you might regret later. If you're happy to talk, that's fine with me, as long as you're sure.'

'I'm hung over and feeling desperate. If I wait until Wednesday, chances are I'll be sober again and telling myself that I can cope and so I won't say anything.'

'I'm still not sure that it's a good idea to talk now. I'm prepared to wait until you feel better about it.'

'God, you sound so smug.'

'I don't mean to and I don't know whether you'll talk or not, but if you do, I'd rather it was when you were feeling better.'

'When I'm sober, you mean.'

'No, you're sober now.'

Sally Barnett hesitated, then blew her nose hard. 'Yes, you're right. I'll think about it tomorrow, when I'm feeling better, and let you know by Monday.'

'That's fine, and I might see you again. I'm going back now to let my joy be uncontained, though maybe not as Byron envisaged. I usually do four sessions in the steam room and I've still got two to go.'

She got up and holding both towels very firmly, one in each hand, made her way back to the warm room. At the door she turned and looked back, but Sally Barnett didn't look up from her glass of Perrier.

She sat watching as the bubbles rose and burst.

God, why did I say anything to her about drinking? I don't even drink that much, at least, not always. Anyway, it comes out of my own money. I still don't see why Dave was always so uptight about it. If I'd financed his toy workshop he would have grumbled that I owned him. Anyway, it would have robbed him of the chance to moan about always being broke. And I'm sure he enjoyed making his own money. He did. And he probably wouldn't have been any better than Daddy if he'd had a lot given to him.

Your father can get through money faster than locusts through a maize crop, Sally. She remembered her mother sitting on the terrace. A chill wind was cooling the early summer day. There was a spattering of rain and her mother said, We'll go in out of this wretched weather and join your father who'll be slumped in misery somewhere. We'll all be in misery if he doesn't sort his finances very soon and heaven knows, when I say so it must be bad because I'm not one to panic, but I haven't paid a bill in months!

That had been the last time she had seen him before he died.

It wasn't my fault I wasn't nice to him. I didn't know he was going to die, she thought angrily as she made her way back to the baths, clutching her cold wet towel.

She opened the door. Clouds of steam hissed at her and the bench rose very slowly to meet her.

Mansell sucked the end of his pen thoughtfully. He'd never made much of a fist of letter writing, and this was a bloody tricky one. He'd been tempted to give up several times, but his perseverance had paid off so far. He'd got the address written at the top of the sheet and *Dear Joan*. It would be a pity to stop there. *How are you?* That would be all right. What next? *I expect you are surprised to hear from me. I just thought I'd drop you a line.* No, she'd wonder what was wrong. *I know I don't write as often as I should but with the farm and everything, it always seems to be your mam that does the letter writing. I hope this finds you well. We are both well but your mam's arm is giving her a bit of bother.* He wouldn't mention running out of diesel or milking by hand. There was no need to worry her. *I wish you'd come home some time. I'd like to see you. Or how about me coming for a holiday?*

That was about it. There was no point in telling her about the heifers or the ewes. They had never interested her. No, he'd leave it at that. He signed it carefully *Your loving father,* then folded it, creased it sharply and tore off the empty bit of paper at the bottom of the page. He didn't know if he'd ever have any use for it, but it didn't look right, hanging at the bottom of the letter. He gazed with satisfaction at what he'd written. It was a good letter. Now all he had to do was find an envelope and get her address from Maggie.

That would be the hardest part, damn her. She was in a mood.

'Yes, I've got our Joan's address. What do you want it for?'

'What do you think; what does anyone want an address for? Are you going to give me it or not?' It was a good job he'd got the letter finished while she was doing the evening milking or he wouldn't have had a minute's peace.

'It's in the book in the sideboard in the front room. You can find it for yourself, seeing as you're doing nowt else.'

The sideboard held years of bills and paid-up insurance policies. The address book was held together with a rubber band. Torn-off addresses from the tops of letters spilled out and floated to the floor.

He'd look under J for Joan and Jowett.

Nothing. It must be among the scraps that had fallen out. He groped around under the chenille tablecloth. Damn Maggie, there were three different London addresses.

'There's three London addresses here,' he called upstairs. 'Which one is it?'

'None of them. Get a pen. Have you got one?'

'Yes.'

'It's Flat 14 . . .' she rattled on. 'Do you want the post code?'

'Hang on, damn you, I just want the address. Tell me it again and slowly this time so I can write it down. What's after Flat 14?'

'Greenways, d'you want me to spell it for you?'

'Then what?'

'Riverside Estate. You should have learned to do joined up writing.'

'Quit that, woman, what's next?'

She gave him the remainder of the address.

'Right, and the post code?'

'I haven't got it.'

'So why did you ask me if I wanted it?'

'Because if you did, I didn't have it.'

'You're a bitter old goat, just like your mother,' he muttered. He'd make a copy of the address then he wouldn't have to go through all this again. He'd use that scrap of paper he'd torn off the bottom of Joan's letter. He knew it would come in handy for something.

He tucked it into his inside jacket pocket. He'd better put his name and address on the back of the envelope, just in case Maggie had given him the wrong one for Joan.

That done, he pushed it into his other inside pocket. It would have to wait until the road was cleared and the post could get through. That might take another week or more; if there was no more snow in the meantime.

Karin fiddled with the tuning on Dave Barnett's radio alarm and the Radio One Breakfast Show blasted into the bedroom:

AND NOW, the FABULOUS Michael Jackson and B-A-D: 'Bad'! The DJ dropped his voice.

She looked at herself dispassionately as she swung the tins of butter beans above her head in rhythmic circles, each elbow brushing an ear in turn.

She continued through the long introduction, then sang along under her breath.

Standing in front of Dave Barnett's wardrobe mirror, dressed only in a pair of his boxer shorts tied in the middle with a dressing-gown cord, she watched critically as her biceps responded to the weight on each outstretched arm. Her body was small and thin but perfectly proportioned with that ideal ratio of muscle to skeleton that distinguishes potential athletes.

Then, still holding the tins, her arms outstretched at shoulder level, she began to do squats. In some ways it had been easier to be ill, she thought. Now that she was better she fretted because the weather confined her to the house. The only thing that she enjoyed doing was the exercises. Besides, they made good sense. They kept the reality of London alive because she would not only have to be fit enough to walk back to the main road when she left but maybe even walk miles between lifts, as well as trekking round looking for somewhere to live when she got there.

For the first two days after she had found the fuse box and restored the electricity supply, she had left the light on day and night and just lain on the sofa, with tins of cold food open on the floor beside her. It had been like a never-ending winter evening, punctuated by odd intervals of sleep, waking to the television's empty humming or drifting off during a quiz show and waking to a test card on the screen.

Her mam was happy to stay like that; lying in bed for days, curled up, dozing or just staring; in a world of her own. But two days of inertia had been enough for Karin. She worked out the ratchet mechanism that allowed the mouse to run backwards. After that, she got into a routine of exercise and activity because there wasn't much else to do, except play with the toys. She'd found more in the window seat. All animals, all like mouse; wooden and on wheels. She lined them up and turned the empty coal scuttle on its side as the Ark. But they were boring. Apart from making them all run backwards by tugging sharply on their strings, there was nothing else to do with them. Other than that, there was only a bit of housework and going to the door.

That was important: to see real daylight. Having the electric light was infinitely better than candles in the house but having it on all day made her feel strange. She needed daylight.

She would have preferred to read rather than do housework, but couldn't find any books. It didn't surprise her. There had never been books at home. There were no books in Tracy's house either. Come to think of it, she didn't know anyone who did have books. Tracy said she was funny: not mad, but queer, sort of, for liking them. Tracy didn't mind, but some of her mates would if they knew. Karin said it was her own business and she didn't give a damn and Tracy said not to worry because she was her best mate and she wouldn't tell the others anyway.

Her exercises finished, she washed quickly and got dressed. She had abandoned her own clothes for some of Dave Barnett's, which were enormous, but clean and warm. She tucked each trouser leg into a sock and held everything together in the middle with a belt.

Downstairs, she paused only long enough to put the kettle on, then went straight to the outside porch door. It opened inwards to reveal huge drifts of ice-glazed snow. The view from the woodshed window was much the same, with similar waves rising up and out of sight. This was another world, the real world.

The kettle's whistle summoned her inside, and she returned moments later, clutching her mug, her arms across her thin chest. She stood shivering in the sharp cold, breathing the iced air, totally absorbed by the winter sunlight, her mind empty.

The light danced off every ice crystal and blinded her. The sky was an intense blue, which darkened to navy as she forced herself to stare at it, her eyes screwed into tiny slits. When she turned her gaze back to the snow, the light exploded and bounced and there was a moment's total blackness before smooth white billows refocused at the corner of her eye.

Her tea cooled quickly and it remained untouched as she

struggled to find the words she wanted. I'm never going to be the same as Tracy and that lot at school. I don't know how they can be happy doing nowt and just watching the telly. I don't want to be like them. I can do other things.

That was it. They had no choice because they couldn't do anything else. None of them in the remedial class could even read properly. But she could. She didn't belong there. She was clever.

She gazed ahead of her to where the snow rolled away, pristine and untouched. I've got my whole life to live when I get out of here. I've got to stop looking back. I can't do anything about what's happened. I never could. Her mind shut like a trap.

She was going to start again. Now that she had left Tracy and everyone behind her, she would be a different person in a different place. Her future lay beyond her like the snowdrift, unmarked by any other person or event, belonging entirely to herself and under her control.

NINE

'. . . unless your journey is really necessary.' Dave Barnett switched off at the end of the weather forecast, then switched it on again as a counterblast to the wind.

He didn't have Gwen's number. He'd rushed out, half asleep, roared down the M4 through driving sleety rain and was now struggling north from Carmarthen to Llangeler, Coed-y-bryn and Maesllyn. He didn't dare stop, or he'd never get started again; but he was going to be forced to stop any minute now and be stuck in a snowdrift and left to die undiscovered.

His breath was already freezing on the windscreen. He scraped a hole and forced himself to sit back, pulling a scarf up round his mouth. Snowflakes whirled, leaping in and out of the headlight beams from all directions, hypnotic in their relentless chaos. The wipers were beginning to fail, unable to keep even a small arc clear of the thickening blanket. His wheels spun repeatedly and the car slithered from side to side. He forced himself to relax and tried to breathe deeply. He switched from the World Service to Radio 2 and back again.

Bloody Gwen, she must have known what the weather was like. She'd be so intent on running a guilt trip on him, getting him to the bedside for a final chastisement, she wouldn't give a damn. He wiped his eyes with the back of his hand. His tears were causing a double distortion of his headlights, already refracted by the snow storm. He swiped his face roughly with the end of his scarf, and screwed his eyes shut to squeeze them dry, but the glare was increasing. He tried again, but it got worse as it focused into five huge lights bearing down on him. It hadn't seen him; it couldn't.

He braked and spun across the road into a snowdrift; then viciously reversed out and came to a halt.

Above the shrieking of the wind he could hear the roar of a heavy motor settle into a steady idling cough, and then he saw a man in yellow oil-skins jump down and head towards him.

'Where the hell do you think you're going on a night like this?'

'I'm trying to get to Maesllyn; my mother has had a stroke.' He winced as the snow blasted through the window.

'Well, from Maesllyn she'd be in Cardigan most likely, wouldn't she? Anyway, you've no choice. The road to Maesllyn is closed but the A484 to Cardigan is open: or at least, it was an hour ago. Turn left at the next junction about half a mile down the road and you'll join it. I'll pull in and let you past. It'll take me a couple of minutes to clear myself a layby, so wait until I signal. Good luck, then.'

Before he could say anything, the man had turned and was struggling to climb back into the cab of the snowplough.

Reluctantly he wound up his window, and eased his way past the flood of light on the road, until the way ahead was pinpointed once again by his own headlights. The road improved marginally, and he wondered if it might be possible to struggle on; but it was closed at the junction, and he obediently turned left to Cardigan.

An hour later he stumbled out of the car and into the hospital. It was seven o'clock, and the silence was broken by distant sounds of rehearsal for the day ahead. He wandered lost through an empty waiting area, past a glass-fronted reception desk, outpatients' toilets and a children's corner with a paralysed rocking horse. He must have come in the wrong door. He'd go back and start again. He turned and blundered along a corridor, exhausted.

'Are you all right?' She looked about fifteen years old: a black fringe, blue eyes, no make-up and a little cap perched unsteadily at the back of her head.

He tried to focus on her fob-watch. 'I think so. It's my mother, Mrs Winnie – Winifred Barnett. She's had a stroke. She was staying with my sister in Maesllyn and I think she might be in here. I've driven from London. I'm a bit tired.'

'Women's Medical is at the other end. Look, why don't you sit down for a moment and I can check for you. You look about as tired as I feel.'

He turned away, desperate in case she would see him cry.

At first he thought she was just deeply asleep and snoring. But her breathing never changed, nor the twisted face. There were no sudden gasps or breaks, just a relentless laboured dragging of air through her lop-sided mouth.

An hour later, the staff nurse came back.

'I'm going off duty in a few minutes, Mr Barnett. I just wanted to check her before I go. I promised your sister I'd ring her if there was any change.'

'Why isn't she here herself?'

'Because she's been here for days and I made her go home. She's got her business to run and her family to look after.'

'Business; a few goats?'

'I don't know about goats – she could have those as well – but she employs a lot of people round Maesllyn.'

A rota of cleaners, he thought, remembering the chill squalor of those November days more than ten years ago and his final attempt to forge some sort of link with Gwen, then twenty years old and already boasting two children. Already. *Still* boasting, she had done it all her life; dismissive, God-sure, certain Gwen: able to sway people.

Look at her husband Philip, five years older and in a safe job with good prospects, brought to wild Wales and penury and supposedly blissful fulfilment.

'Mr Barnett,' the staff nurse said again.

'Yes. Sorry, I was miles away.'

'Why don't you phone your sister now? She needn't be in such a rush if she knows you're here.'

'I haven't got her phone number.'

'Well, I can give you that: it's in the office.' She controlled her voice. She didn't like this man, she decided. She was beginning to understand Gwen Thomas's reluctance to contact him. She wanted to say to him: stop snivelling, forget about your own problems for a moment, your mother is dying. He hadn't even asked for details of her condition; just sat for the past hour, looking through her, lost somewhere in his own mind, only moving away when the night staff came to check her and turn her. Funny man, but not her problem, she decided. Her problem would be getting home through the snow in time to snatch some sleep before tonight's shift.

She took control, 'Come on. The day staff will be coming on the ward in a minute and then I'll be busy giving the report. You can use the phone in the office if you're quick,' she relented.

For one moment Gwen's voice was sleep-thick and distant; but as soon as he spoke she was instantly alert. 'Oh, it's you, Dave, oh good, you're there; good, hang on till I arrive. The road: is it? Oh God, how will I get out then? I'll have to ring for the plough. They may have cleared it anyway by now. I'll check and ring you straight back.'

Philip turned and grunted in the bed beside her. 'That the hospital?'

'Yes, love. It's Dave, sounding badly done to, to make me feel guilty.'

'Mm.' He settled back under the duvet. 'Is he still at that game?'

'I expect it's still what he does best,' she said wearily,

groping for her dressing-gown and pushing a slipper backwards around the carpet with one foot.

Minutes later she was back on the line. 'Dave, the road's open, so I'm coming. Can you hang on there till I arrive?'

'If it's open I'll come straight out to Maesllyn.'

'But that'll leave Mum on her own.'

'Well, she won't notice, will she?'

'It's not that: what if . . . Is the night staff nurse still there? Put her on, please.'

'There's been no change in her condition, Mrs Thomas. As I told you, she could last more than a week yet.'

'There you are,' Dave said when she handed him the receiver. 'So I'm coming straight out. I need some sleep.'

Outside the office, a pale sky was beginning to compete with the electric light in the familiar late moments of a winter dawn.

He was trembling with exhaustion and felt sick. He turned towards the stairs and the exit; then back again to the side ward. She still lay unmoving on her side as the nurses had arranged her. He stood at the bedside. 'Mum,' he said; then cleared his throat.

'Mum,' more loudly now, 'it's me, Dave. I came to see you. I'll come again tonight.' He tailed off in embarrassment.

At the door he took one final look; then headed unsteadily for the exit and the car park.

He squelched through a thin layer of slush to reach the car, but once out of the hospital grounds the road was clear as far as Newcastle Emlyn. Then the whiteness increased, until, on the last four miles to Coed-y-bryn, he was driving along a single track between walls of snow on either side, their ice glaze highlighted by the sun.

He negotiated the sharp right-hand oblique junction to Maesllyn with great difficulty, and began to crawl slowly uphill in first gear. The hard-packed snow was deeply rutted and he swayed from side to side, until a crunching, grinding noise stopped him: wheels spinning uselessly, stranded on a frozen rut, his exhaust smashed. He switched off the engine and got out. He hadn't a shovel, and without one no hope of moving the mound of snow under one side of the car.

Ahead of him, the track continued to weave upwards through multiple banks of snow. He stumbled and slithered until, fifteen minutes later, he saw the house in the distance and willed himself to reach it.

Gwen was her most matter-of-fact self.

'First thing to do is get your car moved, or no one will get in or out. William!' she called, and a lanky sullen boy of about sixteen appeared.

'William, this is my brother, Dave. He got stuck on the road coming up and lost his exhaust. See if you can find Joseph, there's a good boy. Ask him to take the tractor and the tow rope down and move the car. If he could bring it here for the moment,' she hesitated, 'yes, that would be best. Tell him to put it in the yard at the back and be sure to bring the exhaust if it's lying on the road.'

William turned without a word.

'That's that bit organised, then,' she said.

'How do you know? He didn't say he'd do it.'

'No, William doesn't talk much: he's not like that; but he'll do it, don't worry. He's been with us for a year now. I'll tell you about him some other time. Now, breakfast first, or just bed?'

'A cup of tea, then sleep.'

'All right, I'll show you where everything is and you can help yourself. Philip should be here in a minute. He's just at the office.'

'The office?'

'Oh, what used to be the old byre and dairy; that's the office now, I'll show you it all later. I want to get in to be with Mum as soon as I can get down the road. I spoke with the staff nurse just before you came.'

He didn't reply, but stood looking around in disbelief at the oak kitchen units and the copper extractor hood above the island in the middle of the room which housed twin gas hobs.

Gwen controlled her irritation, 'Oh, here, look: tea bags, mugs, milk in the fridge, sugar in here.' She opened a cupboard door brusquely, 'And you can sleep in the boys' room, they're away at school unless . . . never mind.' She rushed on: 'You'll be okay there, for today at least. It's through here,' she said over her shoulder, striding towards the door. 'I've put clean sheets out. There are towels in the bathroom cupboard. I think that's everything. Okay?'

He shrugged and turned back to the kitchen. It wasn't.

'Right then, I'm off. Oh, biscuits are in the cupboard and there's bread if you want toast. Mavis will be in later if she gets through. She's our housekeeper and she might take pity on you, but I'd better warn you, she's a bit fierce.'

'I won't bother with anything,' he said. 'I'll just go to bed.'

'Okay, just as you want. I'll see you later. Don't worry about the phone. I'll switch it to the office and Philip will answer, so you won't be disturbed.' She breathed out sharply and looked round, 'Right, this time I think that's everything. We can talk later. I'm off.' With that she swung through the door and left him.

She could at least have made the bed, he grumbled, as he struggled to tuck the bottom sheet in against the wall. Typical bloody Gwen; bossy as ever, sod her. He'd leave tonight, maybe this afternoon. He couldn't do anything here. Mum didn't even know he was here. She could lie in the hospital for weeks. He'd done his duty and there was nothing else he could do, he thought as he spun slowly downwards into sleep.

When he woke it was four o'clock and nearly dark. He lay and listened. Someone was moving about in the kitchen: otherwise nothing. Good, he could leave without anyone noticing. Oh no, he couldn't. He'd forgotten the exhaust. He'd better sort out a garage immediately or he'd never get away.

Mavis swung round majestically from the sink and eyed him calmly. 'You'll be David then: I'm Mavis.' She wiped her hand down her apron and held it out, but he ignored it. 'I must phone a garage.'

'Is it about the car? There's no need. Joseph ordered you a .iew exhaust this morning, and it should be here tomorrow, so he'll fix it then.'

She turned back to the sink and plunged her hands into the dish of potatoes, expertly paring wafer skins with an old kitchen knife.

'I need to make another call, a private one, to London.'

'The phone's on the wall. You can be as private as you like. I'm not listening.'

He glared at her broad back while he waited for Social Services to answer.

'Could I leave a message for Maureen Wilson?' he said guardedly, 'I had an appointment to see her this afternoon, but my mother is ill. She's in hospital in Wales, and . . . No, I'm here now. No,' he said sharply, 'there's no need, I'll get in touch when I get back. Besides, I'll be out most of the time, and there'd be no answer, so there's no point,' he finished lamely.

'So you'll be staying for dinner, then, I take it,' Mavis said dryly. 'I'll do another couple of spuds.'

She ignored him after that and he wandered outside, cautiously footing it over frozen slush to the old byre. Philip glanced up. 'Oh, hi,' he said awkwardly. 'I'll be with you in a minute. Did you sleep? Good, I'm just sorting this program out,' and turned back to one of the computers. Dave walked over and an old mangy dog growled from under a desk.

'Take no notice, old Shep's in with the fittings. Did we have him when you were here last? If we did he must only have been a puppy then. He was the children's first dog when we had the goats.'

'I was going to ask you about those,' he began, then peered over Philip's shoulder at a sales graph on the screen.

An hour later they stopped.

'That was great,' Philip said. 'I'd forgotten you qualified in this line of business; your speciality, wasn't it? Are you still in computers?'

Before Dave could answer, the phone rang.

'That's the garage to say your exhaust will take an extra day. There isn't one in stock locally.' He replaced the receiver and it rang again.

'Oh no,' he said very quietly; then, 'Oh Gwen, has she? I'm so sorry, love. All the staff will be as well. Yes, I'll tell him. He's here with me now. He's been helping me with that bug in the catalogue sales graph. So you're coming straight home. Good. Okay, get back here as soon as you can. I'll start making arrangements.' He turned to Dave.

'It's all right, I heard,' he said, and turned quickly to the door.

Sitting at the table in the kitchen that evening, Dave still wanted to run away. Gwen was talking softly and wiping her eyes, her meal untouched in front of her. William sat quite still, staring into space. Mavis was fussing quietly and Philip voicing disconnected thoughts: 'I've rung the Minister and the undertaker. It'll be on Friday at the chapel; then at the crematorium. The staff want to come. Kate rang to say she's traced that batch of sweaters; she'll be in tomorrow. There's no point in putting it in the papers, is there?'

Dave rehearsed his line: I've got to get back to London, I'm afraid, I can't stay; but couldn't face Gwen's outraged insistence that he return for Friday.

She turned to Philip. 'Have you rung school?'

'Yes, the boys will be home tomorrow. Joseph will meet them. He'll take William along as well.'

'What about everyone else?'

'It's all in hand. Look, love, if you're not hungry, why not go and lie down, catch up on some sleep? Everything's okay in the office, and Dave here wouldn't mind helping out for a couple of days, would you?' He turned to him and Dave shook his head: 'No, of course not. I can't leave anyway.'

Gwen shot him a look. 'You can leave at any time: there's a taxi, and you can get a train. Your car can be collected later if that's what you want, so don't say you can't go.'

'You're tired, love: you both are. He didn't mean it like that. He wasn't thinking of leaving; he was only thinking about his car.'

'Don't you believe it. If he faces Friday it'll be the first time in his life he's faced anything.'

'Look who's talking about facing things – sitting half-way up a bloody mountain with a couple of goats.'

Gwen's voice was cold and steady, 'In case you hadn't noticed, we haven't any goats. I expect you'll still be reminding me of them in ten years' time. I remember when I was fifteen and you were still talking about my sixth birthday party when I wet my knickers. It must be hell living with such a perfect memory.'

'No worse than living with you when you were always so bloody smug about everything. Anyway, I don't have to sit here and take any more of this.' He got up to leave.

'Fine, but before you go, I just want to put the record straight for you. We now employ thirty-four people. We produce top-of-the-range and designer knitwear and we've done it not by snivelling or moaning, but by honest hard work.' Her voice dropped. 'And neither of us ran away, or left our children, and that wasn't just because Aunt Cissie didn't leave us her farm house up North to run to. Oh that surprises you, does it? You thought none of us knew where you were? Well, Mum didn't, because I didn't tell her, but I told Sally long before you did because I heard from the solicitor.' She clenched her teeth and got up from her chair. 'You're in no position to criticise us, Dave. All you've ever done is make people feel guilty. Mum worried herself sick about you. Well, I don't give a damn. Never once,' she banged the table, 'not once in your life have I ever heard you say you wanted something; just that, plain and simple.

You've manipulated, whined, manoeuvred and sneaked to get your own way, but you've never had the courage just to ask and risk being refused like the rest of us.' She was panting, and William began to cry with a soft, high-pitched sobbing.

'It's all right, William. I'm not angry with you,' she turned to him, 'you're a good boy. I'm not telling you off at all. Look at me,' but he turned his head away. 'Ask Mavis here, ask Philip. I'm very pleased with you, especially this morning, getting Joseph and the tractor. That was great.'

William rocked backwards and forwards, unheeding, and Mavis crouched at the side of his chair and gathered him into her great bulk until he was still.

'I'll stay in Newcastle Emlyn until Friday,' Dave said quietly. 'I'll go there tonight if I can get a taxi, or if someone can give me a lift.'

No one spoke. Mavis was still crouching, holding William and stroking his hair.

'I'd rather you stayed,' Gwen said, cautiously breaking the silence.

'And I'd rather not.'

'Oh, Dave, come on. It might be our last chance to talk to each other. What I said just then is what I've bottled up for years. I'm sure your feelings about me are just as bitter.'

He sat, his head turned away, his face set.

'Come on, Dave,' Gwen urged.

'It doesn't matter any more. I promised myself years ago that I'd cut all ties once Mum was dead, and it still seems like a good idea. There's nothing to talk about. We've got nothing in common.'

'Except anger. But if you feel you can carry it for the rest of your life, fine.'

'After Friday, I'll be able to leave it behind.'

Gwen opened her mouth to reply, and Philip nudged her carefully under the table and shook his head almost imperceptibly.

'You'll do whatever's best, but you're still welcome to stay here, whether you have anything to say or not. It would be easier to make arrangements and settle up Mum's things if we were in the same place.'

'That sounds reasonable to me,' Philip said quietly. 'There'll be a lot of things to sort out: the house in London, for a start. I think it would be easier to make arrangements together.' He started to gather the plates, 'Another thing, you're tired and upset. Sleep on it. If you still feel like staying in Newcastle Emlyn tomorrow,' he turned to Dave, 'then we can book you a room. Visitors are very seasonal in this part of the world. If you go tonight, the room might be damp.'

He was spared a climb-down by Mavis, who got up purposefully and said: 'That's settled then, I'll put a hot-water bottle in Mervyn's bed and you can have an early night.' Then, turning, she said confidently: 'Now William, are you going to help me make apple fritters, there's a good boy?' He got up and followed her to the stove.

Lying in bed that night he saw the scenes at the table again: Mavis rocking William and William's radiant smile when everyone enthused about the apple fritters. Then that moment when he'd looked round and picked up the dish and held it to his chest, whimpering.

You can have more if you like, William, Gwen said.

Yes, help yourself, Philip urged; but William shook his head and continued his small mewing cries.

Do you want to save some of your fritters for the boys, William: is that it? asked Mavis. But it wasn't. For Granmum: that's it, isn't it, William? You want to save the rest for Granmum, she said, and the boy had nodded in relief.

His mother had never mentioned the boy.

Granmum. It was strange to think that everyone could be so fond of his mother; even more that they could all be bothered with William.

And that one persistent memory, of great hulking Mavis, stroking him like a little bird, calming his flutterings. At that memory of her tenderness, he turned his face to the pillow.

TEN

Her tea finished, Karin bolted the door and returned to the kitchen. After breakfast, she'd bring some snow inside and build herself a snowman in the porch. She grinned happily. It was just another bit of daftness.

Now, there's porridge or *porridge*, she giggled. If Mr Littleburn could see her now! Every time she made it she thought of him and that first morning at the Field Study Centre.

She had stood shivering in the queue at the hotplate, and Sir was dolloping it out of a big aluminium cooking pot, shaking the ladle furiously to transfer it to each plate.

Did you scrape it off the footpath last night, Sir?

What do you mean, Karin Thompson?

Nowt, it's just that it looks like sommat the drunks heave . . .

Everyone groaned, and Jean Caspar said she was going to be sick, and Karin quipped: It's good of you to offer, Jean, but I think there's enough in the pan.

Some of the lads started to flick bits off their spoons, and soon there was chaos as they chased each other under and around the tables.

The warden came in, picked up the two nearest lads by the shoulders of their jackets, and banged their heads together. They scraped the porridge off the floors, re-set the tables and sat down in silence.

You've done it now, Thompson, Tracy whispered.

Mr Littleburn tried to be reasonable with her: It's like a holiday here compared with school, and you're still mucking it up.

She said nothing.

Is there anything wrong at home, anything you want to talk about?

Silence.

Then just make up your mind to settle down and enjoy yourself. He cleared his throat again. His voice was failing fast and his throat was getting very sore. I know it's raining, but being happy doesn't depend on the weather, does it?

Nowt as simple, she thought sullenly, driving her finger through the last crumbs of toast.

The memory caused her no embarrassment.

She shrugged. It wasn't her fault that he'd been an idiot. Anyway, it would be his turn to laugh now if he could see her eating the stuff. It still wasn't her choice. It was Hobson's, whoever he was, poor bugger.

By mid-morning she had tidied all the kitchen cupboards and wiped the shelves. There was only the dresser left. Going through every drawer and cupboard in the house kept her busy and fed her curiosity.

The right-hand drawer of the dresser held balls of string and a tangle of rubber bands.

The left-hand one tilted menacingly with the weight of an old box file labelled Household Accounts. She lifted it out, settled herself at the table and started to sort through. He was certainly methodical, this Dave Barnett. All the bills were pinned together in groups, and at the bottom, there were four gas bills inside a coloured brochure.

Holding her breath, she scrutinised them. The first two detailed the supply and installation of a thousand-litre tank and the cost of filling it. The other two were for annual re-fills, the last, a little over a month ago, on 8th December for

800 litres. So that was it! Not little cylinders at all, but a big bulk tank. She should have known he couldn't run radiators off caravan-size cylinders.

She'd been worried about lighting the oven, and there was almost a whole year's gas supply sitting outside. She was a lucky bugger and always had been. She just forgot it sometimes.

She hugged herself and grinned. Now she'd be able to wash her hair, and have a bath and wash her clothes and switch on the central heating and do some baking. She whooped and punched the box file gleefully: then sucked her knuckles. She stood up, danced, raced to the wall, lit the pilot light on the boiler, and jigged for the required ten seconds before turning the control knob to the final position. The gas jets flared; then steadied into a comforting blue glow, bobbing like a well-trained corps de ballet to accompany the hum of the motor.

Maureen Wilson looked at the clock above her door again. It was twenty-five past four.

The traffic must be very heavy. It's not like him to be late, she thought as she opened his file again. Of course, he could have backed out. She doodled inside the manila folder, trying not to think of the two biscuits in her top drawer.

At half-past four the phone rang. 'Maureen, Dave Barnett's just rung from Wales. His mother's ill. No, he didn't say anything about next week. That was all he said. I don't suppose he knows yet. No, he didn't give a number.'

She brushed the biscuit crumbs from the unread file, closed it and prepared to leave.

She had just reached the door when her phone rang again. She left her bags and went back to her desk. 'Hello, Social Services: Maureen Wilson speaking. Oh, hello.' She sat down in surprise. 'Mrs Barnett! Yes, tomorrow will be fine. Yes, just as we arranged, first thing. No, I was planning to come unless you called to cancel, but thank you for ringing. I appreciate that. I'll see you tomorrow then. Bye.'

That's a turn up for the books, Wilson me love, she said to herself, and shimmied to the door.

Sally Barnett woke with a headache. She eased herself out of bed and made her way slowly downstairs to the kitchen. Seeing Maureen Wilson didn't seem a good idea now. She shouldn't have rung yesterday. Was there time to cancel it? She'd try in a minute, as soon as the office opened.

She sat down heavily at the table and picked up the airmail letter again. She scanned it, searching for a loophole.

We'd both love it if you could all come and visit us.

She strained to read her mother's racy scrawl:

We could make a holiday of it.

Was that what she'd written? She fingered the four open return Qantas tickets. As usual, her mother was giving her no choice.

How could she get out of it? What could she say?

She'd have just one drink to get her going, then phone Social Services and cancel Maureen Wilson. Then she'd sit down and write. She couldn't put it off for ever. She'd have to think of something.

On her third attempt to ring the office, a woman answered the phone. No, Maureen Wilson wasn't in. She had an appointment at Muswell Grove Road and was going straight from home that morning. She'd be in later. Would she like to leave a message?

It was a dull cold morning with a sharp thin wind. Sally Barnett opened the door almost immediately, clutching an oversize pink cardigan around her; smiling. Her mousy hair was greasy and hooked back behind her ears.

'Oh, come in, it's freezing out there. Go straight in. We're in the kitchen again; you know the way.' She followed Maureen along the hall. 'Same old mess as last week.' It was said without apology or embarrassment.

'Last week I only noticed the loaf of bread.'

'I've got toast if you'd like it?' Sally smiled.

'I'd love it,' said Maureen with such conviction that Sally laughed.

'Okay, you put the kettle on and I'll make toast. I'll put two slices in for a start, shall I?'

'Are you having some?' Maureen asked.

'No thanks; I never eat in the morning.'

'In that case . . . oh, go on, I'll manage two nicely.' She piled dishes into the sink to clear two spaces at the table and waited for the kettle to boil, breathing with relief at the change in Sally Barnett.

When they sat down Sally sipped her black coffee slowly, while Maureen munched the toast and cleared the plate of crumbs with her finger.

'That was good: thanks; and thanks for ringing the office yesterday and confirming today's visit.'

'That's all right. It seemed a bit more positive than the arrangement you suggested at the Turkish on Saturday, that's all.'

'If all my clients were as helpful, I'd suffer a lot less. I'd probably eat a lot less as well.'

'It's nice to see someone enjoying food.'

'Most of the time I don't enjoy it. I don't even taste it because I haven't swallowed one mouthful before I'm stuffing the next one in. Sawdust mixed with sugar would go down just as well.'

'Ah, but it makes you more approachable. If you seemed perfect you would be too threatening. No one would confide in you.'

'Gawd, you've got me blushing now. I can't cope with flattery.'

'No, it's a compliment: I mean it.'

What a kind thing to say, Maureen thought. I never expected that. She's nicer than I gave her credit for. She rushed in, 'Do you remember at the baths on Saturday? You said you thought that you'd never get the children back. Well, would you like to see them? Have you thought about it at all?'

There was a small pause; 'If you mean, have I fantasised, yes.'

'And what have you imagined?'

'At best a tearful reunion with everything forgiven and forgotten; a big production: music, choirs, clouds and dancing, the lot!' She grinned in embarrassment. 'Most frequently an utter catastrophe: they scream at me and denounce me publicly, refuse to speak to me and I'm left desolate while they are shepherded away.'

'And what do you think might really happen?'

'Probably a mixture of both.'

'Mm; you're probably right. Would you cope with it?'

'I honestly don't know. Part of me aches for them, but another part remembers how furious I was when I couldn't control them, and the relief when they spent more and more time with the Hammonds. I wonder if I'd be any better the second time.'

Maureen smiled. 'I'm going to see Anna and Megan this afternoon. Shall I find out how they feel about seeing you?'

'Oh, do you think they'll really want to see me after all that's happened? It's not that I don't want to. I'm just wondering about how they'll feel.' She hoped she sounded doubtful rather than unwilling.

'I think there's a chance that they'll want to.'

'I can't imagine it. But if you're sure, well, yes, go ahead.' This could be the solution, Sally thought. I could take Anna and Megan to Australia after all and just say that Dave was too busy to come. Could I? Mummy wouldn't spend time talking to the girls. She wouldn't find out where they'd been.

Why just a holiday? We could stay and start a new life together in the sun and put all this behind us. They'd have lovely countryside to grow up in; they'd be happy. They'd forget all this. I would as well.

Struggling to control her excitement, she rested her heels on the bar of the chair, grasped her knees and hugged herself nervously. 'When will you let me know?'

'Will you be in tomorrow morning?'

'Yes, and I'll be home tonight as well: at least, up to half-past seven.'

'All right then. I'll ring you before you go out.'

'That would be a great relief.' She rocked backwards and forwards on her chair, opened her mouth to say something; then got up suddenly and walked over to the worktop.

'More toast?'

'Ah, no thanks: even pigs like me stop shovelling sometimes,' she laughed.

This was her chance. Sally turned to her slowly. 'Was it always as easy to talk about it, your eating, I mean? Was it worse at the beginning, before you'd admitted it to anyone?'

'Why do you ask?'

'It's funny, isn't it, it's like being in school. If you're innumerate, you can joke about it and it endears you to people, whereas being illiterate is something to be ashamed of.'

'Are you saying that my compulsive eating is in the same league as innumeracy?'

'Yes.'

'What is your equivalent to being illiterate then?' she asked, looking at her steadily.

'Being an alcoholic.' Sally Barnett said the word flatly.

'And are you?' Maureen asked, very quietly.

'Yes, I am.' She held her gaze defiantly.

'When did you realise?'

'Ah, no, the question should be, when did I first admit it? I've always known; accepting it was the problem. Accepting reality has always been my problem. I day-dreamed my childhood away.' She paused. 'And admitting it; yes, that's it: that's been the difficult bit, and terrifying.' She fiddled with her coffee mug, running her finger repeatedly around the rim. 'You can't imagine it,' she said quietly.

'I can try.'

'I'm sorry, I didn't mean it like that. It's just such a muddle. I keep trying to tell myself that everyone drinks. I keep telling myself that, and it's true, they do, but not for the same reasons.' She paused again and took a deep breath: 'And not the same amount.'

When Maureen said nothing, she went on. 'And sometimes I'm still not sure. I still don't really want to admit to being an alcoholic. It seems so hopeless. I keep thinking that someone will say that I'm not, and that I'm only a heavy drinker and maybe should think of giving it up for a while or at least pay me the compliment of imagining that I could.'

'And could you?' Her voice was level, unchallenging.

'I don't know, sometimes I kid myself.'

'You're not lying to yourself or me now.'

'Not about this, no, but part of me wishes I still was.' One side of her face began to twist into a strange smile and she checked it immediately.

'What made you decide to tell me? I mean, now, this morning?'

'Because you've just given me hope. I can see a future for myself and . . . Do you remember when we met at the Turkish on Saturday? Well, I knew then really. I sat brooding for a bit after you'd left, feeling sorry for myself. Then I went back into the steam room and I collapsed just inside the door: which was just as well or I mightn't have been spotted. Anyway, I hit my head on the bench, so I got carted straight off to hospital with concussion and was kept in overnight for observation. I was feeling okay by evening, or rather, I was feeling like a drink, but they insisted that I stayed. It was the first time I'd ever been desperate for a drink and not able to get one. I lay awake most of that night, absolutely sober. I couldn't escape.' She stared at her cup and tears began to well.

'Do you want to talk about it now?'

'Yes, now that I've started.' She paused for a moment. 'As the problems with the girls got worse, so did my drinking.' She stopped, then turned and looked steadily at Maureen. 'I think I was already a heavy drinker three years ago when Anna was referred to the school psychologist.'

'Were you surprised when that happened?'

'No, not really, I just pretended to be. Dave had been telling me for years that she was uncontrollable; and of course, his mother did as well: that really got up my nose. I think I took a perverse sort of pride in it – that I could tolerate her, and at the same time, she dared to do all the things I never had. When she started school and the complaints rolled in I joined the PTA just to show that I didn't give a damn and that I wasn't worried about her. Anyway, it all fell apart when she was referred.

'We finally got an appointment to see the psychologist at the end of October but Dave skipped it and left the following week.'

'And how did you feel then?'

'At first, I wasn't worried. It was easier without him in a way, and I thought I could manage. He had blamed all her problems on me. It was a relief not to have him raging at me. There was silence for the first three months. I wouldn't have known where he was if Gwen hadn't told me. Then a couple of months later, he started to phone quite often, and wanted the children to visit him; me as well. He said he'd moved to the North. An aunt of his had died and left him her house. He was renovating it.'

Sally Barnett stared at the table, 'Pathetic really: in our different ways we both played dolls' houses.' There was another silence and she shook her head. 'No, it wouldn't have made any difference. He hadn't changed.

'Anyway, he used to phone and ask to speak to the children, and I used to lie, because by this time they were spending every evening with the Hammonds: George and Betty Hammond – "Uncle George and Aunty Betty" to them.' She covered the top of her coffee mug with both hands and stared at them. There was a long pause.

'You don't have to say any more.'

'It's all right. I want to go on, but I want to show you something first.' She got up and brought a photograph album from the dresser. 'This is what they said they were doing.' She opened the album and Anna and Megan gazed out from white fur capes and hoods. 'Snow Princesses' the caption read. 'I believed them. They were so plausible.'

'How did you meet them?'

'I met her first, at the school gate. We used to chat while waiting for the children, and walk home together. One night she brought them home when I didn't turn up, and said she would do it every night if I wasn't well. She said it was easier for her to have a couple of little friends for her little girl to play with and if I didn't mind, she'd be quite happy to have them stay for tea. It just snowballed. Then she suggested that they should have a portfolio made. They both photographed well and she said they would enjoy the modelling sessions. They seemed happier with anyone rather than me, and when Anna's behaviour began to improve, it seemed like a very good arrangement.'

'How did she improve?'

'Oh, became quieter, both here and in school. We assumed she was settling down, and when she was brought home every night nearly asleep, I just thought it was healthy tiredness and she'd been playing boisterous games with Betty Hammond's child. Betty usually brought them back, though sometimes her husband did. They seemed a perfectly ordinary couple, and they made life so much easier for me. It increased from two nights a week to four; then most weekends. It might have gone on for ever if the police hadn't raided their house for drugs and found the . . . those photographs.'

Sally paused, took a breath and shook her head disbelievingly.

'Then they came here; and of course I was half cut; so a Place of Safety order was made, and the girls were taken into care.' She breathed out very slowly and she sat quite still, slumped forward with her chin on her knees.

'Have you told anyone else about your drinking?'

'No, not yet,' she hesitated: 'but I'm going to my first AA meeting tonight.' There was another pause and she said brightly, 'So when we go and see Anna and Megan, I can tell them it's going to be different.' She nodded to herself, her chin thrust forward. 'And it will be,' she nodded again. 'And I'll get them back, no matter how long it takes.'

She avoided Maureen's gaze and went on, 'I've thought of AA before, you know, but it didn't seem worth it then. There was no point. But now . . .'

Seconds passed. She was crying silently, her teeth gritted, head tilted back defiantly, the tears running unchecked down her face.

Maureen struggled: 'But . . .' She stopped and Sally Barnett seemed not to have noticed. Maureen took a deep breath, then another. 'How will you feel about all this tonight if the children don't want to see you?'

Sally Barnett's face registered complete disbelief; then anger.

'You said moments ago that they would!'

'I said that I *thought* there was a chance that they would, but I haven't asked them yet.'

Sally interrupted furiously: 'You're going back on your word.' They've got to see me, she thought, we're all going to Australia.

'It's not that,' Maureen reasoned. 'It's just that you're pinning your hopes on seeing the children again and what I'm saying is: they mightn't want to see you.'

'I know what you're saying and it isn't what you said to begin with.'

'It is, but I can't help it if you didn't hear me,' she said flatly. 'And what I'm saying now is: how will you feel tonight if the children don't want to see you?'

'I'll probably feel like having a drink.'

'That sounds like blackmail.'

'Then I'm sorry, but you asked the question and that's my honest answer. It's what I usually do. Why should tonight be any different?'

ELEVEN

Why indeed? thought Maureen as she stood on the doorstep, still shaken. I should never have said anything to her about going to see Anna and Megan. It was just because she paid me a compliment.

She clutched her coat collar, and set off quickly to the car. I'll sort it all out at the office, she decided, as she threaded her way carefully into the relentless streams of mid-day traffic.

'Hi, my love,' Trudi greeted her cheerfully from behind a large sandwich. 'Just in time for the rest of my sarni. I've got to dash.'

'Thanks; but before you go, have there been any messages while I've been out?'

'Nope, nuffink, so now's your chance to emigrate, unless you're going to change your mind and come to the meeting tonight.'

'That sounds like the best idea you've ever had,' she said, picking up the half-eaten sandwich, then putting it down again.

'The meeting?' Trudi smiled.

'No, emigrating. I'm not into politics.'

'You can't not be. The cuts are affecting all of us. Look what they've done to the Barnett children.'

'I know and I'm just about to ring Springfields and arrange

to see them. Look, I'll talk to you again about all this, bu
not now: I'm swamped with work.'

'Chickens and eggs,' Trudi said, gathering her papers. Sh
picked up her coat, gave a cool, rather dismissive wave an
walked out.

Maureen shrugged; then dialled the Springfields numbe

She had always had mixed feelings about Ellen Bramha
and the way she ran the house. She was fair, and her report
were scrupulous, but she was cold and cynical and wa
counting the months to her retirement. One incident sti
niggled: an afternoon when they were standing talkin
together and a small boy approached.

My name is Tony, that's my name. My name is Tony. H
pleaded twice more.

Run along dear and find Maria, Ellen said, and then: he
rubbish, you know.

Tony just stood there and repeated: My name is Tony
that's my name.

She deliberately turned her back on Ellen Bramhall an
said: Hello Tony, I'm Maureen.

You've made your point, Miss Wilson, but I don't believ
in hypocrisy. There's no point in pretending they're an
good. None of them will amount to anything and I won
pretend otherwise, even if you report me.

When Ellen Bramhall answered, her plummy voice was botl
triumphant and defensive: 'Well, yes, of course, Miss Wil
son. Quite frankly, I'd almost given up hope of getting any
one to come and see for themselves, because we cope to
well and we've been left to get on with it.'

Maureen pulled a face, then quickly withdrew her tongue
The woman had a right to be fed up. She'd been in the firin
line for a year. Ellen Bramhall continued: 'You've left i
rather late. There's very little time before the High Cour
hearing, but I suppose we should be grateful.'

Maureen Wilson bared her teeth at the receiver. 'So woul

half-past four be okay?' she said. 'After they come in from school and before they have their tea? Fine, I won't keep you then, Miss Bramhall: I know how busy you are.'

'I wonder if you do, Miss Wilson.'

Maureen mimicked her silently; then said, 'I'll see you later then. Bye.' She put the phone down and groaned.

There was a mute despair about Megan standing with her feet turned in, her head down, slumped against the armchair.

'Hello, Megan. I'm Maureen,' she began.

'She doesn't talk,' Anna said. 'I talk for her. I know what she wants.' She flitted from one chair to the other, unfocused. 'I want a Walkman and when it's my birthday I'm going to get a personal television. I might get two. I might get two Walkmen. I'm always getting things.'

'Megan,' Maureen turned to the silent child.

'It's no good. I told you, she doesn't talk to anyone. Can we go now? I want to play.'

She bombed off towards the door.

'In a moment, Anna; but I'd like to talk to you first. I want to ask you something.'

Anna rushed back from the door, hurled herself at Maureen; straddled, then wriggled off her knee. Her high-pitched giggling changed to an engine sound. She chugged away, then turned and peeped over the back of a chair.

'Anna, I have to go soon and we haven't talked to each other yet. Come over here. I'm not going to hurt you.'

'You have to give me a present if you do. That's the game.'

'What's that game, Anna? How do you play it?' She tried to keep her voice level.

'With my friends, it's doctors and nurses. They say, "This might hurt a little bit."' She spun on one foot, mimicking. '"But if you're brave, you'll get a nice present." That's the game. I have to let them hurt me first and I have to smile; then I get my present. I like that bit, it's good.'

'And what else do you like doing?' She tried to make it sound matter-of-fact.

Anna turned her head away and smiled. 'Ballet. I can do ballet and I can get Megan to do it as well. Shall I get Megan to do the splits for you?' She began to do pliés, using the back of the armchair as a barre. Then she turned towards Maureen, lowered her hands demurely to the top of her legs and stood, her knees slightly bent and turned out, her lids lowered, rimming her lips and smiling.

Maureen jerked out of her seat. 'I would still like to talk to you, Anna. There's still something I want to ask you.'

Anna interrupted. 'If I tell you, will you bring me a Walkman?' She opened her eyes wide. 'If you bring me one, I might get Megan to talk to you as well.' She stood for a moment, still teasing Maureen with her eyes wide and the tip of her tongue just showing between her teeth.

The single question was asked and answered in seconds and Anna bounced out of the room with Megan trailing behind.

Oh God, I've let myself in for something here, Maureen thought as she closed the door behind them.

Ellen Bramhall came out of her sitting-room and stood waiting. 'Do come in, Miss Wilson. I'm very anxious to know what you've decided . . .' She settled into her chair beside the fire. Maureen perched on the edge of the other chair.

'Well, now that you've met them, what do you think?'

'They both need help, but I can't work with them: I haven't the time,' she said flatly.

'So you think we have? If they stay in care, this isn't the place for them. We haven't the staff. Anna is one person's full-time job.'

'I'll make an immediate referral to the Child Guidance Clinic, but there's a waiting list and it's longer now than ever it was, because of the cut-backs.'

'And what do you expect us to do in the meantime? How are my staff supposed to cope? Megan is doubly incontinent and Anna's a monster. They must be moved from here.'

'They are very severely disturbed children.'

'I'm very impressed with your understanding of them, Miss Wilson: particularly as you are about to walk out of here and leave them. It's a pity your understanding couldn't extend to us as well.'

'I sympathise, and I'll try my best to get help for both girls, but I'm not a fairy godmother. Or do you expect me to take them home with me tonight?'

'That might be useful training.'

'I don't need any more training.' She kept her voice level. 'I can understand your anger, and I'll do my best to get help.'

What is it about this woman that makes me so pompous? she wondered. Why can't I just admit to being as helpless as she is?

She sat back in her chair. Her face was roasting in the relentless heat of the electric fire. She tried to rub her scorched legs discreetly and she could feel sweat prickling under her arms. To her relief, Ellen Bramhall said, 'Well, I won't keep you any longer, Miss Wilson. I can see you're anxious to leave.'

Maureen said nothing but gathered her bag and got up. At the door, she turned. 'I'd like to come back tomorrow, Miss Bramhall, about the same time, if that's all right.'

'Of course: even half an hour's relief is better than nothing.'

'If it relieves the pressure, well then, good: but I'm coming to see Anna and Megan, not organise your staffing. I'm sure you prefer to do that yourself,' she said smoothly, as she opened the door.

She closed it carefully behind her. Damn, damn, damn, damn the woman, she raged all the way to the car. She fastened her seat belt and sat shaking. You're just furious with her, because this time she's right, and you've been made to look a fool. And it was more than that. She had told a lie and Ellen Bramhall had not believed her.

As she crunched slowly down the gravel drive, and drove carefully over the sleeping policemen, Maureen decided to give the rush-hour traffic a miss and have a cup of tea. I wouldn't have been able to swallow one anyway, even if she'd offered it, she thought as she drove out into the dual carriageway.

By the time she reached Archway and found a place to park, it was five thirty. There was still time, if she hurried.

She crossed the road below Kouri's to avoid being seen. She couldn't take his effusive welcome this afternoon, with the inevitable cups of thick sweet coffee and plates of baklava. She couldn't take his concern for her, nor his uncritical admiration: that, least of all. She had decisions to make. Elsie's would be better, with its uncompromising and cheerless austerity.

A single tinsel streamer was still pinned behind the door. Inside, at five of the six formica-topped tables, there were solitary customers, each sitting behind the other, all facing the same greasy window in a procession to nowhere.

To one side, the perspex counter front held a wicker basket of crisps and a plate of large doughy scones split and spread with margarine.

At the other side was a chipped tureen of chocolate marshmallows in their red and silver wrappers, like a heap of abandoned Christmas tree decorations. Above them, a Santa Claus face had crumpled in the steam and grease, and curled away contemptuously.

Elsie squirted steam into the large aluminium teapot, grasped both handles firmly, swilled it round twice; then tipped it back and forward to yield half a cup of stewed tea. She repeated the process resentfully and wrung a further inch into the cup.

'And two marshmallows, please,' Maureen said firmly, handing over a pound coin.

She turned to the one empty table and merciful privacy

128

behind the back of the customer in front. Scraping the table legs across the lino, she squeezed herself into the seat, and sighed as the shudders caused waves of tea to slop into her saucer.

Staring into space, she automatically unwrapped the foil from the first marshmallow: cracking the chocolate crust and biting through the foam to reach the biscuit base. She picked crumbs off the table, remembering that other formica-topped table, and the crowd of noisy children shovelling and scraping beans on toast.

Rousing herself, she pulled out her notebook. She'd start at the beginning:

Wednesday
2nd home visit to Sally Barnett. On Saturday S.B. had ex-pressed doubts about further meetings. Was given option of cancelling today's visit, but rang yesterday to confirm. Spoke of alcohol dependency and decision to attend AA meeting, fol-lowing accident on Saturday when she had a fall, suffered con-cussion and was detained overnight in hospital. Was undecided at first about seeing children but eventually agreed to go ahead with meeting if they were willing.

t wasn't exactly untrue. And it was only a summary so she didn't have to put in all the details. She clenched her teeth at the first bitter sip of stewed tea.

Elsie was purposefully collecting the empty cups, and the regulars were beginning to leave in response to her familiar signal. Maureen drained the slops from her saucer back into her cup and bit into the second marshmallow. She screwed both wrappers into a small ball, and began writing again:

Wednesday
First meeting with Anna and Megan Barnett at Springfields

hen put her biro down.

Ellen Bramhall hadn't been exaggerating at the last Children's Centre staff meeting two weeks ago. The children had been at Springfields for nearly a year, and Ellen Bramhall was on record as asking for help at every meeting since their placement. She said that Anna had to be watched carefully with two of the older boys. But all the Authority's homes had boys of a similar age, and so it had been argued that to move her would not solve the problem.

And I can't work with Anna either, she thought, struggling and failing to unfold the silver and red pellet. But someone will have to. The waiting list for therapy is months long and it won't improve until the Family and Child Guidance Clinic are allowed to fill the psychotherapist posts. I'll just have to persuade Springfields to battle on; and worse encourage them to achieve some empathy with the child. She pulled a face at the thought of Ellen Bramhall's reaction to that suggestion, and rehearsed her plea:

No child's a monster without good reason: and Anna has more reasons than most for being unlikeable. Heaven knows what she endured before the Place of Safety order.

But it was no good. She disliked the child as much as Ellen Bramhall did, and Ellen Bramhall knew it.

Her tea was cold, and the strong bitter taste counteracted the sweetness of the marshmallow. Elsie dropped the latch on the door and pulled down the blind as a final hint. After a second attempt, Maureen abandoned her tea, gathered her bag and left.

Outside the café she glanced towards Kouri's, hesitated then crossed the road and kept her head down until she reached her car in the side street. A thin cold rain had started to fall, and she pulled out to join a concert of rush-hour noise and windscreen-wipers. As the lights turned red at every junction she could feel her impatience giving way to bad temper at the thought of the next Children's Centre staff meeting and the work still to be done before she could submit her affidavit to the court. For that, she would have to present information and evidence, suggest possible solutions, and sound convinced as well as convincing. Her boss always said that definite solutions were easy; it was the possible ones that were difficult. And they would be, particularly if the children were returned to Springfields after the High Court hearing.

But first, now, before all that she had to phone Sally Barnett.

She negotiated the North Circular Road, and forty minutes later drew up in the yard behind the office. The cleaners were still there, miming behind brilliantly lit windows that shed rectangles of light and shadows on to the car park.

Her office was empty, and her desk clear except for a note in Trudi's large scrawl:

Maureen: if you're in tomorrow, can you be a love and give me a hand? I'm up to my neck. Hope the trip to Springfields was not as bad as you thought.

Trudi had drawn a heart under her signature with an arrow through it; three drops of blood and two exclamation marks after them. Underneath, she'd written: *Don't let them break it!*

Typical of Trudi. She wasn't that bad. She was quite astute, and a survivor. Trudi might be able to help her. She opened her top drawer and took out a small thin phone book.

She flicked through; then held a page open with her elbow and picked up the phone. A man's voice answered. No, Trudi wasn't at home. She wasn't expected until late. Was she on call? She hadn't said anything. Could he take a message? Thanks, but no, it was all right, she'd see her tomorrow. She replaced the receiver slowly and glanced at the clock above the door. Then, after a final hesitation, she dialled Sally Barnett's number.

Hours later, Maureen lay staring at the ceiling.

This time, the dream had been of wave upon wave of long grass rolling across a valley, pursued by the sky: everything moving, the whole universe in motion and she with it, wind-borne, floating effortlessly, the slightest contraction of her leg muscles sending her soaring, twenty, thirty feet in the air, legs outstretched like a hurdler, before floating slowly to earth again, to reconnect and renew her energy from its infinite source; then spring back up, to stride the universe and reach the stratosphere: completely alone and fearless and free.

The same dream had persisted for years, even after she'd gone to college. Eventually it had faded, and returned only rarely.

Then, a month ago, just after Anne Stevens left, when she had felt trapped again, it had come back. Tonight was the second time in a week. She had thought of it as just a bit of nonsense, but not any more. Now she understood. The dream was about trying to escape.

But why shouldn't the rest of the dream come true?

Because you're too fat and you wouldn't dare, she thought as she turned over and tried to get back to sleep.

TWELVE

o that explained it! All them toys: Dave Barnett had made
hem. Karin sat at the kitchen table with another box file in
ront of her: Pull-Along Toys: Invoices.

She browsed through them. He must be a millionaire; his
rices were sky-high. Fancy charging fifteen pounds for a
ttle mouse. It should shit diamonds for that.

'Hand-made' was stressed at every chance but what sort
f person would pay fifteen pounds for a piece of wood on
our wheels with a string attached?

The last invoice in the box was for 25th November, two
ears ago, to Lakeland Crafts, Appleby:

3 dozen Pull–Along animals, assorted @ £15 each	£504.00	
VAT @ 15%	£77.60	
	———	
Total	£581.60	

Jo it wasn't! Thirty-six times fifteen was £540: so his VAT
vas wrong as well. It was anyway: 15% of £504 was £75.60,
ot £77.60. She'd leave him a note about how to move the
ecimal point to the left and add on half as much again.

Mebbe there was no need. There were no more invoices.
Mebbe he'd stopped making the animals. Mebbe he'd gone

bankrupt. What could he expect if he couldn't do simpl[e]
multiplication!

Mansell was meditating. That foxy girl still bothered him
She'd nearly lost her voice that day. She'd been going dow[n]
with sommat. He sat with his trousers around his knees an[d]
his braces dangling over his boots. The wooden seat wa[s]
warm and comfortably broad and his elbow leaned easily o[n]
the window sill.

'Are you going to be in there all day?'

He looked out of the window. Dave Barnett's house sti[ll]
looked secure enough. She must've gone back home or t[o]
wherever she'd come from; somewhere safe, with a bit [of]
luck. Somewhere a bit better than this, he thought. He s[at]
and held his breath.

'I asked you a question.'

'What business is it of yours?'

'Are you going to give me a hand with the milking [or]
not?'

'Aye, in a minute.'

'You've had twenty minutes already.'

'So one more won't make any difference.'

He heard her slam the back door, watched her pick h[er]
way across the yard to the byre; then returned to h[is]
thoughts.

They were broken again by a small speck on the edge [of]
the fell. As he watched, it grew larger, and soon he coul[d]
distinguish a tall spout and spume of snow flying behind [it.]
The plough: at last! Hastily he yanked up his trousers an[d]
adjusted his braces, clumped downstairs and swung his co[at]
off the back of the door as he passed.

He was half-way across the yard and heading away fro[m]
the byre when her voice pulled him to a halt. 'And whe[re]
d'you think you're going?'

'It's the plough. I'm just going to see if he needs anything[.]'

'Are you feeling all right?'

'Aye, why d'you ask that?'

'I've never known you go to help anyone in your life, hat's why.'

'But you don't know everything, do you?'

'I know a lot more than you.'

'Aye, but not about me, you don't,' he said over his houlder, and struggled on to the road.

He'd had Joan's letter written for nearly four days now nd it was getting a bit crumpled in his top pocket. He'd said e wished she'd come home some time; that he'd like to see er. But she wouldn't come; not if she had any sense. She vas better off out of the place. It was getting to be a snarling natch from one day's end to the next. It wouldn't make Maggie any better with him; it would only keep her occu- ied for a bit, having Joan to fuss over. Then when she went ack, Maggie would be worse than ever.

She'd never liked farm life. She'd be better off going to ve with Joan and it'd please him if she did. He wouldn't niss her, the way she was getting. He'd have to sell the easts, of course, but he would still manage. He could let a ouple of the bottom fields, just keep a few ewes. Naw, that ould mean tramping down to Lower Myers with hay. Jaw, he'd let the whole bloody farm and just manage on ie rent money somehow.

Maggie would never come back. She'd told him once; ie'd said: There are times that I detest you so much, I can ardly stomach you. She'd gone out somewhere and not ome back till milking time. She'd acted as if she'd never said owt but she never took it back. She'd meant it, every word. nd they both knew it.

he snowplough driver was young Harry Bell from North- ate. He stopped the machine and lifted the earflaps of his cap.

'All right then, Mansell? Owt you want?'

'Naw, just a letter here for the post.'

'Give me it here, I'll see that it gets there.'

'How's that brother of yours? Is he still at home?'

'Geordie? Aye, he's jobbing on.'

'Well ask him if he'll do a couple of days for us sometime in the next couple of weeks then.'

'Any idea when?'

'Not yet, not till I get an answer to that letter. Why, is he going away?'

'Naw, he'll be around. I'll tell him that you want him.'

He tucked the dog-eared envelope inside his donkey jacket, and restarted the engine.

'I'll probably be back at the weekend, unless there's a new lot, and I'm called out to clear the main road again,' he shouted above the noise. 'D'you want me to bring your post if there is any?'

'Aye: if you don't mind, it'd be a help.'

'No bother, Mansell,' Harry called, and the machine lumbered forward in first gear.

Mansell watched as the plough continued to blow a narrow track across the high fell road. He watched it getting steadily smaller and smaller, building a wall along the edge of the snow poles, a barrier in a wilderness. He turned reluctantly.

With a bit of luck, she'd be well through the milking.

Dave Barnett had told Gwen that he didn't want to see his mother in the funeral parlour, but she had said, She can't do you any harm now, and the unexpected gentleness in her voice had shamed him into coming.

They stood nervously in the office while the girl checked the register; then followed her into a corridor. She opened one of the doors, switched on the light and stood aside. Gwen and Mavis went in first, followed by Philip. Dave hesitated, hovering at the door before making a move to stand behind Philip and keeping his eyes on the floor.

'Isn't she lovely?' he heard Gwen whisper.

'So peaceful, you cannot be sad for her,' replied Mavis.

He lifted his eyes just as Gwen was stepping aside. The little wax figure in the coffin wasn't his mother. It was just a body: somebody, anybody, he decided. So it wasn't going to be as bad as he'd imagined, and by the day after tomorrow, it would all be over. There'd be no one at the service. Fifteen minutes would see it finished. He was glad he had come. There was nothing to it after all.

It had been two days since Karin had lit the gas boiler and the radiators were still cold. She had tried bleeding them, but that wasn't the problem and, as far as she could tell, there were no air locks in the system.

There was a bloody control panel somewhere, but where? It had to be in the loft. That was the only place left.

She would leave the cupboards under the dresser and the boxes of china. She could sort them later.

At the top of the stairs, the trapdoor was in the ceiling directly above her head, and the loft pole was propped in the corner beside the bathroom door. She craned her neck and aimed the hook carefully at the ring. At the second attempt, it engaged; and when she pulled, the door opened smoothly downwards, bringing a set of stairs gliding towards her on a flood of sunlight. She extended them and with very little pressure, braced them into a locked position. She switched off the landing light, and grinned as she looked up to see cupboards, and a radiator running along a narrow ceiling which sloped away steeply on either side.

Cautiously she climbed the stairs, then turned to face a winter sunrise pouring through an unshuttered window in the gable wall.

The sloping roof on either side restricted the headroom to a central passageway, about six feet wide, that ran the length of the ridge.

On either side were storage units and bookshelves and cupboards, their white formica surfaces all sun-tinged pink.

It was light and it could be warm. There were days of exploration here.

She moved to the window, and gazed out over endless snow, to a pink sky and its reflection on distant hills and in myriads of ice flakes in the nearest field.

She stood, looking at the light falling on her hands, moving her fingers and watching their shadows. Then, drawing back, she bent down and looked out at the landscape again.

The work unit in front of the window opened to reveal a computer terminal, with manuals and floppy discs stored above it.

The tears routed themselves around the Vaseline on her cheeks and ran down the sides of her face in front of her ears.

This is all I've ever wanted: well, nearly. She quickly shut out a memory that threatened to erupt. Stop thinking of that, you dafty. The past is past. There's only now, this minute. Even the future is still in your head. So's the past. The only bit that's real is now, standing here in the loft with all this stuff, in a house in the middle of nowhere and seeing the sun on the snow.

This is what I want. I want to know things; I want to learn, I want peace and quiet to read.

So what are you crying for, you great gowk? Now's your chance. You never had one before. You just had to do what you could. You hadn't any choice.

She took a deep breath, held it for a moment; then roared through a fresh outburst of tears: 'It's true, it is, I'm telling you: why didn't you believe me?'

But Mr Weissbaum had never even pretended to believe her. What had he said when she left?

That is the important thing to remember, Karin, that you always have a choice.

He was a little man, with white hair driven back from his

138

forehead by ruthless brushing. A little man with bottle-bottom specs and a posh voice. A man she had come to respect, in spite of herself.

Mr Weissbaum, Area Psychologist: she had been referred to him at Child Guidance after the cloakroom flood at school.

She intercepted the appointment letter to her parents and decided to go on her own. It would stop any snooping and get her a morning off school.

He hadn't been fooled. She told him that her mam was ill and her dad was at work.

He'd lose a day's pay if he took a couple of hours off to come here. He's not like you lot, you know. If he isn't at work he doesn't get paid. The psychologist had just nodded and said he understood. It was often the case and he was sorry about her mother.

I'm surprised you got this job with a name like yours, was her opening gambit.

Why?

Well, it looks all right on paper, but the way your secretary says it!

Oh, Mrs Forster. Yes, she always calls me Vice Bum, doesn't she?

She changed tack, have you always worn them bottle-bottoms?

Yes, I was always short-sighted. There was a pause and when she said nothing more he asked calmly: If you have no more questions, shall we move on? He wasn't angry. He wasn't even slightly annoyed. He could fend her questions all day.

All right then, but I'm gonna call you Whitebum; that's half and half.

He smiled, Yes: that's a good compromise and also true. My bottom is very white.

He was hard and not going to rise easily to a bait. She'd have to try something else.

Did they tell you what I did?

Your school, you mean? You were referred for disruptive behaviour.

I've been in bother with the police as well. Did they tell you that? I bet they didn't because they don't know half. D'you want to know everything I've done? I'll tell you if you like.

If that is how you want to spend your time, that is your choice. I am more interested in why you did these things.

I bet you are, she thought. And you'll have to stay that way.

I don't know why I do these things. I just do.

If that was true, then these meetings would be to help you understand your reasons. But you already know what they are. What we must discover is whether you are ready to talk about them.

He spoke very calmly and quietly.

By the end of that first visit she knew she had met her match. She couldn't rile him and she couldn't fool him.

Bugger him, he looks like a bit of crumble but he's missed nowt, she admitted grudgingly.

That had been nearly a year ago.

After that, she spent each session joking and wise-cracking, first in response to any question and then as a solil-oquy, a weekly monologue to which he listened with an intent courtesy.

They met once a week for two terms, and at the end of July he said: Well, our time together is over, Karin, and you have refused to look at your problems. I am sure some day, when you are ready, you will sort them out, because you are clever. When you do, you might be happy: and you will find it is better than being clever. You are also very brave. It takes courage to carry secrets alone, to endure that sort of loneli-ness. I am sure you have a good reason for doing it and I respect your choice. The only thing that worries me is this: he looked at her over the top of his glasses: you might forget that it *is* your own choice and that you are free at any time to change your mind and talk to someone. That is the imortant thing to remember, that you always have a choice.

She could have smacked him in the gob. She felt like creaming at him. But I haven't! That's the whole bloody rouble, you idiot. Instead she sat fighting back tears because he was talking to *her*, the person inside the clown, the one who wanted to respond instead of bouncing up and going owards the door with, I'll remember that: I'll work out ome new cracks and then I'll have an even better choice.

But it was no good. He knew she had understood. He just nodded sadly. He knew her through and through, she was certain of that, although she'd been careful to give nothing way. He could have told her what was wrong, but he respected her too much to do that; and besides, he knew she would just deny it. As she opened the door he said, I hope ou'll be happy, Karin. I hope that some day you'll be so appy you won't need to be funny any more.

Suddenly, from nowhere, snowflakes began to whirl at the window. The sun disappeared.

Come on: you came up here to find the central heating ontrol, remember?

She turned angrily from the window and walked back to he stairs, judging that the cupboard on the far side was most irectly above the bathroom and kitchen. She was right. Everything was there, labelled and lagged and insulated. She moved the pointer on the control panel to a spot midway etween heating and hot-water, then set the time switch to ring it on at half-past six every morning. It would be lovely o wake up to a warm house every day. She closed the valves n the overhead radiators. There was no point in wasting eat. She wouldn't be coming up here again until she was caving, and then only to put the time switch off.

She took a last look round. It was no good. Look what ad happened already. She'd thought about old Whitebum nd got herself upset. When she first saw the computer, she'd ven been tempted to change her plan. But that would be the end, she knew. She couldn't change her mind now or she would start to think about everything that had happened, to live in the past, and then she'd be finished. There had been no choice then, and she'd done what had to be done, and it was the same now. Thinking about things wouldn't change them, and wishful thinking would wreck her only chance of a future.

No, this was off-limits from now on. There was enough to do to keep her busy: things to get ready, plans to be made, all sorts of things to think about; real things that would be happening as she thought about them, not things in her head that didn't belong there. If only you could take bits out of your brain when you'd finished with them and didn't want them any more. But you couldn't. All you could do was to keep yourself busy so they didn't get a chance to sneak to the front again.

On the landing, she folded the stairs and pushed them slowly back into the loft with the pole, watching the rectangle of light being tucked away, getting smaller and smaller, until it disappeared altogether, as the trap door closed and the latch clicked firmly into place.

THIRTEEN

Maureen Wilson cruised slowly down the side road, looking for a parking place. Suddenly a van pulled out ten yards ahead of her, and she moved in with room to spare.

About time that something went right, she thought grimly.

It was a bitterly cold evening. The pavement was seething with people: heads down against the wind, skirting promontories of vegetable stalls which threatened to divert them like lemmings into the oncoming traffic. With a momentary loss of concentration, Maureen found herself crushed between a paper seller's stand and a road barrier at the junction of Archway and Wood Lane. Her legs sagged.

'Bloody murder,' the man grumbled, glancing at her briefly as he proffered the *Evening Standard*. 'I'd give up if I were you, love.'

She didn't move, and he peered at her more closely. 'Aw, gawd, I didn't mean you should give *up*.' He emphasised the last word. 'Not like that,' he added. She leaned her head against the booth.

'Come on, now: look on the bright side, eh?' he nagged, worried now.

'I'm okay.'

'There you are, then. Tell you what, you go straight home and put your feet up, right?'

She nodded.

'There's a good girl,' he said with relief as she dislodged herself and straightened up.

The shop windows glared at her as she hurried past, head down against the traffic noise, walking unheeding through vegetable refuse and litter swirling and clinging to her ankles.

Kouri's window was blank with condensation, but Maureen knew she had been spotted before she opened the door. Fingers snapped, a chair was pulled out, and she was eased into the family table in the corner with her back to the wall. A cup of coffee and a plate of baklava were put in front of her, and Kouri hovered, an expression of intense concern on his face.

'You look like you had one hell of day, Miss Wilson.'

She nodded and felt a single tear spill over her lower lid and run slowly down her neck.

'You bring friends when you like this then you not be lone and I no worry so bad.'

He snapped his fingers again, and green figs with cream and honey materialised.

'Ah, Kouri,' she breathed softly.

'Not be unhappy. Eat everything I have, please. Then we both happy.' His worn, crumpled face scrutinised her anxiously. 'You no well?'

'Yes, no; I mean, I'm all right, Kouri, I'm just a bit tired.'

'But you cry?'

'Yes, because I'm tired.'

'No, no tired, you sad. Some sod getting you? I kill him.'

She snorted a bubble of laughter through her snotty nose.

'Thank you,' she gasped, wiping her eyes and nose in one sweep with a napkin. 'I know you would.'

'Is true. I owe you everything,' he said simply, spreading his fingers.

'No you don't. Dimitri was never a bad boy. He just go

into bad company. He would have sorted himself out eventually.'

'No.' His contradiction was emphatic. 'Dimitri was sod because I busy all time and he run wild. Without you, he would be dead or in prison: in hell, for sure. Now he has wife and son and works all day and needs an accountant, he pay such bloody big taxes.'

'So how's that little grandson of yours?'

Kouri's eyes crinkled into a smile and he straightened his shoulders. 'He is bloody good kid: smart, the best.'

Maureen grinned, 'I always thought his father was a good kid as well.'

'I know. That why he turn up good. Everyone rubbish him and I am shamed and angry. But you — you always believe in him. He is not able to collapse so much belief. It lift him up. Your friends must all love you.'

What friends? she thought, and grinned again to hold back her tears.

He smacked his forehead. 'Your cup — is empty!' He signalled and the coffee pot was brought over. Then a glass of wine and a plate of olives were put on the table and the menu was opened with a flourish for her.

'Now I give you menu and leave you to feel it.' He adjusted the napkin on his arm. 'I come back soon. Anything you want — is yours.'

Maureen stared at a blank space on the menu and began to eat the olives mindlessly.

At first, everything had gone according to plan. Sally Barnett was waiting for her as arranged at the office at four o'clock, and shortly after that they set off towards Epping, and Springfields.

I was amazed when you rang last night. I still can't believe they want to see me. But what if they won't speak to me? Sally asked.

They might ignore you, but only to begin with, Maureen

replied. She realised that her attempt to be calm and reassuring just sounded pompous. It won't mean that they aren't pleased to see you, she added lamely.

Forty minutes later, they turned left up the drive thickly banked with rhododendron bushes, to the gravel courtyard in front of the house. It was deserted, but there were signs of children everywhere. To one side was a sandpit, a swing, and a climbing frame with an assortment of buckets and margarine tubs strewn about. A small bicycle was propped against the wall and a discarded doll lay on the step naked and bald, its single arm flung behind its head.

I think they're all having tea, she said as she parked neatly alongside the three other cars. They'll be expecting us. All right? she asked, and turned to Sally Barnett who nodded and clenched her teeth, but said nothing.

Maria answered her knock and smiled cheerfully. Oh, Maureen, hi. And Mrs Barnett, isn't it? Come in. Ellen is expecting you. She'll be with you in a minute.

She showed them into the shabby sitting-room, dominated by an ornate black marble fireplace. That would be a good retirement present for madam, she thought as the door opened and Ellen Bramhall swept in. Miss Wilson, she said; and this must be Mrs Barnett, turning to Sally. Anna and Megan are just finishing their tea. Then they're all yours for half an hour.

Maureen chose to ignore her tone. It was a pity she hadn't chosen to ignore Anna as well.

She reached for another olive, then groped absently around the table. Kouri bustled up. 'I see all olives gone; I get more. I happy that you eat.' He refilled her glass and said, 'Now, you tell me what you want.'

Without looking she said, 'The special, Kouri. That'll be great.'

'Not enough. I feed you more,' and he made his way purposefully to the kitchen.

The second glass of wine went down well, and soon she had a third one in her hand, and the second dish of olives was nearly empty.

If only she had got out then, and taken Sally with her, before Maria arrived with Anna and Megan, and squeezed their shoulders and said: Now, look who's here to see you, in a bright, reassuring voice. Then: I'll be back in half an hour. Enjoy yourselves, and smiled at them all as she left.

But I *said* no, I *told* you, Anna began, her voice rising, ignoring Sally's smile and attempted embrace.

Is she still drunk? she demanded, and looked from Sally back to Maureen; then at Megan, who was edging cautiously forward. Wait there, Megan. We don't know what she's like yet, she said, as though Sally was a strange dog, and Megan retreated, sucking the bottom of her jumper.

Sally put her head between her hands, and Megan reluctantly put one leg behind the other and slid back behind a chair. Anna spoke to Maureen again: If you're our social worker, you should get us things. My Walkman's broken and I want another. My friends at the studio used to give me anything I wanted. She ran her tongue around her open mouth. Well, she demanded, are you going to say something, or are you drunk as well?

Maureen leaned forward and put out her hand.

The crack was sharp and explosive. Sally's head jerked up; Anna began to scream hysterically. Megan sobbed. But Maureen did not stop there. Instead, she slapped her again: this time, getting out of her chair to reach her.

She was still on her feet when the door opened and Ellen Bramhall was standing there.

Is Anna being a pain? she asked.

She slapped me, she slapped me, screamed Anna, dancing in rage, her hands between her legs.

I don't think that could be true, Anna: not Miss Wilson, of all people, she added in her plummiest voice.

Maureen took a step forward. It is. She's right, I did slap her.

Anna's screams intensified and Maria reappeared.

Take Anna and Megan, would you, Maria? Ellen Bramhall said; then turned back to Maureen. I'm sure you can explain everything.

No. There's nothing to say. I over-reacted, that's all.

I'll have to report it, of course. Unfortunately I've got no choice, she murmured.

There's no need, and there's no point as you weren't here. I'll report it myself, and Mrs Barnett was witness, so there'll be no problem confirming it. She tried to sound matter-of-fact.

Sally Barnett was still slumped mutely in the chair. Ellen Bramhall raised her eyebrows. I'm surprised something like this hasn't happened before now with you. You're too involved. If you don't get involved, they don't get to you, she ended triumphantly.

And you don't get to them, she thought as she bit fiercely on the last olive, still seeing the shabby sitting-room, with the scuffed chairs dwarfed by the mausoleum-like mantelpiece.

'Miss Wilson,' Kouri said gently as he laid the plate lovingly in front of her. There was a tiny roast leg of baby lamb, spiked with rosemary, on a bed of rice, with pine nuts and sultanas. Maureen swallowed hard as the table filled up with salad, potatoes, stewed aubergines, pitta bread, and a glass bowl of olive oil that glowed green.

'The oil is special for you. It is our own. My brother bring it. No possible to buy this oil in world.'

Maureen breathed deeply and blinked: but the tears refused to be reabsorbed. Her face was swollen with unshed grief and with the next sip of wine, she began to cry. The lamb was whisked away, and Kouri pulled out a chair and sat down opposite her, shielding her from the other diners with his broad back. He leaned across the table and spread his huge hands.

'You work like bloody donkey. We know you do too much when you no come to see us and to eat last two weeks. We all say then that you need holiday. Now I talk to family. We get ticket for you. We all agree you go to my brother. He has hotel. We take you to airport. He meet you and take you. You stay with him for nothing, like family, and stay as long as ever; but then you come back.' He mutely passed her a second large napkin and she buried her whole face in it again and sobbed.

'Oh God,' was all she could gasp.

'It is okay to cry. We cry with you; you cry with us. We hold you high.'

'Don't pile it on, Kouri. I'm not what you think.'

'Now, you are tired and sad but always you are good. Sometimes happy, sometimes sad, but *always* good. We not *think* this, we *know*.' He opened another napkin with a flick and spread it on her knee. 'Now you eat before you collapse. One of the boys take you home. No worry, just to eat and drink.' He nodded approvingly as the lamb was presented again and she took a mouthful. 'Good, now you live and grow strong for holiday.' He leaned across and expertly filleted the leg.

'You'll be spoon-feeding me in a minute, Kouri,' she protested.

'For you, I do anything,' he replied simply.

The steam rose like a veil in front of her. Maureen slid further into the water and watched dispassionately as the cat jumped on to the edge of the bath and toppled her empty wine glass. Instead of tiptoeing along and rubbing his head against her cheek, he stood, out of reach, his back arched, the distance between them an unabridgeable desolation.

A small part of her brain was still quite clear as she dozed in the comforting warmth. Tomorrow she would see her boss and tell him what had happened.

Sally Barnett had said very little as they drove back, but even that had been ominous: Anna has always known her own mind. Why did you tell me she wanted to see me? Oh, the AA meeting; I suppose you thought I wouldn't go if you told me the truth. That's an insult, to try and protect me from the truth. As it happened, I didn't manage to go because Gwen phoned just as I was leaving to tell me that her mother had died, and we talked for nearly half an hour so I was too late. You must think you're a very superior person. Of course you must, or you wouldn't be a social worker – all in a quiet icy voice, almost triumphant. Once she thought about it, she would be vociferous. Of that she was certain.

That wasn't the point. Even if Sally didn't make a fuss, she deserved a dependable, balanced social worker; so did Anna and Megan. At the thought of them, Maureen leaned over the bath and groped for the wine bottle. Tilting it violently, she drained the last half glass into her mouth and down her neck: then banged it clumsily back on to the floor. She screwed her eyes shut and struggled to make sense of it all, as snatches of conversations and glimpses of places continued to dart in and out, her mind sluggishly trying to hold them. Go back to the beginning. That's what you're always telling other people to do.

The beginning: yesterday, Wednesday, and her first visit to the children after she had left Sally Barnett. First impressions: they looked much older than in the photographs. Megan's hair had grown, Anna's had been cut. A year is a huge proportion of a young child's life, so that had been no surprise.

Megan was withdrawn and Anna provocative, but again, no worse than most children in the same situation. She had expected that, accepted it, almost.

Then Anna . . . Anna had been restless and scattered. She leaned against the arm of her chair; then tried to stand on her

pointes. Ballet, I can do ballet; I used to do it every night.
She twirled around unsteadily; then took up a position with
her hands clasped demurely at the top of her legs. She turned
her feet out, placing them one behind the other in opposite
directions, bent her knees and began to rub herself very
slowly. Her expression had the same dreaming look as in the
photographs. As then, Maureen felt herself drain, go icy,
then flush. I wasn't wrong, was I? She was masturbating?
Yes, there was no doubt about that. Nor about her own reaction.

She lifted the empty bottle and banged it on the floor
again. I bulldozed her then because I wanted her to stop.

Anna, Mummy would love to see you, you know.

No, she wouldn't, Anna said flatly.

You're wrong, she would. She wants to see you very
much indeed.

No, she doesn't and I don't want to see her neither, Anna
replied with complete certainty, lifting her arms until her
hands met overhead.

What I should have said was, *I* want you to see your
mummy, Anna. She still wouldn't have agreed but it would
have been one less lie.

And today, she had been found out. Tonight's opening
protest should have warned her. She should have got out
then. No, she shouldn't have been there with Sally in the
first place.

It always came back to the same point: Anna had been
adamant; Sally had been doubtful; and she – she had been
God.

She shut her eyes again, and saw Anna's face as it had been
at today's meeting: old and calculating, as she rimmed her
lips with the same provocative expression as she had in the
photos on the police file.

And today, she had walloped her; and the slap had been
deeply satisfying.

But for some reason that she still could not fathom, she
had failed to see the vulnerable, confused little girl whose

151

brief childhood had been destroyed. She struggled, but as the bath water cooled, the reason remained elusive. Only the facts were fixed. She had done it, and first thing Monday morning she would have to see her boss.

FOURTEEN

Karin hung in the kitchen doorway, gasping after her fourth attempt to do a chin lift. Come on, one more go before you have a rest. She gritted her teeth and strained, but it was no good. Her elbows would scarcely bend and she moved less than an inch. All right, you can have a breather: but then you'll have to try again later.

She dropped to the floor and rubbed her fingers. She was fed up with being stuck here and having to find things to do to keep her mind off the attic.

Yesterday she'd shrunk two of Dave Barnett's sweaters and four pairs of his socks in hot water. Now they were drying on the kitchen radiators. Today she had started to pack: a couple of his T-shirts, a piece of soap and a towel. Everything was under control except her boots. They were still a problem. She wouldn't get very far with a broken heel on one of them, and besides, they were rubbish. They wouldn't even keep the rain out, let alone snow or slush. She'd just have to stuff his wellies with as many socks as she could find to get to the main road: then get herself a pair that fitted in the first town. It would mean nicking them but that was nowt. She'd ask to try two different sizes and she'd be given one foot from each pair. She'd decide which was the best fit and ask for the other foot. She'd get up and walk around a bit, pretend that they didn't fit and ask for the second foot of the other pair. As soon as the assistant went out the back to get it, she'd just walk out with the first pair on her feet. No sweat. She'd manage it; it would just be a bloody nuisance having to clump round like Puss-in-Boots until she did.

Stop crossing bridges before you come to them. First things first: get back to your sewing. She sorted through the old button tin and found a needle, some thread and a pair of scissors. She spread a pair of Dave Barnett's trousers on the table and studied them carefully before cutting off the legs and ripping open the inside seams to give two pieces of material. Two seams, a hem at the bottom, one at the top and the elastic from his pyjamas slotted through and she'd have a skirt.

Patiently she set to work, moving intently along the first seam with small running stitches.

Pop-riveting was easier and a lot quicker. She liked metalwork and Mr Martin was okay.

Sometimes at lunch she went along to the metalwork shop and messed around. He said he didn't mind as long as he was there. That's what the place was for. She'd been suspicious at first, expecting: what's a clever girl like you doing in remedial? Then she realised that he didn't see anyone like that, either clever or not clever. To him, they were all okay. And for him, they were. There was no fooling around in his lesson on Wednesday afternoons. It was the best thing in the week.

Bugger, I wish Dave Barnett had a stapler!

She sucked her middle finger and watched the speck of blood well into a small globule. It was like the sunrise in the attic. She thought wistfully about the computer. You can go to evening classes for computer studies when you get to London. You have to get a job first, haven't you? There'll be plenty going in shops and factories and that. You'll have your pick so shut up and stop whining about the attic.

She bit off the thread and spread the skirt out slowly. Once it was ironed, it'd be all right.

She preferred straight skirts but this would be easier for climbing in and out of lorries. Anyway, she couldn't be bothered with the faff of putting the zip from his trouser flies into the skirt seam. Zips could be tricky. She giggled at a sudden memory of Tracy wailing, Ee miss, I didn't do it on purpose. How was I to know it was in upside down?

She wondered where Tracy was now. She's probably bigger than ever, just like her mam, she thought. She had intended to rubbish them all, that first day in the remedial class, and then Tracy had pushed her grubby book across to her and said, Here, you can copy mine if you can't do it yourself. I don't mind. A few unpunctuated, smeared, misspelt sentences had been laboriously carved on the page with a biro. Would Debbie end up like that? she wondered. What if she didn't learn to read at all? She had pushed the book back. Thanks, I'd better try and write my own. But I'll see you at break. And Tracy had become her best mate. She was big and slow and not bothered about school or being clever. She didn't have to be: she was happy.

The rest of the day dwindled towards television time and *News At Ten*. She had two more unsuccessful attempts at chin lifts, ironed the skirt, tried it on upstairs and left it hanging on the wardrobe door.

As soon as the news was finished, she turned the sweaters and socks on the kitchen radiators, then went upstairs to bed.

She lay with the duvet up to her neck and looked around the room. The mouse was perched on the bedside table. I'm going to buy one just like you for Debbie with my first week's wage, she said.

But I don't want to leave here, she thought. Wanting has nothing to do with it. You have to and you'll be all right. It's just 'cos you've got used to being here the past couple of weeks, that's all. It's just 'cos it's warm and no one's bothering you and it's safe and you've got enough to eat.

Naw, it's not just that: I don't want to have to get a boring old job in a shop, like Tracy.

That's just till you get qualifications. Then you can do something better, she reassured herself.

One minute she was lying looking at her new skirt and thoughtfully trying to poke one of her big toes through the toes of her other foot and suddenly she was bolt upright, thumping her knees with her fists. You idiot, you bloody idiot! You don't need to go into a shop first. You can get trained on the job; in an office, on a computer, just the same as in a factory.

Ee ee: she bounced on the bed and laughed.

That was *it*. She could teach herself a bit about computers here, then say that her certificates were in the post, and once they realised that she knew what she was doing, they'd forget about them! Never mind old Whitebum and whether she'd had a choice then. *Now*: now was all that mattered. She had a choice now and could choose to use the computer. She'd been an idiot and she'd nearly lost her chance by thinking that what was true then still had to be true now. Whitebum had been wrong then and she'd been right, but if she stuck to what she had believed she'd be wrong now. Funny that; did it mean that nothing was ever right for ever and ever, or that right became wrong and wrong became right? Never mind, Einstein, you can work at the theory later, she laughed. She flung her pillow at her reflection in the mirror and jumped out of bed.

On the landing she was shaking so much that she needed three attempts to hook the door with the pole. She took the attic steps two at a time, reached up and opened the radiator valves on the ceiling. There, it'd be warm for starting in the morning. Satisfied, she switched off the light, folded the stairs and returned to bed.

She closed her eyes and hugged herself. Life was getting better and better. As well as learning all about computers, she'd be able to see the road from the little window and she'd know when it was clear and time to leave.

I'm winning, I'm winning, she grinned.

She lay and stretched her arms and legs as wide as possible and felt herself spinning slowly and safely towards unconsciousness, travelling calmly through infinite space, without boundaries, the edges of the double bed beyond her reach. She'd start first thing in the morning. She was tired now, and besides, she didn't want to do it in the dark.

It was a new life, and she wanted it to start with the sunrise.

It didn't snow on the day of the funeral. Neither did it thaw, but the main roads were already clear and only the Maesllyn to Coed-y-bryn road remained icy.

It had been arranged for three o'clock – just in case the weather worsened, Gwen insisted, and they had to wait for the plough again.

The line of cars on either side of the street didn't register until the family formed behind the coffin and walked slowly into the little chapel.

It was full. The congregation rose in unison for the first hymn. She must have bussed them in, Dave thought angrily, then: oh no, I'm going to cry! He panicked and breathed through his mouth and tried to hold his eyes wide open to absorb the threatened tears; and dug his nails into the palms of his hands for added control.

It worked for the first prayer, but the words of the second hymn started to swell like a summer wind in the trees:

> *Abide with me,*
> *Fast falls the eventide;*

Oh stop it, please!

The darkness deepens,
Lord, with me abide!

But it was no use. It continued to swell.

When other helpers fail,
And comforts flee,
Help of the helpless,
O abide with me.

The voices resonated through the chapel. He knew because, half kneeling, his head bowed and his hands over his ears to try and block them out, he could feel them through the bench and up through his elbows. He briefly unclasped his head:

Who like thyself
My guide and stay can be?
Through cloud and sunshine,
O abide with me.

After that, he was lost. Sod her, sod Gwen: they had won, they always had. And at this rate he'd have no handkerchiefs left. And he'd have to turn round and face the damn congregation in a minute. He'd have to dry up and stay dry, think of something, anything. Anna and Megan – no, not them. Too late: his lovely kids – and he collapsed again for the gut-rotting loneliness of his life.

The last hymn was in Welsh, but the familiar tune to Crimond did the damage, and by then he was past caring. Dimly he was aware of people turning to process behind the coffin, and of someone joining him from one of the benches as he started to walk, head down, towards the door. As he passed under the choir loft, the cold air stung his swollen eyes and shocked him sufficiently out of tears to be able to turn to the person at his side.

'You.'

'I'm sorry I was late. I missed one of the connections and had to wait for a taxi.'

'Who asked you?'

'Gwen rang me,' Sally said, climbing into the first limousine.

Afterwards, back at the house, a buffet was spread and a guard of honour drawn up of women with teapots.

'I want a word with you,' Dave said to Gwen's back.

'Good, I hoped you would.'

He clenched his teeth and shook his head when she turned and offered him a sandwich. 'What did you mean by inviting Sally down here?'

'She was her daughter-in-law.'

'She hated her.'

'So did you, but you both still had to attend her funeral.'

'Why do you have to meddle in my life?'

'I don't, but this is a family funeral.'

'How did you know where she lived?'

'Mum told me, and I called to see her last time I was in London.'

'I suppose you had a cosy little chat about me?'

'No. In fact I don't think we mentioned you at all.'

'Good, keep your bloody nose out of my life.' His voice rose.

'No, keep it in: your nose is very welcome,' said Sally, coming towards them. 'Gwen's the only person who's said anything sensible so far.'

'I wasn't asking for your opinion.'

'You're getting it anyway, and if you care a jot for Anna or Megan, you'll listen to Gwen.'

'What does she know about Anna and Megan?'

'Everything. I've told her everything.'

'That's it. I've heard enough. I'm going.'

'On the run again?'

He turned to her murderously, and at that moment, Philip came up. 'Dave, I've got someone here who's very anxious to meet you: Mark Ross. He's involved with some of his company's design. I was telling him about you. He wants to know if you could do some work on a consultancy basis.'

Sally seized her chance and walked casually away, towards Gwen's two sons who had seated themselves with William in the far corner of the room with a stockpile of food.

Dave was still talking to Mark Ross when Sally moved back towards the buffet.

'You've made a hit with William; most people ignore him,' Gwen said.

'Why, just because he doesn't say much?'

'That and his funny ways,' Gwen smiled.

'I hadn't noticed. I just thought he was a bit shy.' Sally sipped her tea nervously. 'What are we going to do about Dave? Have you mentioned anything to him yet?'

'No, I was hoping Philip would try.'

'Do you think he might?'

'Well it's either him or your social worker.'

'Don't mention her. We got a new one, you know, and she's twice as bad as the other. You should have been with me at Springfields yesterday and seen her slapping Anna.'

'What made her do that, I wonder?' Gwen said.

'I don't know, but she'd better have a good excuse ready because I'm going to put a complaint in as soon as I get back.'

'Here's my card,' Mark Ross said. 'Give me a call as soon as you're back. It should all be finalised in the next week or so.'

Dave was spinning. The director of the biggest toy manufacturer – only the top man, for heaven's sake and he wanted *him*.

'You look as though you've won the pools.' Philip came up smiling.

'Better than that. He wants me to join his design team. Where on earth did you meet him?'

'We were at school together. He's my oldest friend. Always was a genius. He's just here for the day. By the way,'

e said, changing the subject smoothly, 'have you spoken to
ally yet?'

'No, why?'

'Well, Gwen and I have been talking to her. We know
bout Anna and Megan. This is just an idea for you to toss
round, nothing definite, not yet, you understand . . .'

When he'd finished Dave thought it over slowly. 'So what
ou're saying is: Anna and Megan will remain Wards of
Court and neither Sally nor myself will ever be allowed cus-
ody: me, because I'm a man living on my own and I de-
erted them, and Sally because she drinks. But Gwen and
ou are willing to foster them and give them a permanent
ome, and the Court would agree because Gwen's their aunt
nd you've both got a good track record with difficult kids.
ally and me could visit them and I could even live here,
vorking for you and for Mark Ross on the side?'

'Well, yes, a bit bald, but that's about it.' Philip smiled
opefully and reached for Dave's plate. 'You haven't had
nything to eat yet. Let me get you something.'

FIFTEEN

Mansell waited anxiously, moving from one foot to the other as the snow plough lumbered towards him.

'Now then, Mansell, I've got sommat here for you, somewhere,' Harry Bell called out, as he searched his pockets, then the cabin. 'Oh aye, here it is. Just the one, that's all,' and he handed him a postcard.

> *Dear Dad,*
> *In a rush. Got your letter. It must have crossed with the one I sent to you and Mam. She wrote by return and said she was coming. Are you coming with her? There'll be a letter in the post this weekend, just in case you can't make it, but I hope you can. I hope by the time you get this, you've already got your ticket. I'd love to see you.*
> *Joan*

Maggie said nowt to me about getting a letter from Joan, he thought. He stuffed the postcard inside his jacket pocket and made his way slowly back to the house.

'There's her letter, there, on the sideboard. It's been there for over a week.'

'She says you wrote straight back and said you'd be down at the weekend.'

'So I did.'

'Why didn't you say owt?'

'Because I'm sick of asking you. Our Joan's invited both of us umpteen times and you've never once accepted, so I didn't bother.'

'Well, you should have done because this time, I'm going as well.'

'Are you serious?'

'I am. I've already asked young Harry Bell if his brother'll come and do the jobs for us.'

'Lad, you never cease to amaze me.'

She rubbed the crumbs of pastry off her hands.

'I'll have to sit down for a minute. You've stunned me.' She smiled at him tentatively. 'She says she has a very special reason for wanting us to go. Here, I'll read it to you.' She wiped her hands down either side of her overall and picked the letter out of a pile of bills in the rack.

He sat staring at the floor when she finished. 'I was going to ask you if you'd read it when you got in tonight,' she ventured.

'Aye, well, it's just as well I wrote for myself.'

'Yes it is. Now you know she wants to see you as much as she wants to see me.' Her voice was strident.

And that's killing you, he thought.

That's what you get for being deceitful, she told herself as she rolled out the pie crust. Serves you right, lass. You never know, he might get himself some fancy woman on the train or join the Foreign Legion. She smiled to herself.

'It's nice to see you smile, Maggie.'

She tossed her head.

'The break'll do us both good,' he went on, undiscouraged, 'and when we get back mebbe we can think about what we're going to do with this place, eh?'

'Don't jump your fences, lad. Check with Harry Bell' brother first. I'll have to get your good suit out of the ward obe and give it an airing or the train'll stink of mothballs. Go on, take the Land Rover to Northgate.'

I think she's quite glad I'm coming, he thought as he struggled into his wellingtons. He turned at the door.

'Right then, I'm off.'

There was no response.

'Right then, I'll see you later,' he said lamely.

Karin woke at five o'clock, immediately alert, and shivered with excitement. There was another hour before the heating came on and another before it would be warm. She lay and debated whether to get up or go back to sleep. In the end she compromised, made herself a cup of tea, brought it back to bed, then changed the alarm from seven to six thirty.

The wooden mouse grinned at her from the top of the computer terminal. Dave Barnett must be a nutter, she told it. He had to be, to leave a list of his passwords in the drawer. There was no point in having a password if it wasn't secret, was there? Good job for you it wasn't or you'd've been sitting here looking at Password Prompt all day, wouldn't you? You?

You'd never've guessed it: Megananna. Mega Nanna? Some sort of outsize granny?

She peered at the DisplayWrite 4 Menu: Create Document, Revise Document, View Document. That was it, the last one. She'd see what he'd written.

It listed a further choice of Repairs and Renovations, Accounts and Diary. The diary, brill. She typed it in impatiently and 12th January came up. That was no good, it was too recent. She wanted to start at the beginning. Page Up travelled backwards an entry at a time for two years and then stopped.

28th December

I've never kept a diary before, and it feels a bit like talking to myself, but I've got so much on my mind since I left Sally and the children that I'll go mad if I don't talk to someone. I don't know anyone up here except the Jowetts and they might gossip, so this is the safest way of trying to sort things out.

I've been here for 6 weeks now, but it seems more like 6 years. This house doesn't help. It's like an iceberg and stinks of damp. The fire eats coal but makes very little difference to the temperature. As soon as the weather improves I'm going to gut the place and get central heating put in. The contract for the Pull-Along toys is secure enough so I should be able to afford it. My work is all right, the only thing that ever has been.

We could have been so happy if Sally had been a better wife, appreciative, that most of all, but nothing was ever enough for her. I wouldn't have minded that she didn't invest her trust fund in the business, if she'd just balanced the house budget and kept Anna and Megan in order. Instead she made my life a misery.

I'm better off here, as far away as possible, although I don't know how Aunt Cissie survived.

This Christmas has been the worst ever. I thought nothing could be as bad as the one we spent with Mum, when Anna was 2, but this was even worse. I kept thinking – they'll be opening their presents now. Then – they'll be asking for me. I must have tried ringing at least 20 times this past week but in a funny way, it was a relief when I couldn't get an answer because I didn't know what I was going to say anyway. I'm not sorry I left. I would have done that anyway, even if Aunt Cissie hadn't died and left me this house.

I keep wondering why Sally doesn't ring me. She's got my number. She must know she's in the wrong but she should know there's nothing to be afraid of. If she would admit it, we could start again.

I wonder what happened when she took Anna to see the psychologist in October. She's only 7. She can't be beyond help. There must be something that can be done but apart from strapping Anna into a strait jacket, I can't think what. I sympathise with child batterers. If anyone saw Anna they'd think butter wouldn't melt in her mouth. She's so beautiful with those gorgeous brown eyes, like Sally's, and that blonde hair. I don't know who she inherited that from but she's stunning. Maybe she isn't ours. Maybe we got the wrong one from the hospital.

I don't know what's wrong with her but something is and it's serious. Sally always said that I was imagining it, and I wanted to believe her, but I've always known the truth, and so has Mum.

Megan's completely different. She's a little pudding, placid and plump, quiet, easy-going. A lot slower than Anna to walk and talk but maybe that's a good sign. Hopefully, she'll be different in every other way as well.

I wonder who Anna is like and if she'll ever be normal. I doubt it.

he next entry was nearly six weeks later:

8th February

I managed to get hold of Sally tonight, at long last. She said they'd all been away for Christmas. Was very cool and said the girls were in bed and she wouldn't disturb them. It wouldn't be fair. I said it seemed a bit early, it was only 7.00 p.m., but she said things were different now. They must be. As I remember, Anna would never go to bed.

She asked for money but didn't say thank you for what I'd sent already for Anna's birthday and for all of them at Christmas, so she hasn't changed. Still, I suppose she could have just put the phone down on me. She wouldn't commit herself to a time when I could speak to the children. She said they were in and out all the time and said I'd just have to take a chance.

Was very non-committal when I asked how it had gone with the psychologist. She just said airily that they were going to keep Anna under review and that the tests had shown her to be highly intelligent, just as she'd always known.

She didn't ask me how I was getting on. She's probably still mad at me for leaving. I didn't mention the possibility of them coming here. I'll sort the house out first then I'll send photographs. If I wait till spring it won't look so daunting. Sally still hates the cold. She still harps on about Africa although she should be used to it here by now. She's been in England long enough, but she's never left her cloud cuckoo land.

Karin sat back from the screen. He must be an idiot. He married a nig nog, so the kids must be at least half blac and one of them had blonde hair, and he wondered what w wrong with her and why she had problems! She could t him. It must be hell for the kid at school for a start. She have to thump everyone till they left her alone. Then she be referred to the school psychologist and they'd say she w violent. She hadn't any choice. The psychologist wouldr be any help unless he took her to get an Afro wig but wouldn't think of anything as sensible as that. He'd probab just wait for her to talk about her feelings, as if that wou change anything. She remembered big Mrs Carberry, h first-year junior teacher. Wayne Kendall went round kickir everyone in the shins and was referred to the Clinic, but M Carberry just took his shoes off. The first time after that, nearly broke his toes on someone's shin, then never tri again. Mrs Carberry said she wasn't interested in why was doing it or how he felt about it, she just wanted him stop. If Anna had been in her class, Mrs Carberry wou have got her a wig and she would have been okay.

She pressed the Page Down key repeatedly, skimming short daily weather reports until she reached:

16th February
There has been a blizzard again and it has now been snowing constantly since 28th January; three weeks with temperatures ranging from −3°C down to −9°C every day. The water has frozen, also the waste pipe. There have been two electricity cuts and last night the tiny paraffin lamp burnt its wick and covered the bathroom with greasy soot.

I'm fed up having to tramp over frozen drifts to reach the car and road. I've written to New Zealand House for info on emigrating. I could have died driving back in that blizzard yesterday, and the walk down to the house from the road is treacherous.

I'm fed up with this never-ending winter, with doors that don't fit, blizzards in the porch, leaking windows, tramping across the yard to the workshop, days and nights of comfortless gloomy cold. I'm sick of getting washed in a bowl on the fireside, of the kitchen at −5°C with a hole in the wall and howling gales and most of all, with Sally. She's rung once since I spoke to her on 8th January, once in 6 weeks, and then only to ask for money! I've tried hundreds of times to speak to the girls but never got them. I may as well pack up and go. The business is doing well and there's no reason why it wouldn't do just as well somewhere warm and civilised, like New Zealand. There's no need to stay here just because I was left the house. It was useful at the time but I'll tidy it up and put it on the market in spring, whenever that is. Jowett called today to see if I needed anything. He probably just wanted a nose round. I kept him on the doorstep and eventually he wandered off.

Karin gazed out of the window. There was something wrong with him. If he had a car, why didn't he just get himself some camping gas lights and a couple of gas fires that

would run off cylinders? Then he'd be warm and able t
see where he was going. If he got a hot-water bottle an
piled the blankets on, he'd be all right in bed as wel
He could always do a bit of exercise if he wanted to kee
himself warm and save on the gas, even though he didn
need to.

He was lucky, but it was no use to him because he didn
know it. He had a house for nowt, a job and a car an
enough money, but he didn't see himself as a lucky bugge
so really he might as well be on the dole and dossing. I
would be better in a way, because then he'd have real thing
to grumble about. He'd wasted loads of disc moaning abou
things he could sort out easily like the heating and the elec
tricity cuts.

His wife must've been glad to see the back of him. Sh
must've felt like running away herself but there was prob
ably nowhere to go with her being black and the kids hal
castes and especially with that one with blonde hair.

She turned back to the screen. There followed anothe
three weeks of single-line weather reports, then:

11th March
−2°C. Very heavy frost but brilliant sunrise and not a breath
of wind. Heard lark and 1st lapwing. Waste pipe running
again, also water. Path from road to house cleared at the
end of last week. Hopefully this is the end of winter but
Jowett says not, there's still snow lying in the dykes so
more to come. Cheerful man.

Rang Sally tonight for third time since 1st March. I'm getting
sick of her excuses about the children. She said months ago
they went to bed early but tonight, at 8.00 they were still playing, and then at 8.30 in bed. I'd just missed them.

Last week, I put an ad in the newsagent's for someone to
help me with the office work and Maggie Jowett, of all people, called round.

A month later there was another entry:

14th April

−3°C. Another freezing day and bitter NE wind and all the back wall glazed with ice. I watched a lapwing fall like a stone and saw two dead lambs. There was a sick ewe huddled at the gate this morning. It died later. Maggie Jowett, surly as ever, just shrugged and said it was the dying time of year. Will it ever end?

arin tracked through a series of entries listing work done the house. He'd got a damp proof course in and a back orch added, then central heating and insulation, and had pened up the loft and shelved it all. The barn which he was sing as a workshop had also been insulated and had had ating put in.

So in some ways he wasn't daft. She chewed a knuckle oughtfully. He'd sorted out the house okay. But in other ays, he was clueless. He kept on moaning in between jobs at life was pointless, and one day just followed another, d what would he do when all the work was finished? He pt repeating that he was a failure and didn't know how to e and never had known how to live.

What'd he mean? You just breathed in and out and kept doing it. How else was there to live except by breathing? hat's all there was to it, with a bit of eating and sleeping w and then. What was wrong with him?

He didn't seem to know his arse from his elbow. One mite he said he hated the place and was going to emigrate; d the next:

. . . a sense of calm and even a liking for this house. Sometimes, when I am on the road and look at it, I know I wouldn't really like to leave it. Much of it works already and I can easily sort out the bits that don't. This year's projects have proved that.

at was on 6th May, at 5°C cold but sunny, and repeated 7th May at 9°C when it was windy and wet, so it wasn't

really the weather that affected his outlook. Anyway, he ha
enough sweaters and a good pair of wellies, and besides, h
didn't have to walk anywhere, he had a car. Naw, he mus
just be queer. He had to be a bit queer to marry an African
And why didn't he just get in the car and go and see her an
the kids if he couldn't speak to them? Why had he left them
Mebbe he was ashamed of being seen with her and with tha
kid with the blonde hair. But he wasn't any happier her
than he had been there. Mebbe he would never be happ
anywhere. Some people were like that.

She pressed the Page Down key repeatedly and skimme
more grumbling entries: Jowett's cows were in the garde
and he had to clean up their mess; an invoice had been re
turned because there was a mistake in it; he'd have to chec
all the others; Maggie Jowett was a dead loss; and then th
contract for Pull-Along toys with one of the big nationa
chains had come to an end and had not been renewed. H
was strapped for cash and wished he hadn't spent so muc
on the house. Sally was asking for too much.

3rd June
Megan's birthday. I'm getting crafty in my old age. I rang at
8.15 this morning and caught her getting ready for school. She
picked up the phone and I said Happy birthday, 6 year old.
She said Who's that and I said Daddy. There was a long
pause and I thought for one horrible minute that she was
going to say, who's daddy but then she said Oh, in a little
voice and I said again, Happy birthday Megan. Then I heard
Sally shout something and Megan said I have to go now,
and put the phone down. I rang again and Sally answered
and I blasted her. All she said was, They're not your toys,
you know. You can't have them just when it suits you. You
did leave them, remember. Toys! Her saying that to me!
She treated Anna like a life-size doll for the first two years
of her life. I know she might have been difficult anyway but
Sally made sure of it.

I felt like killing her. What did I ever see in the woman? Everything that was different from Mum, I suppose, and Gwen, but then I didn't like Sally any better than them after a while. I thought she was cheerful and had a sense of humour but that was only as long as I was footing the bill.

I hate her. If Anna and Megan had been boys I would have brought them with me but I can't really cope with two girls. It's not fair. I pay for everything while Sally just drinks like a fish and tells lies about me. If I got a divorce, and met someone else, I could get custody of the children.

He was a pig. Where was he going to find another woman willing to take his kids on unless she was blind or daft or both? The big-head, he probably thought he was God's gift. Sally must be glad he'd left. I wonder how much he sends her? Not a lot, I bet, but he probably thinks he's Lord Bountiful with a few quid each week. She should take him to court for maintenance, the way Mrs Taylor did for her and Tracy. Being African, she probably didn't know how to go about it. Mebbe she'd never even been to school. She probably didn't fit in here but she wouldn't be any better off back in Africa, not with two half-black kids and especially one with blonde hair.

Funny, he didn't really like his kids, or his wife and he didn't seem to think much of Maggie Jowett or his Aunt Cissie; so that only left his mam and Gwen and he didn't like them either.

SIXTEEN

As soon as Mansell drove out of the yard, Maggie went upstairs to the bedroom and looked at herself in the mirror.

Her hair needed a good cut. It was straggling and split where an old perm had grown out. She was going grey very fast, she thought. She'd ask Joan about that, wouldn't risk the village hairdressers.

Her face was heavily veined and mottled purple with the cold. Pennine winds had seen to that. You could tone it down a bit, Mam, Joan had said last time they had met. Try a bit of eyeshadow. Of course you're not too old. That bright red lipstick's too harsh. Here, try this brownish-pink. There, that's better. She'd come back with a make-up bag full of new things and never used them.

I'd better show willing, she thought as she rooted in the top drawer of the dressing-table. I've probably forgotten what goes where now. She found her little make-up bag at the back of the drawer and sat down.

What comes first? Moisturiser, that was it. Then that green colour to correct the redness. Oh, that's a bit drastic, she said to herself as an unfamiliar pale face stared sadly back at her from the mirror. A bit of rouge, I nearly forgot that. Funny, blotting out all her colour then putting it back under the cheekbones. But it worked. She smudged a bit of eyeshadow tentatively on her lids; leaned back a little and smiled, then turned sideways and raised a cautious eyebrow at her reflection.

She looked at herself critically. I'm not bad for fifty-eight she thought. Better than a lot of women. I'm as good as the next, she told herself defiantly. Joan said she was sick of telling her that.

Now that I've started, I might as well go the whole hog and try on a jumper and skirt.

She picked the sweater up carefully. Strange colour, purple, not bright, more like slate, more like the bloom on a bunch of grapes. Bit dull, she'd thought when it arrived. The person who looked back at her from the mirror was glowing. Can't be; is that me! Naw, she murmured with pleasure it can't be.

She took the skirt off the hanger and stepped into it, kicked off her slippers and rose on tiptoe. Hang on a minute get your shoes on. There, that's better. Now you can see yourself.

She liked what she saw. She wasn't pretty, never had been, her face was too strong for that. But she was handsome and well boned and carried herself well. It's just my hair, she thought, that's all that's spoiling me.

Blow it, I'll leave them on me. You never know, he might even notice when he comes back from Northgate.

The smell was different: a smell of newness, of wool not yet tainted with sweat and repeated washings. Bit much to call it dignity or self-respect. But it was. It was just that.

She found his suit and unwrapped it. Thank goodness took them trousers to be altered a couple of years back. He'd look an idiot in flares at his age.

Maureen Wilson was in her office by eight fifteen that Monday morning. At eight thirty she rang her boss and asked to see him and five minutes later she was in his office.

'I've come to give in my resignation,' she announced without preamble as she sat down.

Andrew McArdle swung round and lifted his phone. 'I'm tied up for the next hour, Janet. Don't put anyone through.' Then he turned back to Maureen. 'This is a bit sudden, isn't it? Don't you want to talk about it first?'

'No. You'll be getting reports – two, almost certainly. One from Ellen Bramhall at Springfields and one from Sally Barnett. She's the mother. I took her to see her daughters, Megan and Anna, on Thursday evening; and while we were there, I slapped Anna across the back of her legs, twice.'

'She must have provoked you badly.'

'She did, but it's still no excuse. Anyway, Ellen Bramhall said that she would report it, and I'm sure Sally Barnett will as well. She was furious.'

'So you want to get in first. That's sensible.'

'I haven't come to make excuses, if that's what you mean. There's no excuse. I never imagined I could over-react so stupidly: it's frightened me. Even if there'd been no witnesses, I'd still resign. I've had enough.'

Andrew McArdle leaned back and swivelled his chair gently from side to side. She was his best professional, and at a time when morale was at a low and he was short of staff he didn't want to lose her. There had to be a reasonable explanation for what had happened. There would certainly be no need to resign. He wouldn't let her. As she said, she'd over-reacted, but only marginally; probably tired.

He tried again. 'Maureen, something got to you. You've been in this line of business too long not to recognise that, so let's sort out what it was and work out a strategy to make sure it doesn't happen again. There's no reason why it should. I'll give the Barnett file to one of the others, and if either Ellen Bramhall or Mrs Barnett asks, I'll just say you were cautioned. That's all that's needed. Resigning's a bit drastic for a slap on the legs.'

She shook her head firmly. She wondered if she sounded as patronising when she was talking to her clients as he did talking to her. If it had been quiet, observant Dick Turner, she might have considered talking to him, but Andrew McArdle was the new breed of manager, and more interested in managing than listening. With Dick Turner she would have gone to the pub and sat in silences big enough to drown in, secure in the knowledge that he trusted her to swim. Andrew McArdle was giving her a life belt before she got into the water.

'No. Thanks, but no. It wouldn't happen again anyway. I'm sure of that. But as I said, I've had enough and I'm leaving. I'm sick of making excuses for nasty people.'

He sat quite still, watching her. She sat facing him squarely, looking beyond him.

She was four when she was orphaned in the Blitz.

The home had been very like Springfields: a Victorian foundation, strict and loveless in those early days and for years after the war. She had been called out of a game of netball to meet them: Mr and Mrs Wilson – Jim and Lizzie, she later discovered; childless, Lizzie five years older than Jim and looking ten, because he looked younger than his age and acted daft. She had been careful from the start, so that Lizzie, Mum as she insisted, wouldn't feel jealous or left out. Jim would say: This won't interest you, Lizzie, and take Maureen by the hand, bold as brass, and laughing. Always laughing, teasing her out of her stricken conscience. The misery: trying to be fair to the disillusioned woman; trying to evade his constant attention; aware of Lizzie's resentment; trying to be cheerful coming home from school to a load of housework; using it as an excuse to avoid him; to be loyal, grateful, good; to make Lizzie as happy as Jim. And all the time wishing she'd been left in the orphanage.

Once Lizzie said she half expected Mo to turn out a bad lot. Jim put his arm around Maureen's shoulder and answered mildly that Lizzie was letting her imagination run away with her. As far as he was concerned, Mo couldn't be a bad ot because she was his daughter, and as good as a real daughter. Better in fact.

Maureen saw Lizzie's face as she turned away, and knew that neither she nor Jim would ever be forgiven for that. She also knew, without knowing any of the details, that the emotional distance between Jim and Lizzie was permanent and unbridgeable, and that she would never span it. The impossibility of it all, the powerlessness – most of all, the misery, the endless, gnawing misery.

Andrew McArdle shifted uncomfortably. Tears were running down her face and she was still staring into some distant space, unaware of them or of him. She must be overworked; would end up with a breakdown at this rate. She'd better have some leave – immediately.

'Maureen. Maureen.' She still didn't focus. He got up and walked round to her. 'Maureen, I want you to go home now and take a week's sick leave. You've been overdoing things since Anne Stevens left. That's probably what caused that spot of bother on Thursday. We needn't make a mountain out of a molehill. If you have a break now, you'll be as good as new in a week, and then we'll think about a new job description for you. You're too good to lose.'

'No.' She jerked her head towards him and the tears followed, splattered diagonally across her face. 'No, I want to work my notice, starting from today. I've got appointments this week that I want to keep – nothing to do with the Barnetts. I'm going for a long weekend this Friday, and by the time I'm back on Tuesday, you should have heard from Sally Barnett and Ellen Bramhall. I'd like to check their statements. I don't mind them telling you, but I want the truth. There's a chance they could exaggerate. Not deliberately, of course,' she added.

'But you're not giving me a chance to help you. You're not willing to consider alternatives!'

'No.'

'Why?'

She didn't say, Because I don't want your sort of help, but: 'I don't want to help anyone else any more. I'm tired of being the doormat, the dogsbody to the victims of society, as we fondly call them.'

Andrew McArdle winced. This sarcasm wasn't like her.

'But I've been as much a "victim" as anyone else,' she went on, 'ever since I got that Barnett file.' She stopped for a moment. 'I've thought it over long and hard and I want to leave.' She reached into her bag, 'Here's my letter of resignation.'

'I'll keep it for the moment. I still think you're tired. A week's leave will sort it out.'

'No,' she said quietly, getting up to go. 'I'll need the rest of my life to do that.'

Her lunch finished, Karin rushed back to the attic. She'd practically lived there since Saturday. Apart from eating, doing her exercises and sleeping, every other moment had been spent at the terminal. She was beginning to get the hang of it. Most of it was just common sense and the rest was in the manual.

Best of all, she'd started putting comments in at the end of each diary entry. A cinch: just press Insert, then type. Brill, and he'd be gobsmacked when he saw what she'd written.

She was enjoying herself something scandalous.

Now she was up to the following December. In a whole year he'd never once tried to visit Sally or the children, only moaned about them endlessly and about the jobs he was doing and about Jowett trying to poke his nose in, but he'd done nowt about any of them. She switched on and worked patiently through the now familiar checks, then scanned to:

6th December

2°C. Strange to think I've been here a year. So much has

180

happened. I'm sitting here now, in the loft, everything functional and warm and tidy, a central heating and hot water system that work, the house dry and insulated and clean, thanks to no-one but myself. If Sally was here we would still be living in a pigsty.

The biggest disappointment has been the Pull-Along contract. If they'd even extended it for another six months, things would have been easier. They said that the toys weren't selling, felt they were both too simple and at the same time, too complex. How they work that out is beyond me. I've wasted precious hours doing drivelling little jobs for tight-fisted locals, all of them expecting something for nothing. Mending a doll's house takes nearly as much time as making one but no-one expects to pay for all the work that's involved. I've let Maggie Jowett go: I was glad of an excuse to do it. I still have to check all my invoices when I get time.

Karin pressed Insert: then typed slowly and carefully:

What they said about the toys is right. By the time a kid can work out how to use the ratchet handle, she would be too old to want to pull a mouse on wheels.

9th December
8°C. Wind almost at hurricane force and frightening. Two main problems here, expense and loneliness. The Appointments page always brings it home to me how much I'm losing as a freelance. This house costs nothing to run compared with the London one but when combined with Sally's endless demands for money, it's a constant worry. She seems to think I just wave it out of the air.

Apart from all that, I've only just realised how lonely I am. The only person I see regularly now is Mansell Jowett and we've nothing in common. While I was working on the house I hadn't time to think. There was a patch last April/May when I hardly seemed to get to bed, when Pull-Along was hammering me and the house was in bits everywhere, but the light nights seemed to give me bottomless energy with all my thoughts concentrated between the next stage of the contract and the next job to be done in the house. Now everything seems to have come to an end together, all the work and the daylight. Now I find myself wondering what to do with myself, putting on the radio, then the TV and not taking notice of either.

Karin wrote:

You've got a bloody short memory. In April you were moaning that one day just followed another and you were a failure and you didn't know how to live. Now you're saying that you were happy then. Make up your mind.

10th December
−2°C but absolutely still. No wind at all. Great relief after gales.

Spoke to Sally last night. She sounded surprisingly cheerful, probably because the money arrived that I sent her. She said the house was bursting at the seams with all the girls' friends. Anna has started cello lessons and Megan, little Megan, is playing the drums! I asked her if she was sure and she said of course she was and that the peripatetic music teacher was thrilled because too few girls were attracted to percussion!

She babbled on for ages and sounded almost like her old self. She made them all sound so much happier, more settled, lighter somehow. Altogether better off without me, except for the cash. If I was to believe Sally, they grow out of clothes every week and shoes only last three days. I don't mind as long as the money is being well spent on extra classes, lessons, equipment. They'll all help.

She said they've made special friends with a little girl from further down the street who goes to the same school. It didn't occur to me until she'd rung off that if the house is always full of their friends, why can't I ever catch them to speak to them. I suppose they must take it in turns to go to each other's houses. I wonder what they think when they see the mess at our place.

Those kids of yours could be out anywhere, doing anything with anybody and all you're bothered about is the state of the bloody house.

Karin added.

13th December

−4°C. Woke to snow, the first serious fall of the year. I met Jowett and he asked me what I was doing for Christmas. Feel increasingly desperate at the prospect of spending it on my own again. I've spoken to Sally twice more, briefly both times, both times OK although still didn't manage to get the children. She sounds so normal again. I'm tempted to suggest that they all come up here for Christmas especially as she says they're not going anywhere. When I told Jowett I'd probably be here on my own he said I was a lucky bugger.

Karin typed in capitals:

WHY DON'T YOU DO THINGS INSTEAD OF JUST THINKING ABOUT THEM?

She pressed Page Up through a week of brief weather reports, −4°C every day with further snow falls until:

22nd December

−1°C and no more snow overnight. I've decided, no more shilly-shallying. I'm going to surprise them all and turn up for Xmas. I'll take some toys as well. She's always complained that I couldn't do anything on impulse, that I always had to plan it first. Well, now she'll see that I can and maybe she'll try and change as well. I won't give in to her, she's still very wrong but as it's Christmas, I'll relax a bit and she might begin to see things my way.

Karin inserted:

Fat chance. Do you keep your brains in your bum?

'Mr McArdle, I have Mrs Barnett here to see you. No, she hasn't got an appointment. No, she doesn't want to speak to the duty officer. She says she has a complaint and must speak to you.'

'She'll have to wait then, at least half an hour. I'm going through the Barnett file now. Tell her I've got a meeting and I'll see her at eleven o'clock.'

Janet turned hopefully to Sally. 'Mr McArdle is just about to go into a meeting, Mrs Barnett. Can you come back at eleven? He can see you then.'

'I'll wait,' Sally snapped and sat down purposefully on one of the plastic chairs.

Great start to a Monday morning, Janet thought. First Maureen Wilson in some sort of trouble, and now this woman with a very posh accent on the warpath.

Sally Barnett had rehearsed her speech well. She was tired of being ignored for nearly a year; then lied to about her children and humiliated in front of them; then seeing Anna humiliated in turn. The Service was utterly incompetent and she wanted some action.

She wanted Maureen Wilson removed for a start; then the

children moved somewhere smaller where they could get specialised treatment; and she wanted them back again, at least for weekends. After all, she had done nothing.

'No,' said Andrew McArdle slowly, looking up from her file. 'You didn't do anything, did you?'

'No,' she agreed.

'No: you never checked where they were at night or what they were doing, did you?'

'It hardly seemed necessary,' she flustered. 'They were only going to a house six doors away and were always brought home afterwards.' She reasserted herself quickly. 'What I'm saying is; I've had enough of incompetent social workers. First it was Anne Stevens and now Maureen Wilson.'

'Has it occurred to you, Mrs Barnett, that you wouldn't have needed anyone if you'd been a competent parent?'

'How dare you suggest that I wasn't! What happened was a complete accident. It could have happened to anyone's children. They were running a child pornography ring. Anyone was vulnerable.'

'No, not anyone, Mrs Barnett: only children like Anna and Megan who were not collected from school; who came home to an empty house with no food and a sleeping mother. Oh yes, they've told us a lot in the time they've been in care. Anna used to steal money to buy food for Megan and herself. They were ripe for picking at the school gates – a nice mumsy friendly woman who would give them a hot meal and a warm place to stay.'

'I don't have to listen to this.'

'No, true, because you know it already. Anna was only seven years old, and yet you expected her to get herself and Megan to school every morning, feed them both every night, then do whatever they wanted, as long as it didn't bother you. Am I right, Mrs Barnett?'

'You most certainly are not, and I'll see that you are dismissed as well as Maureen Wilson. It's an outrage – a

185

vicious, prejudiced attack. I'm going to see a solicitor and the Civil Liberties people.'

'Good, I'm glad. And maybe you can explain what you were doing instead of looking after your children?'

'I was ill. I was ill a great deal.'

'I'm not disputing that, Mrs Barnett. It's on record that you were very ill when the police called at your home the night the children were taken into care. You were so ill you couldn' speak. Is that right?'

She relaxed, wondering how he would apologise and explain away his previous outburst. And then he went on, 'Bu your illness is self-inflicted, and it takes hours of my staff' time and uses up valuable limited resources. And all you do in return is try to destroy one of the best social workers I've got. He realised he'd gone too far. Alcoholism was officially an illness no matter what he thought about Sally Barnett, but it was too late and to retract it would only make matters worse. He ploughed on. 'Her only mistake was to give you the benefit o the doubt, despite the evidence stacked against you. She fel for your sob story and you knifed her in the back.'

'I'm not listening to any more of this. I half expected cover-up, but I didn't think you'd stoop to a slanderous attack on me as well. That woman hit my daughter.'

'That woman tapped her on the back of her legs for being severely provocative and insolent, and that's not what's bothering you. It's because the children don't want to see you that's why you're out for her blood.'

'I'm taking this further.'

'You can, of course. I'm sure you're prepared for the publicity about your illness, Mrs Barnett.'

'I want Maureen Wilson taken off this case. I want that, no matter what else.'

'You've got that already. Maureen Wilson asked to leave the case this morning. She said she had trusted you and felt she couldn't do so again. There's a Children's Centre staff meeting in a week's time to discuss Anna and Megan. We'll let you know what is decided, and I'll allocate a new social worker to

186

the case. Meanwhile, feel free to contact your solicitor or the Civil Liberties lot. Janet at the desk has a leaflet on complaints procedure.'

He half rose as she left the room and the door clashed behind her. Then he sat down heavily.

I'd better calm down, he thought, it isn't even lunch time, and it's only Monday. At this rate I'll have a coronary by tea time. What a start to the week! I can't stop Maureen from resigning, but I'm damn well not going to see her lose her pension on the say-so of a manipulative alcoholic liar. But she won't take this any further, now that I've called her bluff, I hope; I hope. He sat and swivelled, drumming his fingers. Now all I've got to do is to persuade Maureen to change her mind. I can't lose her. She's got more years of experience than all the rest of them put together.

Maureen worked on automatic pilot for the rest of the day. Trudi worried when she wasn't interested in a sandwich and fussed when she refused a chocolate biscuit.

'Go home and go to bed if you're not well, love.'

'I'm fine. I'm just not hungry.'

'It's none of my business, but you don't look fine.'

'I've been crying, you mean?'

'Well, yes. Do you want to talk about it?'

'No thanks, I've already had offers of ears this morning. There's nothing to talk about. I've just resigned, that's all.'

'That's *all* – *MAUREEN*!'

'Should I have put it in the Court Circular first then?'

'Oh Maureen, don't be sarky. It's a helluva shock. What did Andrew say?'

'Same as you.'

'And?'

'I told him what I'm telling you: I'm okay. I don't want to go to bed or take sick leave. I just want to work my notice. And I'm not here to save the bloody world! Okay?'

'Well, it has to be, hasn't it?' Trudi said, sounding huffed. 'If you won't let anyone help.'

'You've got enough to do without worrying about me, and you'll be late for that meeting if you don't get a move on.'

Trudi fussed around, then left, and Maureen sat staring out of the window, wondering what she was feeling: just ugh, nothing, at an end, not even hungry. The telephone interrupted her analysis.

'Maureen, David Barnett's here to see you.'

'I'm not on that case any more, and besides, he's not due till tomorrow afternoon.'

'He says it'll only take a minute.'

'Tell him to wait and see Trudi.'

'Ten seconds, he says. He's just driven back from Wales.'

'No.'

'He says five seconds would be enough.'

'Oh, all right. Tell him to come in.'

He looked steadily at her desk as he walked across the room, then sat down and looked at his feet.

'Mr Barnett, I have to tell you that I've handed your case to a colleague.'

'My mother died.' He hadn't heard her.

'Ah, no. When did that happen?' she asked gently.

'Last Tuesday. The funeral was on Friday. She died in Wales at my sister's house. No, I mean, she was staying with Gwen but died in Cardigan Hospital.'

'I'm sorry,' she said simply.

'I'm not.'

She searched for some neutral remark. 'Was it sudden?'

'Yes. An unexpected bonus, you could say,' and without warning there came harsh uncomfortable sobs. He bowed his head further. 'I'm not sorry for her,' he gulped. 'I'm sorry for myself.'

'About lots of things or one in particular?'

'The lot: the whole bloody miserable lot of my life and the mess it's been.' He looked at her suddenly. 'There'll be no one to cry for me; no one to fill a chapel and sing their hearts out or me. I hated her, but everyone else seemed to love her, even he handicapped kid that Gwen and Philip are fostering.' He ooked at the floor again. 'But that's not why I came. I want to ay something about Anna and Megan.'

'You didn't hear me when you first came in. I've handed over the case to a colleague.'

'Oh, not again. Why've you dropped it?'

'I took your wife to see the girls at Springfields on Thursday, and I slapped Anna twice across the back of her legs.'

'Well?'

'It's assault.'

'Rubbish: you should have got promotion.'

'I know some people believe that a slap is the answer to most children's behaviour problems, but when a social worker does t, it becomes an assault. I have no authority to hit any child.'

'You have mine. She's needed that since she could crawl. ally would never reprimand her, let alone smack her.'

'That's not the point. I shouldn't have touched her. Mrs Barnett has already filed a complaint.'

'I bet she has. She'd love that.'

'She had a right to complain.'

'I disagree, and I hope no one listens to her.'

'Oh they will – they'll have to; and you'll get another social worker.'

'Well, before that happens, there's something I must tell ou.'

'Not me: it's out of my hands now.'

'Just listen, at least.'

'It wouldn't do any good. I won't even make a note of it, so ou'd only have to repeat it to your next social worker.'

He slumped for a moment, then got up to leave.

'I'm sorry you're giving up our case. As far as I'm concerned, slapping Anna is the best thing you've ever done.' He aused, and when there was no reaction he said, 'So I suppose d better say goodbye, then?'

'Yes.' She put out her hand.

'Good luck, and thank you.' He closed the door quietly behind him, started for the exit, then changed his mind and turned back to the enquiry desk.

'Could you tell me who's in charge here?'

'Mr McArdle.'

'Then I'd like to make an appointment, please. I'd like to see him.'

'Harry Bell forgot to tell his brother that we wanted him,' Mansell began.

Maggie scraped their plates into the dog bowl.

'When did the brother go to Aberdeen?'

'Last week sometime.'

'So why didn't Harry Bell tell you then that he wouldn't be coming?'

'He says he forgot that as well.'

'Forgot, *forgot*. What's he got to think about all day except pushing snow from one end of the dale to the other?'

She banged the kettle onto the Aga and beads of water ran sizzling off the hotplate.

They both sat, listening to the spattering and hissing as it settled down to boil. The afternoon was darkening with the threat of more snow and the Tilley lamp was holding them in the pool of its light.

She poured two mugs of tea and passed one to him. They drank in silence. When he finished, Mansell put his mug carefully on the table and cleared his throat. 'I'm sorry I'll not be going with you after all. You're looking very nice, though. Have you had a new hair-do?'

SEVENTEEN

Maureen joined the slow-moving Friday night traffic heading north for the M1 and settled down with the frustration. It was just after four o'clock and already the cars were bumper to bumper. A fine drizzle was refracting the waves of oncoming headlights into showers of sparks, and causing the lights of the car ahead to explode every time it braked. She tailed lorries cautiously for nearly two hours, keeping as far away from their slipstreams as she could, her wipers barely able to clear the pale brown mud that was flung at them every time one moved out to overtake.

By the time she left the motorway, the rain had settled into an exhausting torrent, gusted by strong winds. The Metro bucked and rocked and she clutched the wheel tightly as she peered ahead, straining to see the road in the inadequate beam of her dirty headlights.

In the failing light, the early February countryside looked bleak. Hedges and trees were still bare, the fields bogged and dead. Lowering clouds shawled the last remains of light over the hills. Every ditch and hollow held defiant traces of snow and a chilling damp enveloped everything.

At five to six she switched on the weather forecast. It was uncompromising: outlook for tomorrow – rain in most places with the band of snow continuing to move eastwards across the country. Continuing very cold. She switched off

Bring warm and waterproof clothing, the acknowledgemen slip had said. *Have a pair of strong boots with good grip and ankl support*. She should have cancelled then. She would only hav lost the deposit. Instead, she'd found her boots growin twenty years of mould in the bottom of the cupboard unde the stairs, and promptly borrowed a pair of Doc Martens They probably were not what the organisers had in mind nor her urban plastic mac. Rural waterproofs were different She had a sudden vision of herself hobbling out like a de ranged Mary Poppins, minus the umbrella. As for th Castro beret that Aristophanes, Kouri's youngest son, ha insisted that she borrow to go with his boots, well; but she' promised to wear it and to bring a new badge back in it a proof. You'll look great, Mo, he said. They'll all know yo mean business as soon as they see you.

But they might wonder what kind of business, she replied struggling to fasten his combat jacket.

You could leave it hanging open, casual like, he reassure her; but in the end, she settled for two of his army surplu sweaters and a padded waistcoat. Her plastic mac just fitte over the lot and as long as she breathed carefully, the popper held.

She must be mad. She was nearly fifty, unfit and unabl to explain herself. She couldn't begin to tell anyone why sh was doing it. No, why should she have to justify it to any one? But a lifetime's conditioning was difficult to shrug off In the end, she said nothing about where she was going. Sh just left the office and said she would see them all on Tues day.

At that moment, there was a series of small rivetin knocks and the steering wheel shuddered. She braked in stinctively and the car slewed towards the ditch. She'd neve had a puncture miles from anywhere, from a telephone and friendly rescue service. She found the handbook in the glov compartment, and the page on changing the wheel.

The rain ran down her neck and gathered at her waist. Th

two sweaters were soaked and clung to her waistcoat in a sodden mess. The wheel brace refused to slacken the nuts and she kicked it viciously, lost her balance and sat down on the road.

It's an omen, she decided, wet knickers on a dark road: the runes have spoken, the gods are angry. She scrambled awkwardly to her feet, picked the torch out of a puddle, then discovered to her great delight that the kick had done the job. Half an hour later, she stowed the wheel in the boot, wiped her filthy hands on tufts of wet grass and drove on.

Her determination began to evaporate again as she sat outside the hostel, dark and looming, watching sheets of rain blasting against the windows and wishing she was warm and dry and back in London. It was all a mistake. This wasn't her kind of place. She was too old and soft to rough it now.

But the weather was foul and she had no spare tyre and she'd paid for the accommodation – and anything would be better than spending the night stranded in the car, so she went inside.

'Nearly given you up for lost,' the warden said cheerfully.

'So had I,' she laughed.

The hostel was warm – that surprised her. The warden showed her where to dry her wet clothes and opened a bottle of decent wine to sell her one glass. Slowly, her spirits began to lift. She would certainly survive one night. Supper was finished, he explained. She didn't mind, she wasn't hungry, she replied; and bought tea bags and milk from the hostel shop.

'Is that all you want? We've got tins of stuff. You can heat them in the members' kitchen.'

'No thanks, I'm too tired to be bothered now,' she said, surprised at her own answer.

As soon as she finished her wine, she made herself a cup of tea, filled her hot-water bottle and went to bed.

The next morning dawned pale and wild. Maureen met the group at nine thirty and Brian, the instructor, introduced them to each other: Dene, Craig and Mike. She was the only woman. Brian said he liked a challenge and the men laughed. Outside, behind the hostel, he invited her to be first on the simulator.

'Just like riding a bike,' he said.

'I've never ridden one,' she replied. Dene disguised a snort as a cough as she demonstrated her ineptitude by spiralling helplessly in the harness.

'Turn your head first then shift your weight across,' Brian said. She fingered the bar lightly until it returned to the neutral position, then turned slowly and smoothly, first left, then right, savouring the delight of being weightless.

'That's it, you've got it. You'll be riding a bike next,' Brian cracked, and they all laughed again.

It was gusting hard on the hill but Brian thought it would be ideal lower down. 'Just enough is what we're looking for, for your first attempt.' They went through the pre-flight checks and Maureen was the only one to spot the deliberate mistake in the rigging.

'Tell the rest of them,' Brian said.

'No need,' she replied. 'I'm sure they've all seen it as well.' Brian straightened the rigging and gave dire warnings of the consequences if such a mistake wasn't spotted and corrected. They all listened solemnly.

'Right then, who's the smallest?'

All the men stepped back and looked at Maureen.

'You're the shortest, anyway,' he said and they smirked. 'Get into the harness and put the helmet on.'

'Do I have to wear it?'

'Yes, it's vital. Tighten the chin strap, that's right. Don't bother about your SAS beret: it'll keep your eyebrows warm.' More laughter. Then: 'I'm going to hook you into the frame, right?'

She lay, dangling happily in the harness, listening to the final checklist, until he said: 'Right, Maureen, stand up, put your shoulders through the frame. Then straighten up and lift it.'

She heaved and strained but remained bent double. 'I can't; I can't lift it.'

'Try again,' he said patiently.

She did, straining every muscle. 'It's no use, I can't. I never will; it's just too heavy.'

'Most days you would have problems holding on to it, it's just that today's a bit difficult with the wind being light down here. I'll tell you what we'll do,' he said smoothly. 'We'll give Dene a try and leave you till later when the wind might strengthen a bit, eh?'

No, she thought mutinously as she stepped out of the harness.

She could have murdered Dene as he came forward to take it. She smirked as he tripped and had to be helped into it. But he recovered quickly and picked up the machine like a preliminary warm-up in a weight-lifting contest.

'Right, now the hang glider needs twenty m.p.h. for take-off. So if this wind's about ten m.p.h. what speed does that mean that Dene's got to run? Anyone?'

There was silence and eventually Maureen offered, 'Ten?'

'Right: ten.'

They set off at a lumbering run, Dene in the frame like a grounded moth, Craig and Mike each with a rope running alongside and Brian running with them, yelling encouragement.

Maureen was left far behind as they careered down the hill, bumping off the ground for a few feet then running again before coming to rest, spread-eagled on the slushy grass. She brought up the rear just as they were lifting the hang glider and preparing to carry it back up the hill. The wind had dropped, but Dene was still determined to get up enough speed for take-off and he got soaked twice more before it began to sleet in unexpectedly vicious gusts.

The torn clouds raged across the hill and then, just as suddenly as it had started, the wind dropped again and a weak sun blinked across the grass.

'I wouldn't mind a cup of tea while we're waiting,' said Dene, still breathing unevenly after his runs.

Brian seized on this. 'Good idea. Right, get your packs and have a break. I'll go and have a word with John and see what he thinks. I'll be back in ten minutes. Okay?'

She opened her youth hostel packed lunch and looked at it critically. Times had changed and not for the better: one cheese bap, one packet of crisps, an apple and two digestive biscuits. What had happened to all the Marmite sandwiches – stacks of them in every pack? She chewed meditatively on the apple and watched the clouds scudding in random sequences across the Peaks.

Brian came back, joined them crouching under the hang glider, rolled a cigarette and announced, 'John says to go back to the Hall; this'll get worse, not better. I'll cover the theory with you and tomorrow, if it hasn't improved, we'll arrange for tethered soaring off the top, just so that you all get the feeling of being up. With the wind the way it is today, you're running your guts out and getting nowhere.'

At four o'clock the group broke up for the day. The men drifted outside together and Brian looked across at Maureen. She might be dumpy but she certainly wasn't dim. 'You seem to have got the hang of it all quite nicely. Is everything clear?'

'Yes, fine, thanks. I'm just anxious to get up.'

'You'll do it tomorrow,' he said comfortingly. 'You'll have no weight to lift. The wind will do it all for you.'

'I know, and I'll be all right once I get up. I've always known that.'

'Of course you will. You'll get up and you'll do it yet. You're not the oldest we've had,' he added by way of reassurance.

'That doesn't bother me. I know I can fly.'

'So you've done this before?' he asked, struck by her certainty.

'No, only in a dream. I've had it for years,' she began.

He didn't laugh. He listened, and when she faltered to a

stop he said, 'I used to have that dream. I had it so often that I just got myself a second-hand machine and started throwing myself off the tops of hills. I didn't know anything about it, except that I could do it. Then once I started doing it, the dream went. I suppose I didn't need it any more. Doing it is better.'

She thought back to her own dream of flying. It had started shortly after she had left the children's home and gone to live with the Wilsons. For the first few months she hadn't thought about anything, she'd been so busy. She had been determined to be good, tried her best from the very first day – washing up, tidying, running errands, sitting quietly, being polite and never, never forgetting how lucky she was.

Then the dream had started. She knew it was only a dream, even while it was happening, but she didn't mind. It had taken her to another world, one where she could be carefree and careless, where she was safe from criticism. And it had been different from her reality in another way as well: she had been happy.

'Even if it's just as good as my dream, it'll be out of this world,' she said.

She wandered outside. Between the showers, the pale sun had the quality of a stage spot, lighting first a snow-speckled field, then a clump of shivering trees, then panning the ancient route of stone wall climbing the hillside, before dimming in the onslaught of another shower.

She was content to wait, irritated neither by the weather nor the delay. She was aware of an absolute certainty in her now, that bestowed a very deep and new serenity. She was possessed.

Maureen had had the dormitory to herself the previous night, but when she went upstairs that evening, there was an elderly woman in tight cord trousers and high heels, struggling with a massive suitcase.

'Here, let me help you with that.'

'Ta very much. It's good of you, I'm sure.' She had a strong Black Country accent and confided that she'd never stayed in one of these places before, but her sister-in-law wasn't well and couldn't do with them staying with her, but they had gone to visit her and would only stay one night, and she wondered what had happened to Lawrence.

'He'll be in the men's dormitory, I expect.'

'Do you think so?'

When she opened her suitcase, packs and packs of toilet rolls tumbled out.

'Well, yer never know, do yer?' she said, embarrassed.

Maureen smiled, suddenly warming to her. 'The food isn't that bad.'

There was a pause, then: 'Oh, I see what you mean. Like Spain and them places?' and she laughed.

She insisted on having the bunk above Maureen, despite reassurances that she could have any of the other lower ones.

'No, I'd rather be on top of you, just in case anything happens in the night. Then I can hold yer hand.'

Not any more, thought Maureen: those days are finished.

The next morning, she got up early, and when her dormitory mate hadn't appeared by breakfast, she collected a cup of tea and went to find her. The woman was suspended helplessly, half in and half out of the bed, one foot a mere two inches from the edge of Maureen's bunk and safety.

'I'm stuck,' she said, sounding desperate.

'No you're not. Hop back up and have this cuppa. Then we'll get you down.'

She grunted and clambered on to the bunk and lay there, gasping. 'I've been trying to get down for the last half-hour. I thought I'd be here for ever. And Lawrence must be wondering where I am. I've never had a head for heights, you know.' She wriggled round and sat up, and accepted the cup of tea that Maureen offered her. 'Thanks love, that's just what I needed. I slept well enough, yer know: quite comfortable really, isn't it? The worst bit was yesterday, trying to make up my mind to risk it.'

'Same here.'

When the tea was finished, Maureen brought a chair across and she stepped gratefully to the floor.

It was wild and gusty on the hill. 'Perfect for tethered soaring,' Brian enthused, then: 'Right, Maureen, you're first again today.' He turned to them all. 'This is very different from yesterday. On no account must any of you let go of your rope. Have you heard that? Today the wind will be sufficient to launch you from a standing start, so it could snatch you just as easily and take you out of control. So if you're holding a rope on the ground, keep hold of it at all times. Got that?'

The hang glider buffeted and rocked in the wind, as though anxious to be aloft. Calmly, she held the frame. Her beret was crushed to her eyebrows again under the helmet. Her Doc Martens were linked to her stretch Lycra trousers by a pair of sea-boot socks, and her sweaters were tucked into her waistband. Over everything, her pink plastic mac fluttered wildly and threatened to burst open. She waited, oblivious, utterly still.

Brian let go of the struts and stepped aside. The men braced themselves, holding the ropes, and she rose in the air, just as he had said and as she had known she would. Pure joy bubbled from the bottom of her guts to her shoulders. Her dream had been an omen after all, and she had been right to follow it. She hovered twenty feet above them, securely tethered, safe and calm, the ropes stretching tautly away from her to the men below.

'Right, try your bar, Maureen. Ease it towards you. That's it; feel yourself rise. Good. Now back to neutral and hover . . .' Brian's voice drifted up.

What happened then was never clearly established. Dene said he got something in his eye and tried to wipe it and lost his rope. Craig said he saw what had happened to Dene and tried to grab hold of his rope but let go of his own. Mike said he tried to hold the glider with the remaining one but was forced to let go just before Brian got to him.

Maureen, who moments before had been tethered like a child's balloon, shot into the sky, upwards and outwards, away from the hill. As she rose, she could see Brian waving his arms and cupping his hands around his mouth, trying to tell her something. 'Oh, hell,' he raged, watching helplessly as her small pink figure continued to rise, now like a demented barrage balloon, the ropes flying behind her. Above him, Maureen shook her head firmly; then turned her attention to the hang glider.

For a moment, she considered the landing procedure, but remembered Brian saying that it needed eighty feet to recover from a stall, and she couldn't be sure of the walls. Below her now, they looked small and harmless, but she didn't want to risk hitting one. So instead, she pulled the bar towards her a fraction, rose smoothly on a thermal, then returned it to neutral and began to hover.

Now she knew how the elephants danced! This was something deep and unacknowledged in her own psyche, of which her dreams had allowed her only a glimpse.

She had escaped at last, was free from a lifetime of irreconcilable conflict: of being a reproof of Lizzie's childlessness and the daughter Jim had always wanted.

Jim argued for her to sit the Eleven Plus, and when she passed, he insisted that she took her place. Lizzie just sniffed and asked who would buy her the fancy uniform, and what would he do when she got ideas beyond herself?

He said that he would do overtime to get her whatever she needed, and it was daft to talk about her having ideas beyond herself. How could she get them? If she was doing the thinking, then the ideas would be in her own mind, not outside them. He was wrong there, but it didn't matter because he managed to get Lizzie's grudging agreement on condition that she still did her whack in the house and didn't expect to be waited on just because she was going to the Grammar.

Lizzie wanted her to leave as soon as she was fifteen and get a job, but Jim held out and she got through to college. No one saw her graduate. Jim died six months before her finals, without warning, in his sleep. Lizzie said Maureen had killed him; he'd done so much overtime to keep her. She wouldn't come on the day, of course, but then, she had never intended to.

And she'd spent her life proving that Jim was right and Lizzie was wrong.

And now it was an irrelevancy at last, as were all the opinions and judgements Maureen had bowed to all her life. Now the only reality was herself, neither good nor bad but just as she was; just being – just that – and that at last enough.

Far below, the men now looked like models in a child's game. The tiny fields were mottled green and white, and the stone walls were thin black lines edging the white ditches.

She knew that, just as in her dreams, she would have to return to earth. But not yet, not now that she was here. She'd waited years for this.

EIGHTEEN

'Bring the Land Rover to the back door so I can get in without getting up to my ankles in muck.'

For once, Mansell was content to let her be, seeing as he'd be on his own for a week. It'd be more than a week: it'd be nine days if she stayed away till Sunday. The diesel had come yesterday, so the milking machine was working again and he'd be through them cows in a crack every day. The rest of the time would be his own to do nowt in. If he wanted just to sit and think, he could, or he could stand and look at things.

'Right you are; got your case, your bag?'

'Course I have. I've had it ready for over a week.'

They bumped cautiously over the half-thawed ruts in the road, not speaking, he with his chin nearly on the wheel, Maggie holding the door with one hand and the edge of the seat with the other.

'I suppose Dave Barnett'll be back soon,' he said as they passed the house on the right, below the road. 'The plough would've cleared that track in for him if he'd been here, but he'll most likely tell them when he's coming back, so as he can get the car up to the house.'

'If you don't keep your eyes on the road, we'll be up to the house as well,' she snapped.

They drove the remaining miles to the crossroads in

silence. He was tempted to leave her down to wait for the bus, and turn round, but he didn't dare lean over and open the door and she made no move, just sat, looking out of the window.

The bus was on time, and stopped to Mansell's frantic signals. Maggie watched her case being stowed, then climbed in and looked straight ahead until the bus pulled away.

Mansell stood and watched it go, breathing deeply, savouring the moment, before being startled by a blast on a horn, and jumping to one side as the red Post Office Land Rover drew up behind him.

'Now then, Mansell, thou can save me a trek, lad; I've got a letter here for you.'

He recognised the writing and tucked it into his jacket pocket. When he was safely alone on the fell road, he stopped at the junction for Dave Barnett's house and opened the letter:

Dear Dad,

    Sorry about the rushed p.c. earlier, but I was up to the eyes with school things and I wanted to write to you properly when I had more time.

    I was surprised to get your letter and very, very pleased. It made me wish once again we'd kept more in touch. Anyway, your letter came at a good time for all of us, and I hope my news will please you and make Mam a lot less anxious about me.

    I've got a special person I want you to meet, someone who shares your love of farming. There now, I bet that's a surprise for you!

    We're living together and I've never been so happy in my life.

Mansell pushed his cap to the back of his head. So she wasn't married – leastways, not yet – but she'd be getting married; and to a farmer! Maggie and him could retire, go to Canada to see his brother! Aw Joan lass, well done, well done, he breathed. She was thirty, just right – old enough to know her own mind and still young enough to start a family. Mebbe she'd call him Mansell if it was a lad, or Maggie if it was something else.

I've had lots of friends at college and at work, but Alison is very special. I cannot believe how lucky I am, and I'm sure Mam will love her.

Alison? Who was she talking about now? What was the lad's name? She hadn't said. And who was this Alison?

We're hoping to come up at Easter, both of us. We don't want to spend the rest of our lives in secret, and I want to show Alison the North Pennines and have her meet everyone.

He tried to focus on the words but couldn't. Naw, couldn't be. He'd read it again slowly and it would all be clear. He'd missed a bit somewhere. He read it aloud from the beginning, then again, and sat staring out of the window.

She was mad. She'd gone crackers – got that from her mother's side of the family of course. Maggie had always been too soft with the lass: delicate, she'd always said, and this was the result. If she'd let her help on the farm as he'd wanted, it'd never have happened. She'd have married a local lad and they could have moved into the other end of the house that Maggie kept shut up, and now he'd have help with the beasts and everything. And instead, he had a daughter who was soft and had gone mad and was going to live with another woman and didn't seem to know the difference.

I know you'll soon come to think of her as one of the family. I don't want us to be distant with each other any more. I want, oh, it's funny writing this, not knowing whether or not you'll get off the train with Mam. This is just in case you don't. I want you to have the news now and not have to wait till Mam

*comes back to tell you, and have you feeling left out as I think
you have been in the past. I've never said it before and now
I wish that I had, and often: I love you, Dad.*
                                   Joan

And I wonder what Maggie'll make of that, he thought.

Karin sat looking out of the window to the road. She'd jus
seen a Land Rover go past, and then come back and park o
the road for a bit. It could only be a matter of days befor
the track to the house was clear. Dave Barnett mightn't wa
that long: he might just park up there as well and wal
down.

It didn't matter. She was nearly ready to leave. She'
nearly finished reading the diaries and she'd got a bit of prac
tice with the computer, so she wasn't grumbling. It woul
have been nice to have had another couple of weeks to ge
really good with it, but she'd manage with what she'd don
Besides, she needed to get away: the diaries were beginnin
to get to her.

Come on, there might be a happy ending yet, with Sall
and the kids.

She switched on, got December, then began to read.

27th December
Well, so much for my great plan. What a fiasco. It was
doomed from the start. 24th December and I set off, planning
to surprise Sally and the children. I'd just drop in, I'd decided, without warning. It wouldn't matter if the girls were
in bed. Sally couldn't object, especially as I'd always been
the inflexible one, according to her. Anyway, it'd be a good
start. It'd show her I'd changed and could be spontaneous.

Driving down I was imagining what it would be like, tiptoeing into the girls' room, waking them gently. Them, shy
at first, then all over me, daddy had come home, laughs and
cuddles and tumbles. I'd piggyback them both downstairs,

and when the excitement had died down, I'd carry them firmly back again. They wouldn't make a fuss, they'd know I meant business. Sally would turn to me outside their room and put her head on my shoulder and say in her little-girl-lost voice, I'm glad you're back, Prince, Piglet's missed you, and I'd just say, it's all over, Princess, we're going to start again. We'd giggle and snuffle and tiptoe past the children's room and I wouldn't bother checking the doors or lights. I'd allow Blackpool illuminations and the whole street as audience as a demonstration of my goodwill. So much for the fantasy.

I stopped at the Services just north of Hatfield, and then I wished I'd planned it more carefully. Their shelves were nearly empty. In the end, I bought a Miss Piggy for Sally, not quite Piglet, but she wouldn't mind, I thought. She'd know I'd tried. In the cafeteria, there were muzak carols and I felt like Scrooge when he discovered he still had a chance to celebrate Christmas. I was choked. I was so ready to make a new start, but not for what I found when I got there.

Sally was drinking, and there was no sign of the children. At first, she was very elusive, pretending to be vague. Said they were out playing with their friends but she didn't know where. It was nearly 9 o'clock. I kept hammering at her, and gradually she changed her story, and said that sometimes the father of one of their friends used them as models, and maybe that was where they were. Maybe, I yelled, don't you know, and what sort of modelling? She said for high-fashion magazines, but she hadn't been to any of the sessions. She was told it was better not to be there or else they got embarrassed and self-conscious. It was best if she just reassured them that it was fine with her for them to do it, then they'd relax and enjoy it more, and that would show in the pictures. She hadn't seen any of the photos in the magazines, only the test shots in their folder, and they made Little Miss Pears look poor. How often has this happened? I asked.

Then she admitted that it wasn't just an occasional session. They were at the studio at least twice a week, and that she got paid on their behalf. She got very defensive then, and said that the children were well looked after while they were there, and if they didn't do it, I'd be grumbling because she'd be asking me for more money every week, and that it was already like getting the back teeth out of an elephant to get the dribbles I did send. Her trust fund was only intended for her, she said.

I was furious. I'd sent her as much as I could afford. She seemed to have forgotten her stories about the cello and the drums and all the friends always at the house. When I reminded her, she denied ever telling me and then said maybe I'd imagined it, she'd never mentioned it! The truth has always been on a sliding scale with Sally but she's much worse now. She doesn't even try to cover her tracks.

I was really mad with her and said it was the equivalent of prostitution to allow the girls to work, just so she could keep herself in booze. She threw a glass at me, and I grabbed her and shook her and demanded to know where they were. She still said she didn't know. I got her round the throat and shook her again, completely out of control, yelling at her for being such an ignorant, greedy, idle slut, that she'd let strangers take the children away without knowing where they were going.

She was screaming. I let her go. They weren't strangers and she could explain. She'd met the woman at the school gate one afternoon, and she'd remarked how beautiful Anna and Megan were, and explained that her husband was a photographer, and always willing to consider new faces, and she would get a lovely portfolio for free, even if he decided not to use them. The children would be well looked after and the rates were excellent, more in a session than I sent in a week, she said.

So why didn't you go along and see for yourself? I got hold of her again and I rattled her with every word, still not believing her. She grabbed a photo from the dresser. It was Anna and Megan in white fur things. She waved it at me and repeated what she'd already said, that she was told that it was important for the girls to relax and be natural, and know that they wouldn't be interrupted until the end of a session. It was very busy, and if they had to spend time getting them into the right mood it meant that they would lose money, and Sally's best way to help was to say that it was important for them to learn all the new games that they'd be taught, and how pleased she was that they'd been chosen as very special little girls, and very clever ones, to be able to do everything they were asked. They said that games were the way they got the children to relax, they were fantasies, like in playschool. But once they were home for the night, she should allow them to unwind and not to make them go through everything they'd done. It was sufficient to reassure them that she knew and approved. This was better than turning up to a session, and causing the girls to become self-conscious and shy and waste expensive studio time.

Rubbish, rubbish, rubbish! I still had hold of her and was yelling, how could you tell them that you approved when you didn't know what they were doing, when the bell rang.

It was Anna and Megan, both very quiet but apparently OK. They'd been brought home by a very ordinary-looking woman who seemed completely at ease with me as well as with the girls. They seemed quite happy with her as well. She thanked Sally profusely for letting them go to the studio and when I asked why they'd been needed on Christmas Eve, of all times, she said it was to meet a deadline for an overseas catalogue her husband was working on, for the Gulf, she thought; they didn't celebrate Christmas there.

I asked her where the studio was and she said it was just a couple of doors away, but as all the staff had gone home, she couldn't show me round. I was welcome to visit any other time, except when the girls were working. She kissed Anna and Megan, and wished us all a very happy Christmas. Megan suddenly said, Will Uncle George make me play that new game again? I didn't like it. And Anna interrupted and said, Don't be a baby, Megan, you got a super present from him because it's a big girl's game. I tried to ask Megan what she meant, but she slipped behind the woman's back, and the woman just laughed and said they had worked very hard, and were very tired little girls, but they had played beautifully and would get lots more lovely presents. Then she handed Sally two parcels, all ribboned and bowed, and said they were a little extra for their stockings, and then left.

Sally was triumphant. There you are she said. Nothing sinister going on after all. As you can see, she's a perfectly ordinary nice woman, and I trust her completely, and so do the children. If anything was wrong, Anna and Megan would soon let me know. I pointed out that Megan had just tried, but she dismissed this as Megan being difficult. The woman had explained that she had to be firm, as well as encouraging with them. So you can manage to be firm when there's money at stake, I said.

I still thought there was something wrong: neither of them would come to me, but Sally said, What did I expect? They hadn't seen me for a year, and as far as they were concerned, I had abandoned them. Then she added that I had complained when Anna was hyperactive, and I was still complaining now that she was so quiet.

It was very odd, she wasn't just quiet, she was lethargic, until Sally told them to get ready for bed and put them in the bath, and I went in to dry them. Then Anna went off like a rocket. At first I thought she was having a fit of some sort and I ran outside and shouted for Sally. Anna calmed down as soon as she went in, and seemed OK then. Megan is more pudding-like than ever, so placid and dreamy, she hardly seems to be aware of anything. But Anna, she's completely unpredictable, despite Sally saying that she's much better and much quieter. That old tendency to explode is still in evidence, to me, at least.

Karin sat staring at the screen. Her whole inside was churning and the back of her neck was cold and sweating. She didn't know these kids. They had nothing to do with her. It was just that little Megan sounded so much like her Debbie. No she's not, she's nowt to do with Debbie, so stop being daft. You're getting too involved. It's none of your business how they bring up their kids. There's nowt you can do anyway and it probably all works out all right in the end. You'll just have to see.

She returned to the screen.

I said to Sally that I thought we ought to patch things up, even if just for Christmas Day, for the sake of the girls. She said she didn't care one way or another. As far as she was concerned I had left for good, and she was managing fine, and so were the girls, and I wasn't needed, but if I wanted to stay, then she couldn't stop me.

I should have just turned round then and walked out. Christmas Day was a shambles. The girls hardly looked at their presents. They were tearing the paper off one before they'd properly opened another, a sort of gluttony that nothing satisfied. Anna dismissed what I'd brought as being for little girls. We play grown-up games now, she said. It was frightening to watch them, unfocused, somehow unaware of the day or that it was supposed to be special. They just strewed paper everywhere; then lost interest. The house was the usual pigsty, with no attempt made at Christmas decorations or a tree. And as usual, there was nothing in to eat.

I took them all to Oxford Street to see the lights, and we ended up eating hamburgers and chips from a disgusting

Take-Away. We must have looked like refugees. I remarked to Sally, quite mildly, that she might have made a bit more effort, if only for the girls' sake and she turned to me outside the Hamburger Express and said very quietly, I WISH YOU WERE DEAD. I thought I hadn't heard her to begin with, but she went on, we'd all be better off dead, but you in particular, and first, so we could enjoy a little bit of life without you. So I had heard her, and she had meant it. I was freezing cold.

That was it really, the bottom line. There was no point in kidding myself any further that there was any reason to keep in touch. I had only ever been a cheque book, and now I wasn't even needed as that.

Karin stared into space. If she could believe him, Sally wa just as bad as himself. Fancy doing nowt for the kids fo Christmas: a bloody hamburger – and if he hadn't turned uj not even that, yet she was keeping herself pickled on wha they earned! Mind, he was too soft, he should just've packe them a case each and took them away. Naw, he wouldn' Anna would probably throw a wobbler on him, and he wa scared of her; and anyway, he'd said earlier that he couldn really cope with them, so he was just as cruel in his ow way. That only left one choice: to put them in care. H should, if he wasn't prepared to look after them and his wif wouldn't. She pressed Insert and began.

Those two kids didn't ask to be born and if you won't look after them, you should give them to someone who will. If I was you, I'd investigate that photo place. You never know what sort of photos they are posing for and they would be more relaxed with Sally there and anyway, they shouldn't work at night, not for more than a couple of hours at a time and not after 6 or something like that. I'd check if I was you because that's the law and you could be in trouble if you get found out. You will be found guilty and it will serve it right. They would nearly be better off if they were slaves. At least they wouldn't expect any kindness. You sound like a right pig and she sounds like a bitch and the kids cannot have done anything bad enough to deserve you as their mam and dad. She gets away with murder because you cop out of everything. You should be ashamed of yourself.

here, that'd tell him.

The entries for January moaned on about ghastly weather and financial problems, as though the Christmas episode had never happened. There was a leak in the attic from a loose slate and an electricity cut – all single-line entries. Then came a block of text.

4th March

Sally rang last night. I couldn't believe it for a minute. For a split second I wondered, hoped, if she'd thought things over. Then she came straight to the point without any pre-amble, and I am still reeling from it.

Anna and Megan have been taken into care. A Place of Safety order was made over a month ago and the Local Authority have applied and had them made wards of court. Their photographs were found in a file of child pornography and again in a reference file with their address. When the police and social worker visited Sally, they said there were prima-facie grounds for issuing the order, so presumably she was drunk as usual.

She's left me winded. I haven't slept all night. Not a word of concern for the children. She only rang to say not to mention anything about her getting money for the sessions or she'd implicate me as well, and she was sure that the other woman would remember that I'd been there on Christmas Eve and knew what was going on. It's blackmail. I think I'm going mad. I'll have to get proof that I was here all the time. But how? I can go for weeks without anyone seeing me here. Worse, Jowett knew I was away. He told me he'd seen me come back on Boxing Day.

She's left me speechless. In all the years I've known her, I've known she was utterly selfish and self-centred and greedy, but I've never realised just how ruthless she is. It's almost worth going to prison myself, just to nobble her once and for all. But knowing her, the chances are that I'd end up behind bars and she'd sell the story to the gutter press: Husband Rented Wife and Kids for Porno Mags.

I just want to kill her, to strangle the woman. It's over twelve hours since she rang and I still can hardly breathe, I'm so angry. I think I'm going mad.

I told you you should have checked that studio. It's your own fault but it's not you that's been hurt, it's your kids, right.

Dave Barnett continued to rant on:

Now it's all clear to me, Anna's erratic behaviour, Megan's remark about the game and her reluctance to talk about it, their indifference to their presents, Anna saying they played grown-up games, her reaction to me in the bathroom. I'd been an idiot not to see it, not to have had Sally arrested, imprisoned. I'm so angry, SO ANGRY, and what will my mother say? I told you so. I can't bear it. She's always known that Sally was no good but I can't stand hearing her tell me. And bloody Gwen, she'll gloat no doubt, if she finds out. I'll have to keep it a secret, have to go down and see Social Services myself, say Sally is getting treatment, tell them I'm in charge, will take the children just as soon as I can, when everything is running smoothly here. There'll be no more problems. It was all just an isolated episode. That's it, just an isolated incident, an accident that could happen to any family. They needn't know I was there on Christmas Eve, surely. I'm ill, can't sleep, can't eat, have got diarrhoea, can't think straight, or concentrate, and most of all I'm AN-GRY – ANGRY. I daren't go near Sally or I'd kill her, be done for murder. I'm going to a solicitor to file for divorce. I'll sell the London house. She won't get a penny and she'll be homeless. I'll show her.

September, the accounts of each visit to Social Services d meetings with Anne Stevens started. On each occasion e'd driven there and back in one day, eight and a half hours riving for a fifteen-, twenty-, or at most, thirty-minute in-rview; each time getting nowhere, saying nothing, giving othing away and never satisfying Anne Stevens.

8th September

She asked me if I knew what was going on, and I said no, and I was sure that Sally didn't either, she'd been too ill, and had been taken advantage of. I said that whenever we'd spoken on the phone, she had said the girls were playing with a neighbour's child. The girls had never said anything about what was going on, and they were always brought home safely at night, so there was no reason for either of us to be suspicious.

Anne Stevens persisted. So why was I so adamant that I should have sole custody, so determined that Sally shouldn't be allowed even to see them again, if she was as innocent as me? Why did I want to penalise her?

Because she was ill and couldn't be trusted and had failed to discipline the girls, I told her.

But discipline wasn't the problem. We were discussing abuse she said.

But it would happen again if they went back to her, I replied.

What was the connection in my mind between lack of disci-pline and abuse she asked me.

If she couldn't see that then she shouldn't be in her job, I said.

Why did it take you from March to September to get up enough bottle to go down and see about them?

Karin read on, page after page, all much the same, until t final entry, made less than a month ago, just a week befo she'd set out for London and got here instead:

8th January

I've just about had enough of this monthly marathon to try and get Social Services to see sense, and more than enough of the winter here, so I'm going down for a whole month this time and will sort everything out. A month should be enough but I'll stay longer if necessary. I've wasted more than that already in travelling up and down and got nowhere.

Presumably Sally is still at Muswell Grove Road, but I'll see my solicitor about that as soon as I get down. I'll have to stay with Mum. I don't know what I'll tell her but I'll think of something to keep her off the scent. I'll say the house is being decorated and Sally has taken the children to Norfolk. Mum will drive me to the edge of madness even without knowing about the children. She'll fuss and faff like a de-mented hen, utterly deaf to my needs or wants. She's always been the same and won't have changed.

I met Jowett, scattering his cows with the help of his lunatic dog, this morning, so I told him I was going away for a bit but that I'd be back at intervals to collect post and so forth. That might keep him off my premises. He offered to keep an eye on the place if I left him a key! I said it was as secure as Fort Knox once I locked the shutters, and he said that I might think so now but I might get a surprise. What an idiot.

I feel clear in my own mind at last. I'll divorce Sally, and get the girls back. I'll threaten Social Services with the Civil Liberties people. That should do it. It won't be easy with the girls but I'll find someone else, sell the London house, and this one, and start again somewhere new, a new beginning for all of us. The first thing will be to get myself a job. I need a steady income.

I know that's a lot to do in a month, to practically sort out my whole life, but I feel ready to do it. This time I'll make better choices about everything, the type of house I buy, the job I accept and the woman I allow to live with me, and just that, not marry, at least not at first, not until she's proved herself with me and the girls. I won't be hurt again or made a fool of ever again. This time, I'll choose someone who believes in discipline, someone thrifty, responsible, that most of all, reliable and responsible. I don't know where I'll begin to look, but there's bound to be some woman who appreciates and wants what I've got to offer.

arin wrote:

You must be joking. Do you have to take your head off to get it through the door?

ne read on:

There might be a problem with Sally. If she tries blackmail, it will bankrupt me. And if I call her bluff and tell Social Services about her taking money for the photos, I'll lose custody of the girls because she'll squeal on me. But if push comes to shove, I'd rather lose them than pay her maintenance. As for the girls, being in care might be the best thing for them, if they won't let me have them. At least they'd get some discipline.

'hat a sod he was. He was the absolute pits. She wanted to rite, *You are vicious*, but wasn't sure if the spelling was the me as in Sid Vicious. 'Wicked' wasn't strong enough, nor as 'cruel'. In the end she wrote:

I'm not sure how to spell the word I want to describe you but it means you are utterly rotten and cruel as well and both together. You have no decency in you and have never been any good to anyone in your life. You don't know how to be. All you can think of is yourself and because of that no one will ever give a damn about you. No one does now. Not Sally or your kids. With a bit of luck they'll get adopted by some nice people and then forget you and start again. And you'll never find another woman to bother about you because anyone can see what sort of pig you are. Women aren't soft. You only think they are. Sally doesn't sound very nice but you never helped her to be any good. All you ever did was criticise and it must have been very hard for her coming from Africa. I bet she needed all the help she could get and you just knocked her all the time. No wonder she drinks. She could be on drugs as well. I was as mad as hell with her when I read about the kids being used in those photos but you are just as bad and cruel thinking that being in care will be good for them. It's not them that needs to learn and they've done nothing to deserve what's happened to them. It's you two that should be put away, in prison.

She was shaking. It served her right for poking her nose ir his private life: now she'd added all his shit to her own, a: she hadn't enough already.

The last month had been tough enough: never being al to think of home, always having to keep busy, looking f ward, never back except to the funny bits at school, shutti all the others off, all the bits she wanted to forget.

It had been a constant battle. Even doing somethi simple like washing up: she'd see little Debbie again, sitti on the draining board with her wet knickers, laughing a playing with the empty squeezy bottle. She'd been like t man who walked a tightrope across the Niagara Falls, exc that he'd got across and she was going to slip. It would been easier if she'd managed to get to London straight aw as she'd planned. She could've forgotten everything that l

ppened then, because there would have been so much to
ink about. But being here, with nowt much to do and then
ading that diary . . . It had been like shitting into a full pot,
d now it was going to overflow, and she couldn't control
any more.

She could do with a good night's sleep. Her mind needed
reak. I bet my snowman does as well, she thought. She'd
ent hours building him in the back porch. Then she'd
cked him to death. She'd rebuilt him twice more and de-
olished him again each time and each time she'd told him
e didn't mean it. You could do that with snowmen.

Mebbe she wasn't getting enough exercise? Naw, it wasn't
t. She always wrecked things when she felt like this. She
oked around. She could always smash the computer. Daft
a: he'd never get to read her comments then. She'd never
eak the mouse or the other toys. That would be a pig-
ful thing to do. And if she flooded the house or burnt it,
ere would she stay? Anyway, there was no point in com-
g to the attention of the police. They hadn't caught her so
, not even when she'd started that fire in the flats.

e allowed her memory to roam back. They'd been her re-
at: hundreds of empty rooms, echoing stairwells and rub-
h chutes, here and there a shred of wallpaper; once, a bit
old carpet tossed into a bath. She'd rescued that and made
orner for herself in another room. It had been good. She'd
n the only one there, in an empty building standing in
ck mud and rubble in the middle of nowhere.

t was like that picture at that art exhibition they'd gone
from school. *Figure in a Landscape* it was called. It was a
man with a white face among a whole lot of ruined build-
s. Everything was grey, as though it was raining. The
man's face was twisted, like she was crying but not mak-
any noise. As soon as Karin saw it she wanted to leave.
Can anyone tell me what the theme of this painting might
Mr Littleburn asked.

She's all by herself, Sir, Jean Caspar said. She looks sad
Can anyone think why that is? he asked.

Has she got BO, Sir? she quipped. He rounded on her.

Are you going to joke your way through everything
life, Karin Thompson? Being lonely and alone is no jok
Being lonely, having no one to talk to – you think that
funny, do you? he demanded.

No, she thought, it's bloody awful. That's what's wror
with me and I'm fed up with it.

That sod Dave Barnett had the same problem. That w
why he wrote it all down. He had to get rid of it and I
couldn't tell anyone.

She couldn't either – not Tracy or Mrs Taylor becau
they might think it was her fault. The teachers? Naw, ev
if she could find one who remembered her. Naw, they
probably make comments because they wouldn't understar
what it had been like to live like she had. Even if they didn
she couldn't tell them everything, at least not the importa
bit at the end, or else they'd shop her.

Weissbaum! Old White Arse? Naw. Why not? Naw, I
said I had a choice, that's why not. Go on, why not? I
never said owt else to you and he listened. I know, he di
but naw, I couldn't go back.

She sat, turning the idea over in her mind. Well, I coul
I suppose. I could give him a ring and ask him how he wa
like, then see how he sounded. I needn't tell him anythin
I needn't tell him he was right.

I'll do that, she thought. Today's Sunday, I'll ring hi
tomorrow at the Clinic. He'll get a surprise.

Naw, he wouldn't. He wouldn't be surprised, but I
wouldn't say I told you so, neither. He'd just be pleased
hear her again and he'd sit and listen.

NINETEEN

ndrew McArdle sifted quickly and decisively through the
ost on his desk, then lifted the phone. 'Janet, ask Maureen
o come and see me, will you? As soon as she gets in.
'hanks.'

'What in heaven's name have you done to yourself?'

'Just sprained a wrist.'

'How did you manage that?'

'Jumping off the top of a hill.'

He laughed. 'I'm glad you are feeling a bit more cheerful.
know you probably felt like doing that when you left here
n Friday, that's why I've asked you in. I've got a few bits
f news that might cheer you up.'

'I'm still going to leave, if that's what you mean.'

'All right, but before you do, could you just listen to what
ve got to say? Just give me a chance to tell you, okay?'

'I'm listening.'

'Right: first, it's been no fun for any of us being two and
half people below strength and there's no one else to take
ie Barnett case, so even if you're determined to work your
otice, you'll have to stick with it. I wouldn't normally do
iis, but I haven't got anyone else with enough experience
o do that affidavit. It'll be a tricky one. And second,' he
ined his hands, fingertip to fingertip, and pointed them

towards her, 'your position is not as bad as you think. Ellen Bramhall rang to confirm the children's centre meeting – this should reassure you – she never mentioned that Thursday night, just wanted to be sure that you would be there because she was depending on you. She's hoping she'll be called as a witness at the hearing.'

Maureen raised one eyebrow. Andrew McArdle leaned back and began to swivel. 'As well as that, you needn't worry about Sally Barnett. She came to see me, and I sent her away with a flea in her ear when she threatened me with the Civil Liberties lot. I told her what she could do. I was worried about it for a bit, but then,' he smiled, 'then, Dave Barnett came to see me, and he told me everything. He went to visit her last Christmas and discovered then that she was taking money for the photographs. He swears that neither of them knew what sort of photographs they were but admitted that he didn't bother to find out. He only stayed one day. They had a bust up.' He leaned forward again, 'And here's the best bit, though he doesn't think so: his sister and brother-in-law want to foster the children. At least it gives us a choice. They already foster for their own Authority and take Special Needs children as well; and they know that these two have problems.'

He swung back in his chair triumphantly. 'So, come on, Maureen: the solution's been handed to us on a plate, with no complaints from Ellen Bramhall. What d'you say, eh?'

'Hobson's choice, from the sound of it. I'll have to see it through, so I'll do it as part of my notice.'

He sighed to try and hide his irritation. 'It's none of my business, but why are you so determined to leave? You do the best job of anyone I've got.'

'I know I do, but not for the right reasons. I never have.'

'What have reasons got to do with results?'

'A lot. If they're out of synch, you can lose your sanity.'

'That's a bit dramatic, isn't it?'

'No, I don't think so, not for me.'

'So okay, you're the best, and a perfectionist, but what's wrong with that?'

'I slapped the opposition, that's what.'

'Oh, come on, Maureen. The Barnett child was only one mistake, for heaven's sake.'

'I haven't explained myself very well. I'll try again.' She started to speak very slowly. 'I've spent all my life trying to be so good that no one would ever be able to say that some-one else should have had my chance. I've been the best, yes: I set out to be that, to be the one who could do the imposs-ible, then more besides. I've been a Bodhisattva: that god with all the arms. And do you know why? Just to earn my place on this earth, to atone for being clever, to show my gratitude for being taken from a children's home, even though my adopted mum and I both wished I'd been left here, and most of all to apologise for the fact that my adopted dad liked me.'

She was breathing hard. 'That's the only reason I went into social work. I'm not going to go through all this again. I've decided that it's not my job to save souls and it's time to enjoy myself. It probably sounds selfish and it probably is and I don't care,' she said defiantly.

'And I know now why I slapped Anna. It was because she dared to defy me, to answer back. I couldn't control her. I've only ever paid lip service to client autonomy. I've been the benevolent dictator.'

'But you've worked longer and harder than anyone else to keep this office running,' he encouraged.

'Same thing; being indispensable, all-powerful, instead of just yelling that we were snowed under. I kept muddling through, feeling like Boudicca.'

Andrew McArdle tried to suppress a smile.

'You don't know what size or shape she was, so don't assume she was tall and thin,' she retorted. 'Anyway, she took on the Romans against hopeless odds, instead of going to get help!'

He leaned forward eagerly. 'But now that you know why

you got yourself into this mess, you needn't do it again.'

'Exactly. That's what I've been trying to tell you. Slapping Anna was the best thing I've ever done, at least for me. It made me look at myself, and I realised that I wasn't that way because I'd been born like that – it was the way I'd made myself, the way I'd chosen to be.' She smiled ruefully. 'It's funny, really, after years of trying to get clients to recognise their scripts, to realise that I had one of my own! Now I don't need to be a damn Bodhisattva any more.'

'Well, if you were one of them, Bodhiswhatever-they-are, one sprained wrist wouldn't matter so much. As it is, it's half your assets.'

She smiled for him.

'That's better. Seriously, Maureen, will you change your mind?'

'No. And that's final.'

'Well, maybe you're doing the right thing, leaving and starting again at something else.' He sighed. 'God knows, the job is getting to most of us these days. Just as long as you know how much you'll be missed, that's all.'

'That's the first thing I've got to do, to stop thinking that I'm indispensable.' She got up. 'Right then, if there's nothing more, I'll get cracking on the Barnett file again and finish the affidavit. I take it Dave Barnett's sister will be coming in some time? Fine.'

He watched her leave. Another morning was beginning to crumble.

Outside his office, Maureen stopped at reception. 'Jane, as soon as Mrs Gwen Thomas arrives, show her in, will you? Andrew says she's coming today to see me. I'll be waiting for her.'

Gwen Thomas was not at all like her brother. She was an unfashionably big woman and confident with it. Blooming would be the word to describe her, Maureen decided. Hers was a real confidence: not strident or defensive, just utterly sure and serene. All this and she had only walked across the room! She sat down and smiled. Maureen eyed her warily, then returned the smile. On a plate or not, she was going to scrutinise this solution of Andrew McArdle's. She wasn't going to make any more mistakes. She'd grill the woman.

'Mrs Thomas? I believe your brother Dave Barnett called yesterday, when I was away, and said you wanted to apply to foster his children?'

'Yes, that's right,' she said.

'Fine. I just need a few details, then. If we can get this tied up, we might have the first happy solution since they were taken into care.'

'I hope so. I'll answer any question I can. What do you need to know?'

'When did you start fostering?'

'Oh, good heavens, pass,' she laughed. 'I'm hopeless at dates. Ten years ago? Something like that. We seem to have been doing it all our lives. I've never really kept a record of dates, except for their birthdays in the photograph album. I've got it here. Would you like to see it?'

Maureen nodded. Gwen pulled it out of her bag, put it on the desk between them, leaned one half of her huge bosom beside it, and started to turn the pages.

'That was our first, Tammy. She only stayed with us a month, just while her mum was having a rest. That was to give us an easy start, I think. We thought then it was going to be a doddle; we didn't know what was in store!' She turned the page. 'That's Dale and Ben on the beach with my own two. They were a couple of terrors – nearly wrecked the place. Not that they could do much harm, except to the goats. They were nearly as fast, and my heart was often in my mouth. They'd just started to settle down a bit when it was time to leave.'

She continued to turn pages and Maureen found herself looking at the undistinguishable beaming face of a Down's Syndrome child, tongue lolling.

'Now that's our Helen, our first special child. Isn't she

gorgeous? She is a treasure,' she went on. 'She was nearly thirteen when she came to us. You know, she'd never been in an ordinary house or gone upstairs to bed, little things like that. She had to learn everything. She was the one who persuaded us to concentrate on Special Needs children after that. They're the bottom of the heap, aren't they?'

'Does that mean you feel sorry for them?' Her Achilles heel at last – but no.

'Oh, no, it's not like that. It's just that they're often overlooked. We were the same. We wouldn't have chosen Helen ourselves. We were asked as a special favour and at first we had a lot of misgivings. After her, it's been a bit like a treasure hunt ever since. There's the first moment of bringing them home and thinking: This is it, kid. From now on you're going to blossom. The first mealtime is usually an uproar because no one's taught them to use a knife and fork. They're used to grab and shovel with a spoon at most. Bedtime is just as bad. They'll sleep anywhere but in the bed. But even then we know that in a couple of months, we'll be seeing the first little signs of change. It's worth all the effort. The ones we've had so far have all done so well.'

'And where are they all now?' thinking: Go on, surprise me further, tell me they're standing for parliament!

'Well, Helen and Dale are in a community village and Dan is in a sheltered employment scheme. William came to us a few months ago so he's still with us. They're all looking after themselves with a little bit of help. That's the whole point I think, to teach them to be independent, not to baby them – that's no good at all.'

'And your own childhood, is that when you learned all this?' she asked, not bothering to disguise the cynicism in her voice.

But Gwen just laughed. 'Yes, but the other way round. My mother was the world's worst fuss. She did too much for us. That's why Dave is the way he is. He never escaped. Dave was her favourite when we were little because he would let her faff on. He's paid for it since. I could never tand it – being told what to do, what to wear, as though I adn't a mind of my own. I was the rebel. I wouldn't even et her do my hair. She was always wanting to put big daft ows in it and I always made sure I lost them. Funny, isn't t, Dave was the favourite but it's me that's most like her. I nherited her bossiness.' She laughed again.

'And what did you do with it?' wishing she could punc-ure the woman's self-assurance.

'Well, Dave might have told you. We started with goats, ut it was before the cashmere boom and there wasn't a lot f money to be made. So then we hit on the idea of handi-rafts and organised some local people and eventually we ormed a co-operative. You might have heard of us: the Red Dragon?'

'That's yours, is it?' Maureen was impressed, in spite of erself. 'Everyone must have heard of you. One of the Sun-lay Supplements did an article on you last year, didn't they?' 'hen, archly: 'So how do you find time to do all that and ook after foster children as well?'

Gwen still wasn't thrown. 'It's no favour to have them hink that the world revolves around them. They get a fair hare of my time and a share of nearly everyone else's time s well. Some of the staff are great, so they're not neglected.'

'You sound like a miracle woman,' Maureen said. 'And vhere does your husband come in all this?'

Gwen still ignored the tone. 'He's the miracle bit, not me. 'he power behind my mouth, we always say. I couldn't do without him.'

'Mm.' Maureen raised her eyebrows and looked down at er desk.

Gwen looked straight at her. 'I think that's enough of this, on't you? I can tell you don't like me. I think maybe you refer people with problems, people who have to depend on ou? Well, I'm not going to apologise for being happy. It's ecause of that that we can help a few children. I'm not say-ng that we're saints or anything, but we are happy and we're aankful for it.'

That's me told, Maureen thought, and I asked for it. She looked up. 'You're right. I'm sorry, you're absolutely right. I was feeling jealous, that's all. In this job, I don't often meet people like you. I usually get the inadequate ones. I'm not used to feeling inadequate myself.'

'Ah,' Gwen said slowly, 'you're the second person that's said something like that to me in the past two weeks. Dave said I was too smug and certain about everything. If I've made you feel inadequate, I suppose it's the same thing. I didn't mean to.'

'No, I'm sure you didn't. It's just that you sound so confident.'

Gwen laughed. 'Philip always says I head for the rocks like a galleon in full sail.'

And that was it: the matter closed. Maureen hesitated this time. 'I have to ask you this, but what about your own two boys? How do they feel about sharing you with a business and handicapped children?'

'You'd have to ask them, and you're welcome to, but from what they've said, they'd gladly fill the house to the attic with more. I was a bit worried about them in September, when they went off to boarding school, but they've both settled well and went back okay after Christmas, so hopefully they'll be just as successful at flying the nest as all the others have been before them. When that day comes, Philip and me are going on a world cruise.' She threw back her head and laughed again. 'They can all come to the docks to wave us off – the two old fogeys, safely despatched.'

That settled it. 'Would you like a cup of coffee?' Maureen asked.

'I'd love one. I've got a couple of chocolate biscuits somewhere here in my bag,' she said as she rummaged on her knee. Maureen chuckled. Gwen looked surprised. 'Don't you keep supplies handy, then?'

'Yes, but I thought I was the only one. You're like a breath of fresh air to me.' She hadn't meant to let that slip.

'That's a lovely thing to say. I love a compliment. Comes

228

from having been rationed as a child,' and she laughed.

Maureen noticed that Gwen also picked up the crumbs with her finger and realised that she liked her as instinctively and as irrationally as she had first disliked Sally Barnett. It was against all the rules of good social work practice and she didn't give a damn.

'About Anna and Megan: would there be any trouble transferring them to us?'

'No, provided the Court agrees.'

'Oh I realise that. Mr McArdle has already explained about the High Court hearing. Can I see the children before then?'

'I don't see why not. How about this afternoon? I'll just ring and check.'

'Would you? I'm here sorting out my mother's house with Dave. She died a week ago while she was on holiday with us.'

'I know, Dave told me, I'm sorry.'

'Yes, I'll miss her,' she said quietly. 'I never thought I'd say that but we got on better and better as she got older.' She was on the point of tears. 'I'd better stop blathering and let you make that phone call.'

Ellen Bramhall answered the phone quite cordially: Yes, of course their aunt would be quite welcome to come and see the girls any time, whenever it suited her; and Miss Wilson too, of course. They could even be kept away from school. Maureen breathed deeply. The old dragon was human after all; maybe she'd been hang gliding. She smiled across at Gwen Thomas.

'Would after four suit you, when they come back from school?'

'Fine, if I come back here about half-three? I should be finished by then.'

She got up gracefully from her chair and glided out, leaving Maureen staring after her.

She'd got the number from Directory Enquiries and was waiting impatiently for it to answer.

'Family and Child Guidance Clinic. Can I help you?'

'Can I speak to Mr Weissbaum, please?'

'No, I'm afraid he's left. He retired last August. Can anyone else help?' Karin put the phone down, and after a pause picked it up and rang the number again.

Again the same voice and 'Can I help you?'

'Yes. Can I have Mr Weissbaum's number, then, the one where he is now?'

'Oh, no, dear, I couldn't give you that, unless you can find it in the directory. Are you a past client, may I ask?'

'It's none of your business,' she said and heard the woman say, 'Obviously, with a rude reply like that . . .' before she put the phone down again.

She was stuck. She didn't know his address, not even the town.

To her surprise Directory Enquiries were sympathetic but they couldn't help her unless she could get an address, even though the woman agreed that it was an unusual name. If Karin could get the town, she'd be glad to try and help.

That was it. It was her own fault, she should have trusted Weissbaum. It was only her stubbornness that had stopped her. She had known then that he would listen but she was determined to solve everything all by herself. This was what she got for being a clever-clogs.

The tube train rattled emptily between stations.

'You're very quiet, Mam,' Joan said uneasily.

Maggie said nothing and continued to look at her own reflection in the window.

'I'm sure Dad is coping fine, you know. You shouldn't worry about him like this. And it's a shame to leave so soon just when you're getting to know Alison . . .' she tailed off

Maggie snorted.

'What's that for, Mam?'

'I know as much about that Alison one as I need to know.'

'What does that mean?'

'I went to take a cup of tea in to you that first morning and –' Maggie stopped, her mouth closed in a straight line.

'Go on, and . . .'

'I saw the two of you lying there . . . asleep,' she spat the last word.

'Where did you think Alison would sleep?' Joan asked quietly.

'On the sofa, like any decent woman.'

'You mean conventional woman,' Joan said.

'The same thing,' Maggie said grimly.

Joan sat, trying and discarding every reply she could think of. At King's Cross, she reached for Maggie's bag but Maggie snatched it away.

'I'll manage myself. I know the way to the train.'

'Mam, wait,' Joan pleaded, hurrying to keep up with her. But Maggie's face was set and without another word, she turned resolutely and followed the signs for the mainline station.

The early afternoon traffic was still light as Maureen and Gwen made their way to the North Circular road and headed towards Springfields.

For the first time that year, the February sun held the imminent promise of warmer days.

'Fancy another one?' asked Gwen, mooching in the packet.

'Mm, please.'

'Any special colour?'

'No, as long as it's not green. I don't much like the green ones. I don't like green fruit drops either.'

'We've finished all the black ones. Here, have a red one. Jelly Babies were always my favourite sweets. When I was little, I used to bite their heads off, then cry my eyes out and send them to hospital in a matchbox ambulance.'

'So what did you do with all the half-eaten Jelly Babies?'

'Oh, I ate them afterwards. I couldn't think of what else to do with them all.'

Maureen laughed. 'So you showed early ability for crisis management.'

Gwen noticed a scattering of daffodils on a bank and above them, a forsythia blazing gold against a blue and white sky. She turned back. 'That's one way of looking at it. I only hope I can show some ability this afternoon, not only for the children's sake, but for Sally's as well.'

'You're fond of her, aren't you?'

'Yes, I am, in spite of all the daft things she's done. And still think she'll sort herself out. She'll get to AA eventually.'

'I hope you're right. Did you know that she was getting money for letting the children be photographed?'

'Yes. She told me everything when I phoned her about the funeral.'

'And she told you why they were in care? She must trust you a lot!'

'Yes, she does. And she's quite happy for Philip and me to foster Anna and Megan, if we can.'

Crocuses gleamed among the grass. Like so many discarded Cadbury's Roses wrappers, Maureen thought. She turned to Gwen.

'But Sally said nothing to me about this when I took her to Springfields.'

'Maybe . . .' she hesitated. 'That was when you slapped Anna wasn't it?'

'Who told you that?'

'Sally.'

Maureen said nothing.

Gwen sensed her embarrassment: 'I said I wondered what made you do it.'

Maureen still didn't answer and Gwen continued: 'To get

232

back to the children – Dave wasn't as keen as Sally on the idea of us fostering them.'

Maureen was glad to change the subject. 'But don't you think he knows in his heart of hearts that it's for the best?'

'Maybe, but he'll never admit it, even though I think he's desperate about them. When he saw the way our two behaved with William, I'm sure he knew we wouldn't make such a bad job of Anna and Megan.'

'So you do know that Anna and Megan are difficult?'

'Good Lord, yes. If they'd been mine, I would have taken them in hand years ago. Sally couldn't do a thing with them. She just let them do as they pleased. Having no rules must have been like playing at the top of a cliff.'

They were shown into the same sepulchral lounge, and the girls were again ushered in by Maria.

'You slapped me last week,' Anna said immediately to Maureen.

'Yes, I know I did.'

'Why?'

'Do you know why?' Maureen asked.

'Because you were angry with me?'

'Yes, I was.'

'Are you sorry?' she demanded.

'I'm not sorry I was angry, but I'm sorry that I hit you to show it. I should have told you instead.'

'Mm, but that wouldn't have made any difference. Mummy used to tell us things all the time and we never listened. Uncle George used to slap us as well sometimes,' she said matter-of-factly, and turned to Gwen, leaving Maureen dumbfounded.

'You're our aunty, aren't you? You used to come to our house at Muswell Grove and tell us funny stories if we sat down and listened properly.'

'That's right, Anna. You have got a good memory. I'm sure Megan remembers me as well,' she said, turning to her.

'She doesn't talk to anyone any more. I have to talk for her.'

'That must be a bit of a nuisance for you, having to talk for both of you. Maybe Megan will start talking for herself again soon? She used to, didn't she?'

'Yes. I wish she would. I get tired of her. Are you going to tell us stories again?'

'I'll tell you one now if you like.'

'All right then. But not a very long one.'

Gwen laughed. 'You can tell me when to stop. Once upon a time, there were two little girls called Anna and Megan.'

'Oh, that's us. This is going to be a story about us.'

'These two little girls had an aunt and uncle who lived in Wales. The aunt was called Gwen and the uncle was called Philip. Aunty Gwen and Uncle Philip lived with their three children in a lovely old farmhouse. They had a dog called Shep and an old pony called Neddybumps.'

'I'm sick of this story. It's for babies,' Anna said.

'Wait and see what happens first. Anna and Megan went to spend a holiday on the farm. They came all by themselves because they were quite grown up and everyone knew they were very sensible. The first morning there, they got up with the sun and looked out of their window. In the paddock, Neddybumps was eating windfalls from the old apple tree. They hurried downstairs and out into the warm sunshine. Neddybumps was waiting for them and he whinnied softly as they ran to the paddock.

'"Come on, Megan," said Anna. "We can both get on and go for a ride. I'll help you onto his back."'

'I want to go on my own!'

For a moment, no one spoke. The Gwen turned to Megan.

'Oh, so shall I change the story, Megan? You want to ride Neddybumps yourself?'

'Yes.'

'So can you tell me what happens next?'

Megan hung her head and sucked her cardigan.

'I don't know because I don't know the story.'

'Do you know what happens next, Anna?'

'Megan goes for a ride and Neddybumps runs away and Megan falls off and gets killed and I run after her and say the magic words and she comes to life again and then she says, "How can I ever thank you, Anna?"'

'I don't want to be dead,' protested Megan.

'Don't be silly, it's only for a little bit until I say the magic words. I wouldn't never ever let you die, not really.'

'Promise?'

'I promise, but you have to be good and do what I tell you.'

'I will,' breathed Megan.

On the way back, Maureen couldn't stop smiling as she listened to Gwen in full flow.

'Oh, I don't suppose the honeymoon would last longer than a day, not even that if I know my Anna. There would probably be a snarling match as soon as she arrived. She reminds me of myself at her age: so bloody-minded. And another thing, I don't know how she would get on with William. He hasn't been with us long. He's as bright as a button, knows every word that's said to him. Just hasn't a word to say for himself yet. We were told he was handicapped but I don't think so, somehow.'

'And if he is, after all?'

'He'll still be better off if we're optimistic about him.'

'And being realistic?'

'Fine, as long as it's not an excuse for putting the boot in and saying it's for the child's own good.'

'You must have met my mother,' Maureen said.

'Needed a bit of remodelling, did she?'

'Mm, she was never very happy.'

'You don't sound bitter about her.'

'No I'm not – and I've just realised that,' Maureen said with some surprise. 'I used to be, but not any more.' She smiled to herself and they drove on in silence.

'Are you hungry?' Maureen asked suddenly as they approached the North Circular, unwilling to part company.

'Starving, as usual.'

Maureen laughed, 'Then I know a great place. He's a friend of mine, Kouri's his name. I'll take you if you like?'

'Ah, I'd love that.'

Mansell stood staring at the milking machine. He should've made a start an hour ago, but he was feeling a bit under the weather. He had got another letter, this time from Maggie. She was coming home early, and he had to meet her off the bus at five o'clock and to be sure to be there. That was all. So Joan must have told her.

TWENTY

Maggie scarcely glanced at him as she climbed into the Land Rover.

Had a good trip? he thought of saying, then decided against it, driving with all his concentration on the road instead while she sat looking out of the side window. At last he cleared his throat. 'Snow's getting away nicely, I see.' There was no reply.

'Did you see her then? You didn't say much in your letter.'

'Yes, I saw her.'

'She wrote to me, you know.'

'Yes, she said she had,' Maggie replied grimly.

'Canny letter, I thought.'

'You would, seeing as you cannot think past your nose. What d'you think people around here would say if they knew, eh?'

'And who's to know?' he said slowly.

'I'm a respectable woman. I'd be the laughing stock of the dale if anyone was to find out.'

He changed tack. 'Are they still going to come up at Easter, then, the two of them?'

'They most certainly are not.'

'Who said that, them or you?'

'I told them exactly what I thought.'

'I think they should come,' he said, sliding open his window.

'What did you say?' she demanded.

'I've had time to think about it and I think they should come. When I die, this'll be her place. So as far as I'm concerned, she's welcome to come any time and bring who she likes with her.'

'Have you gone mad?'

'Naw, one's enough.'

'And what does that mean?' Her voice was ominous.

'You can take it however you want it to mean, but I'm going to write to her and tell her that she can come.'

'You do that and I'll leave. And you can shut that damn window while you're about it.'

'Just as you want.'

'If you write to that lass, your life won't be worth living.'

What a bloody woman. He drove the rest of the way telling her that in his head.

As they turned into the yard she snapped, 'And I don't suppose you've done the milking yet?'

'Naw. Why do you have to ask if you know already?'

'Just in case I was wrong.'

'How could you be when you're perfect?' he muttered as he slouched into the house, and upstairs to the toilet, and safety.

He sat meditating for as long as he dared, wondering how he would break the news: I've sommat to tell you, sommat that concerns you, so you'd better listen till I've finished.

She went on cooking, her back to him, giving no sign that she had heard. He cleared his throat. I've sold the farm.

You've what? she spun round.

Just what I said. I've sold it.

Who to?

To a mining company and I've got a good price for it as well. I'll be fair with you and give you a bit and then you can go your own way. I've had a lifetime of being gnawed

238

and of your snarling matches and I've had enough. There's no reason to stay together.

She put the spoon down and gripped the rail in front of the Aga, and where are you going like, when you leave me?

To my brother in Canada.

Canada? You – Canada? You cannot even get yourself to Newcastle. How'll you get yourself to Canada?

I've seen the travel agent and he says he'll arrange everything: the ticket to London, then the plane, and all I have to do is to sit till I get there.

He must know you, the only bloody idiot likely to get off afore it lands, and she began to laugh.

Naw, I'm not an idiot: it's just suited you to think I was. You made me in your mind so you couldn't, wouldn't have to love me, 'cos you're so bitter and loveless yourself.

That was the bit he'd waited for. That stopped her laughing.

There'll be enough to get you a room or sommat somewhere, mebbe near Joan.

You sly little sod. If it'd been in our joint names, you couldn't have done this.

Naw, you're right. And if you'd put your father's money into it, it would've been in both our names.

He smiled. He'd won, at last.

But it was a brief moment of triumph before his favourite fantasy was interrupted.

'Mansell, are you still up there? Come on, man, are you making your will or sommat? Them cows will be busting.'

He got up reluctantly, sorted his linings from his trousers, pulled them up, settled his braces and went slowly downstairs.

She was sitting at the table. 'I'm not feeling too good. This business with our Joan has knocked me back a bit.'

'I know,' he said quietly. 'It took me a while to get over the shock. The way I read her letter at first, I thought we were getting a farmer for a son-in-law, not another lass.'

He peered at her closely.

239

'D'you want me to do the milking, then?' She was looking a bit off colour, he thought.

'If you would.'

That wasn't like her. She must be bad. 'Make yourself cup of tea then, and stay where you are,' he said nervously

She made no move.

Bloody hell. 'D'you want me to make you a cup afore go?'

'Aye, if you would.'

Aw God. She was definitely bad. 'I think I could do wit one myself.'

'Well, make one then: make it in the pot and we can bot have one.' Her voice wobbled and two tears were poised o her lower lids, ready to fall.

At this rate she'd be no use at all at the lambing and it wa due to start any day now.

She put her head in her hands and slumped.

She must be going to die. He turned from the stove, kettl in hand, to try a few rough words of encouragement, an the water poured in a steaming curve on to the floor.

'You great cack-handed lump. Give me it here. I cannc even trust you to make a pot of tea.'

'Aw Maggie, lass, that's better,' he breathed. 'You had m worried there for a minute.'

Sally clutched the letter from Dave's solicitor. She shouldn' be surprised. Dave had threatened as much on Friday.

She had been late. She couldn't find the Court and the she hadn't dared to go inside. She was making her way ner vously along the corridor and he'd surged through the swin doors behind her, nearly knocking her over.

Ha, you: you can go home. You haven't a chance. I've tol them everything. His voice loud and triumphant.

She had leaned against the wall and looked at him.

There was no need to do that. They already knew it, sh said.

He faltered for a moment; then recovered. Just the sort of lie you're good at.

She steadied herself against the wall, then walked gratefully towards a door being held open by a woman who seemed to be expecting her. Someone from Social Services? Maybe from the Court?

Just wait, he murmured as he brushed past her. Just wait until you hear from my solicitor. You'll wish you'd never been born.

She struggled to think clearly. She needed to talk to someone before she phoned a solicitor – someone who would be on her side. Gwen, she'd phone Gwen. She would help.

'Hello? Oh, Philip, it's Sally. Is Gwen there? I see – at her mum's house. And Dave's there as well, is he? Okay, thanks. No, no message. Fine, thanks; bit low but fine really. No, honestly, I'll be all right.' She put the phone down slowly and brushed a fresh flood of tears across her face. She couldn't stop crying; they just kept leaking out, without her noticing.

I must have cried on to the photographs, she thought as she ran her finger over a splattering of blisters. One had distorted Anna's lovely face so it looked as though she had mumps. On another, Megan had a huge hydrocephalic forehead. Her beautiful, beautiful babies – ruined. They were all she had. She had made them. They were hers, no one else's. She tried to dry the photographs but only raised more weals as she swiped the tears with her sleeve. Oh, Gwen! She'd ring her. If Dave answered, she'd just ask to speak to Gwen.

She stood listening to the ringing tone, and jumped when she heard Dave's voice.

'Hello, hello, who is it?' he asked. She stood holding her breath and then replaced the receiver very carefully.

Dear, sensible, comforting Gwen. Lovely warm fat Gwen. The only person who knew everything about her and still liked her. No, that wasn't true.

There was Mummy.

Be brave, Sally, she'd said at the port. You don't want th
captain and all the crew to see you crying, do you?

At first, there had been the distraction of being on a big
liner and of finding her berth and the games room. And then
as she watched, everything began to disappear: firs
Mummy, and then the port buildings; and finally the land
itself until there was only the shimmer of sun and sea in al
directions.

After that, her sense of loss and loneliness grew as insidi
ously as the cold. The North Atlantic was sunless and wild
the English Channel fog-bound.

It was November and everywhere was grey. The boardin
school was on the Sussex coast, a long, slow train journe
from Southampton past rows of dull brick houses and fla
muddy fields under a freezing rain.

The other girls were horrible. At first they teased her mer
cilessly about her accent and her clothes and then they ig
nored her.

On Sunday walks along the beach, they would link arm:
heads bent against the wind; or laugh and whirl with it lik
savages racing along the shore, in and out of the great sno
of foam blown by a bitter east wind.

And she trailed behind them, aching with cold, fightin
back tears, willing Mummy to write and say she could g
back to Kenya.

And Mummy did write.

Don't moan, Sally . . . work hard, there's a good girl . .
make the most of it . . . be cheerful.

But every letter always ended: I am still thinking of yo
darling, with fondest love.

So Mummy *had* liked her, she supposed. Maybe she st
did? At least, she'd sounded as though she might in h
Christmas letter.

She whirled round to the dresser and snatched at the ai
mail envelope protruding from *Paradise Lost*. The boc
tumbled against the Famille Rose bowl and sent it crashir

o the floor. She kicked the pieces under the cupboard and
scanned the letter.

*I've tried so many times to ring you, darling. I hope every-
thing is all right. It's such a long time since we've heard from
you. If you're very busy, why not ring me here at Booligal
when you get a moment and then we can agree a time for me
to ring you back?*

*Life on the station is good. We're coming up to shearing
soon. We'd both love it if you could all come and visit us. We
could make a holiday of it. Do think about it and talk it over
with Dave. The tickets are open returns, a present from
Vincent. You can book any date to suit yourselves. Give me
a ring as soon as you've decided.*

She could always ring her now. Of course it wasn't quite the
same. Mummy didn't know anything. But that didn't matter. It would be better than nothing and she might even manage to tell her everything.

The international calls operator said that Booligal was nine
and a half hours in advance of GMT. To hell with the cost;
if she phoned now, she'd probably catch her mother settling
down to a pre-dinner drink. She wiped her hands on her
skirt as she listened to it ring, then gasped when she heard
her mother's voice.

'Mummy, oh Mummy, it's me, Sally, calling from London. Oh, Mummy . . .' She began to cry again.

'Sally, this call must be costing a lot of money; don't waste
it by crying.'

She gulped. That Mummy of all people should worry
about the cost of a phone call! The voice continued, 'Is everything all right? Nothing wrong with Dave or Anna or
Megan, I hope . . .'

And me, Mummy, what about me? She pleaded silently.

'Sally?' her mother's voice insisted.

'Everyone's fine, Mummy. I just wanted to talk to you,'
she said flatly.

'About coming out? Have you fixed a date?'

'No, not yet. I just wanted a chat.'

'Well, that would be lovely, darling, but can we arrang
some time next week when the shearing is over? I was jus
going out the door when you rang. We've got the gang her
at the moment and they need feeding and I'm just about t
fly up to the North Station with supplies. It's lovely to hea
you, darling, but I must rush. I can hear the engines.'

She put the phone down clumsily and tried to grab it as i
teetered on the edge of the table and fell to the floor. He
kick was sharp and savage and the phone rose in the air; the
checked by the cord, it ricocheted back and narrowly misse
her face. She killed it with her foot, grinding and hacking a
it with her heel, then turned and blundered towards th
dresser cupboard.

It was nearly eight o'clock, and time to leave. Karin sat a
the attic window cradling the mouse against her face. Th
smooth wood fitted the hollow of her cheek. Our Debbi
would love you, she told it.

The sun rose slowly, hanging like a lost red balloon. Th
thin skin of overnight frost was beginning to glow pink
She'd better go.

At least she was warm. She had found two thermal vest
as well as his sweaters, and put them all on to bulk out hi
waxed cotton jacket. She had pushed her hair under hi
bobble hat and wound a long scarf around her neck. It wa
just her skirt and the wellies that were the problem. Th
jacket was nearly as long as the skirt and then there was
funny looking bit of bare leg before the wellies started so
looked as though she wasn't wearing anything. It might rais
enough curiosity for someone to call the police. She had n
doubt that they were still looking for her.

She checked the few items in her bag for the last time
then zipped it and went downstairs, carrying the woode
mouse. She closed all the doors behind her, climbed th

wood pile and let herself out through the little shutters.

She clumped up the field towards the gate, climbed over it and then stood for a moment, looking back. She wished she wasn't leaving. London scared her, even though she knew a bit about computers now.

She wondered again about the things she had written. She knew she should have wiped them off to be really safe. But Whitebum had been right all along.

This was the best time of the day, Mansell thought as he settled himself more comfortably on the wooden seat and leaned his elbow on the window sill. It was quiet, watching the sun come up and before Maggie got her teeth in. The early morning must suit Dave Barnett as well. He'd just seen his car turn up the road.

He topped the last rise on the fell, stopped the car and got out.

Above him, two lapwings were hurling themselves to the ground, then turning at the last moment and wheeling upwards again, ringing in triumph. It was windless and brilliant, the sun scattering the heavy overnight frost with light that was refracted in the still air. The whole fell and sky were sprinkled with sun stars that dazzled and merged into one deep blue light as he stood and stared.

He had driven overnight from London, only stopping once for a brief rest in a lay-by when he had felt his energy flag. Usually he liked driving in the small hours on deserted roads and arriving at the beginning of a new day. But not this time. He was tired. It had been an exhausting fight.

There'd been that row with Philip after the funeral: He'd jabbed his empty plate at Philip's chest. Then stuff it. Forget it. Get your sticky fingers out of my life. No one's going to pull my strings, including your bloody Mark Ross. Who put him up to that? Gwen and Sally, I bet. Offer him a job then he'll have to say yes in gratitude, he mimicked. Well, I don't want your bloody job or your home or your fostering. And if you're so bloody good with kids, why don't you teach that idiot in the corner to talk? he'd shouted, pointing to William.

Then Gwen had said quietly, We're going to apply to foster Anna and Megan, whether you like it or not.

I'll object, he had told her.

Do, but it won't make any difference, except to your access. Think about it, she'd replied. He had. Then he'd gone to see Andrew McArdle, who was much the same age as himself. That had unnerved him. As he tried to tell him about Sally, the man had sat back and swivelled in his chair. It had been distracting. When he'd finished, he'd said, This won't affect my application for custody, I hope?

I doubt it. We consider everyone on their own merits, Andrew McArdle had replied laconically.

So he had felt that there was still hope and his hopes had continued to rise at the High Court.

He recognised Andrew McArdle, Maureen Wilson, the probation officer and a police inspector. And besides these, there were his own solicitor and barrister and, he presumed, those for the Local Authority. He was thankful that no public or press were allowed.

His legs were trembling as the usher called the court to order and they all rose as the judge came in and took his seat.

. . . M'Lord, this case concerns the future care and control of the wards Anna and Megan Barnett . . .

His feelings pitched from wild hope to despair as the evidence was presented and the witnesses called. Ellen Bramhall seemed nervous and not at all intimidating; Gwen less boisterous than usual.

Time dragged and raced. He could smell his own sweat and sat with his arms folded, dreading the moment he would be called.

His voice shook. It took a lifetime and was over in

seconds. He could hardly walk back to his place and could remember nothing of the questions or of his answers.

Then mercifully the judge intervened . . . I don't need to hear more . . . The evidence presented so far is sufficient . . .

. . . I have considered Mr Barnett's application for custody very carefully. He is a toy maker, a self-employed craftsman. His income is erratic but that would not deter me in this case.

That was the first hurdle. He had relaxed visibly.

. . . I have also noted that he lives in a rather isolated part of the North of England where there might be few friends for the children outside school and little social life . . .

He held his breath.

. . . But again, many children live in similar circumstances and are happy so this has not affected my judgement . . .

He risked a glance around the court.

. . . Nor is it a factor that he is a man living alone and would therefore be a single parent of two small girls. Although it's not a common situation, it does occur and the arrangement can work well . . .

He smiled.

. . . brings me to my decision about this case and perhaps I should say that . . .

He'd been about to get up and shake his hand. It could have been done ten months ago and he couldn't forgive them easily for the stress he'd endured, but . . .

. . . I have two insurmountable objections.

There had been a moment of disbelief. Shafts of light from the high Victorian windows immobilised specks of dust in their beams. Tears sprang again at the memory of it all.

. . . first, that although he knew his wife was being paid by the Hammonds and although he had serious misgivings and doubts, he did nothing about it . . .

– If you'd let me finish, Mr Barnett –

. . . secondly, his disappearance for three months without trace . . .

– Please, Mr Barnett –

. . . and connected with this, the fact that he only visited the children once in two years and then only for one day . . .

– I'll finish if I may, Mr Barnett –

. . . and despite being worried by what he found, he left without doing anything about it . . .

There had been quite a lot more said but he hadn't heard it. He'd turned and blundered out of the room.

And even then, he'd still been so sure, so sure, that they'd all be proved wrong once the children saw him again.

We're going to live with Aunty Gwen, Anna had said, full of her own importance. You can come and see us if ever we want you to, but not to stay.

I want you, Megan had said.

Yes, but not to stay, Anna corrected her.

No, not to stay, Megan agreed fervently.

And that had been that.

He had been out-manoeuvred by bloody Gwen and now he was coming back to nothing except humiliation and defeat. The memory of the past week still choked him.

He'd never had a chance.

He turned abruptly, got back into the car and drove on. There was no one about. Jowett's house had a thin stream of smoke rising from one of its chimneys. That was all. His own house lay sleeping below him.

He parked on the roadside, took his bags from the boot and set off to walk the last quarter of a mile.

It was only afterwards that he remembered seeing footprints leading back towards the road.

Inside, he opened all the shutters, then turned the water on at the stopcock. He started to fill the kettle for tea, realised he was using the wrong tap, began to turn it off and noticed that it was warm. Surely he hadn't left the heating and hot water timer on for a month? He rushed upstairs to the attic. No, of course not, the controls were just as he'd left them.

It must have been his hand that was cold, making the water seem warm.

Back in the kitchen, the dishes in the drainer were still wet. The food cupboard was nearly empty. He hurried from room to room, noticing small signs of disturbance everywhere. The computer! He hadn't checked! He raced up to the attic again. Relief, it was still there! He'd check it later – no, now. He'd better do it now, just in case. Breathless, he switched it on and read the last lines of the text in front of him with disbelief. He pressed Page Up rapidly until his own last entry appeared, saw that comments had been added to it, scanned them with amazement and read on:

Dear Mr Barnett

I'm leaving in a couple of days because the snow is nearly gone and I want to get to London before you come back and catch me. I know this is where you write your secrets. I have read them. I have a secret as well and I want to get rid of it. I never told anyone before because it was about all of us and I had to keep it. Now it doesn't matter any more and I don't want to go on keeping it because I will keep thinking about it and when I get to London I will be too busy with everything and it will be no good if my mind is up here and not with me. So I am going to write it in this diary and then I will leave it behind for good. This is my secret.

He pressed Page Down. There might be more to come.

I hitched a lift and the lorry broke down and I started to walk then I got lost. A man in a Landrover gave me a lift as far as here. I was only going to stay the night but I must have caught a cold or flu or something but I was not well for nearly two weeks. I must have had a high temperature. I had funny dreams and did not know if they were real or not. Then it snowed so I was stuck. I have been careful with everything. I am not as bad as you think. I have read your diary and you are not much good yourself. You said you were going to get Anna and Megan when you had everything sorted out but you have had time to clean the carpet with a toothbrush up your nose and you haven't even got a room ready for them. I hope they get somewhere else to live. I hope they are happy soon. Some foster homes are not bad. I've been in some. You wondered in your diary when the lapwings and curlews would come back. They came two days ago. I think that's what they are. One of them has a long beak and the other looks as if it has white underneath and is a floppy flyer. I have eaten a lot of your tins of food but if I hadn't I would have starved. I will turn the water off again at the stopcock and I'll close the shutters to the woodshed when I leave. I've taken two of your jumpers, two vests, two pairs of socks and a pair of your trousers and your jacket because my own aren't warm enough. I've also got your wellies but I wish they were a bit smaller.

You should have gone through your copy invoices. You got diddled in some of them because Maggie Jowett didn't add up properly. Also, there is an easy way of working out 15% for tax. Just move the decimal point one place to the left then add on half as much again. But if you are not very good with figures either, you'd better use a pocket calculator.

You are a brilliant toy maker, even though they are no good for children. But the Pull-Alongs would be brilliant for adults if they wanted to play with toys but there are not many of them like that because even if they wanted to be children for ever they have to grow up.

The rest of the page was blank.

This was all he needed. He straightened up from the desk. He'd have to see what else had been taken. It wouldn't be just his clothes.

In the bedroom, the duvet cover and sheets and pillow-cases were lying folded, perfectly ironed, and beside them were two neatly folded towels. His wardrobe was still tidy and his summer clothes hung in polythene bags. His drawers had even been sorted and rearranged. Whoever it was had polished as well – even the brass finger plate on the door that he'd always intended to do.

Downstairs it was the same. All the kitchen shelves had been washed and tidied and the boxes of his aunt's old china unpacked and sorted. On the window seat, all the animals stood in a line gazing at the mouse who was holding them at bay.

Apart from the food and clothes, nothing seemed to be missing. And whoever he was, at least he wasn't a complete yobbo. The boy was obviously from a good home.

When he switched on again, the last text that came up wasn't about his wellies. The boy must have added some more. He backtracked rapidly, found the wellies bit, then moved forward:

You are probably mad at me but I don't care. There is no point in telling the police. They will never find me. If they did, I would get put away for the rest of my life. The night before I came here I went to see my dad. He was in bed. I sloshed paraffin over him. Some splashed on his face and he woke up and saw me standing there. He was mad. He chased me. At the top of the stairs he tried to clout me and I ducked. He tripped over the paraffin heater and fell straight over the top of me down the stairs. He was lying funny. I went down. His eyes were open but he wasn't blinking or breathing and I knew he must be dead. All his back and shoulders and head were stinking of paraffin. I knew that the police would know it had been me because the home would have told them I'd run away.

They might think I'd pushed him then I'd get done for murder. I was going to murder him I was so mad but I didn't do it in the end. He did himself in and he would have murdered me if I hadn't have ducked. I knew the police would not believe me because I've been in trouble before so I decided to go to London where I could hide and get myself a job then get our Debbie back as soon as I could buy her a Barbie doll. Then she would come and live with me.

I am not sorry about anything. There is no point in being sorry about things afterwards because they are done and being sorry can't change them. It would still not make my mam or dad be alive again and it would not help me to get Debbie back. My dad is better dead. He was a sod. I think my mam is better off as well. She was always crying and taking tablets.

Only sometimes I am a bit sorry about our Debbie and for her kitten that my dad killed to show me he meant what he said. I wish she was with me but if she gets fair turns with the Barbie doll she will be all right. She was always happy as long as she was playing. I don't think she ever knew what was going on. She just thought my mam wasn't well and my dad didn't bother her as long as I was there. She was a bit slow and my mam never looked after her properly. She never wanted her. I would have left but I was scared he would start messing with her and my mam wouldn't bother if she was feeling very bad and was in bed. Sometimes she stayed in bed for weeks. Our Debbie was the only one I loved and I hated her as well because I used to think I couldn't stand any more of it and I had to put up with it because of her.

When she was a baby, I looked after her most of the time and looked after my mam and dad and he used to say I was better than a wife and I liked that. Then he started touching me. When he started to have it off with me I really hated it but he said it would get me ready for boyfriends and if I didn't do it he would get our Debbie to do it. I thought about going to the police but if he told them I was telling lies they might have believed him and then he would have belted me afterwards. Even if they had believed me they would have put him in jail and split us all up and sent my mam back to that hospital and my dad said he would kill me if I told anyone so he would just have waited till he got out of jail then he would have got me. The other thing that stopped me telling the police was that my mam knew what he was doing and said that as soon as she was OK again he would stop and go back to her and I was helping her. But she never got any better and he didn't. I went to get myself put on the pill and the doctor said I was too young and I said I was sleeping around a lot and he put me on it.

I used to go mad at school thinking about it and smash things up and cause floods and then they got mad at me and sent me to see Mr Weissbaum. I flooded some old flats once and fired some others but I wasn't caught. So it's no good telling the police about me because they won't catch me in London either. I will just disappear and change my name and get a job and then send for our Debbie if I still feel like it. I am still a bit mad with her that I put up with everything for her sake and then she wouldn't come with me. But I know that if she had she would have died because she could not have looked after herself when I had flu. So it turned out best in the end that she stayed in the home. If she stays there a long time, she might even forget me. If she doesn't and if she's not happy and if she wants to come with me then I'll get her.

It could not have gone on much longer at home but I did not see how it would ever end until Debbie was old enough to leave. I knew my mam wouldn't ever get better because she didn't want to because she didn't like my dad.

At first he used to come into my bed. Then at Christmas he told my mam to swap with me because he was sick of her like a big lump in their bed and there wasn't room in mine for two of us and he wanted to stay put in the one bed all night. She never said nothing. I wanted her to but she didn't. The night we swapped beds I went for a wee when he'd finished with me and to clean myself up. My mam wasn't in my bed. I told him but he said the silly cow had probably gone out somewhere.

Someone found her at the back of the old Co-op the next day and told the police. She was dead. When they came he was *out and I said I didn't know where he was and they believed me so we were taken to the children's home. I stayed one day then decided to leave. I waited until it was dark then went to get our Debbie. She wouldn't come because the aunty in the house had said it was her turn for the Barbie doll the next day so I had to leave her and go on my own. I was so mad I decided to set fire to him for everything he had done. I was going to slosh paraffin all round the house but when I got back there was only half a can in the shed.*

I thought he might manage to jump from a window and escape before he got burnt so I went inside and just put on the stairs and landing light and then went up. I could see him lying asleep in bed. I would have put a match to him if he hadn't woken up.

I don't think I'll get everything sorted out straight away because there's a lot to do. I don't think I'll find a job and somewhere to live all in the same day. I might but I might have to live rough as well for a bit or join a squat. Then I'll have to have enough money to go and see our Debbie and see how she's getting on. It has been good here. I hated it at first but when I had to put up with it I got time to think about things and sort things out in my mind. Reading your diary helped.

It might not be any better in London but it could not be much worse than it was at home because at least I won't have to worry about anyone else and that should give me a chance and that is all I need.

Outside, on a late February day, it was mild and calm, winter truce. The sun was brilliant on the high fell. Clou shadows dappled the lower slopes. Above and through it a lapwings were wheeling and whooping.

What sort of chance did she have? He'd seen a televisic documentary about missing children. There were one or tw safe refuges in London, run by the Children's Societ

Otherwise it was hostels, squats, cardboard city or prostitution. He'd switched off at that point.

If this girl could make it, anyone could; he could, Anna and Megan, Sally – even Sally. He brushed the back of his hand across his face. Don't get caught, whoever you are . . . I want . . . His tears took him by surprise.

He turned back to the screen and read the last sentence again.

It could have been written for him, for all of them. Another chance was all he wanted. It was all any of them needed.